CAN

"YOU ARE STUBBORN, MY LITTLE ONE, BUT THAT ONLY MAKES THE WINNING SWEETER!" ANTONIO MURMURED.

Freya smiled seductively. "I'm just trying to make the game more tantalizing."

Antonio's eyes glowed with fire. "I'd be careful if I were you. If you make this evening any more 'tantalizing' than it already is, I will be forced to break your will to resist me right here and now."

Freya felt her heart throb at his delicious warning. "All right, I'll behave for now. But later on, where will you take me to break my resistance?"

Antonio let his gaze rake over her face, then down to stroke her figure like a caress. "Why don't you wait and see, my curious kitten? As they say, the element of surprise is critical to the success of any attack. And this is one attack I want to be successful!"

CANDLELIGHT SUPREMES

ROMAN FANTASY

Betty Henrichs

A CANDLELIGHT SUPREME

Published by
Dell Publishing Co., Inc.
1 Dag Hammarskjold Plaza
New York, New York 10017

Dell ® TM 681510, Dell Publishing Co., Inc.

Candlelight Supreme is a trademark
of Dell Publishing Co., Inc.

Candlelight Ecstasy Romance®, 1,203,540, is a registered
trademark of Dell Publishing Co., Inc., New York, New York.

ISBN: 0-440-17451-1

Printed in the United States of America

November 1986

10 9 8 7 6 5 4 3 2 1

WFH

To all my friends, who make each day more beautiful than the last. Thank you.

To Our Readers:

We are pleased and excited by your overwhelmingly positive response to our Candlelight Supremes. Unlike all the other series, the Supremes are filled with more passion, adventure, and intrigue, and are obviously the stories you like best.

In months to come we will continue to publish books by many of your favorite authors as well as the very finest work from new authors of romantic fiction. As always, we are striving to present unique, absorbing love stories —the very best love has to offer.

Breathtaking and unforgettable, Supremes follow in the great romantic tradition you've come to expect *only* from Candlelight Romances.

Your suggestions and comments are always welcome. Please let us hear from you.

Sincerely,

The Editors
Candlelight Romances
1 Dag Hammarskjold Plaza
New York, New York 10017

CHAPTER ONE

As Freya Davidson was led into the domed chamber her eyes were drawn from one naked couple to another. After quickly scanning the incredible scene her gaze returned to the first couple she'd noticed. The woman, reclining against lush satin sheets, was obviously waiting for her lover. The man, whose bare chest rippled with powerful muscle, impatient for her love, eagerly tugged at her sandles. To Freya's surprise there were nude youths surrounding the two. Some were embarrassed, shielded their eyes. Others watched the couple with rapt attention.

Sensuality soaked the air, bringing a warm flush to Freya's face as her eyes were drawn to another couple. As eager as the first to share the passion of love, the man, older and bearded, gently drew the woman to him. As she neared, her robe slipped from her body, leaving her breasts bare. His hand, sliding up her naked thigh, pulled her onto the bed.

Freya swallowed, shuddering slightly at the sight of the third couple. Naked to the waist and obviously sated by lovemaking, a young man slept. Fair, with muscles hard and glistening, he was cradled in the arms of his lover. Freya couldn't draw her eyes away from his beauty, and she felt a stab of envy for the woman who'd possessed his love.

She was so enthralled in the scene before her that she let out a startled yelp when the man beside her tapped her arm.

"*Pardon,* Mademoiselle Davidson, I didn't mean to startle you."

"No, it's my fault. I shouldn't have jumped, but I've never seen anything like this in my life," Freya confessed.

The Frenchman puffed up his chest in pride. "There is nothing like it in all of Italy. This ceiling fresco, *Love of the Gods,* painted by Annibale Carracci, is second only to the Sistine Chapel, and *we* own it!"

Freya turned on her most persuasive smile. "But don't you see, Ambassador Maromme, that's why you should open the gallery to honor the fortieth anniversary of the Italian Republic. In a way it would return part of Italy's heritage to the people in this, their special year."

She linked arms with him as they strolled through the magnificent gallery. Stopping under the fresco of the bearded Jupiter in bed with his wife Juno, she commented, "How can you deny the world this splendor? Jupiter was the most important Roman god. Wouldn't it be a generously appropriate gesture to let him bless the three-day festival Ambassador Whittiker has planned?"

The French ambassador shook his head. "Mademoiselle Davidson, it is impossible. Ever since we French bought the Palazzo Farnese to use as our embassy, this gallery has been closed to all but a few. It has to be. One terrorist bomb and not only would the world lose this *magnifique* example of baroque art, but our embassy would be gone as well. We dare not risk it. Not in the Italy of today."

"But don't you see," Freya insisted, "that this is the perfect time to 'risk' it? You know the plans. Ambassador Whittiker came up with this fantastic idea of exhibiting three of the greatest documents of liberty in the world, to celebrate the fortieth anniversary of the Republic. Your government has already agreed to send a copy of the *Code Napoléon*, signed by the emperor himself. We are sending a copy of the Declaration of Independence written in Jefferson's own handwriting, and we are waiting to hear from the British on the Magna Carta."

Freya's voice dropped to its most seductive level. "Now, Mr. Ambassador, think about it. With those three documents here and all the prominent guests who'll attend the three-day event, this gallery will be swarming with police, probably even Interpol. Trust me, with all that activity, a terrorist couldn't get within a mile of the Palazzo Farnese. This gallery will be safe, and so will your embassy." She softened her argument with a smile. Pointing upward to the sleeping shepherd, she joked, "With all that excitement, even Endymion might wake up."

Even with all her persuasive arguments, the

French ambassador still looked uncertain. Then Freya remembered one of Ambassador Whittiker's favorite sayings: "When in doubt, you can always rely on Maromme's ego."

She sighed, pretending regret. "Well, I suppose I can understand your reluctance. When Ambassador Whittiker suggested this celebration, I immediately thought of holding the festivities in this magnificent gallery. I was hoping to convince you, but I see I've failed."

She glanced at him out of the corners of her eyes and sighed again. "It's just so unfortunate that neither the United States nor the British own anything to compare with this, but I'm sure we'll find somewhere suitable for the ceremonies."

With one last lingering glance at the reclining Venus and her lover, Anchises, she reluctantly turned to go.

She was halfway across the gallery when Ambassador Maromme's voice stopped her. "Mademoiselle Davidson, wait, *s'il vous plaît.*"

Freya concealed the tiny smile of triumph as she turned back toward him.

The French ambassador spread his arms as if to embrace the gallery. "How can I deny that you are right? Neither the British nor you Americans possess anything to rival this. I can see that it is our French duty to help our less fortunate allies. Plus," he said, preening proudly, "as you said, it will honor our Italian friends to let them see again with their own eyes one of their greatest baroque masterpieces, which, unfortunately for them, they had to sell to us."

An hour later, after the usual harrowing ride through Rome's congested streets, Freya arrived back at the American chancellery, the official residence of the American ambassador. Her blue eyes sparkled with excitement as she rushed through her office and past her assistant, Emilio's, desk without stopping. After knocking, she pushed open the door to Ambassador Marshall Whittiker's private office.

When he saw her radiant smile, he clapped his hands. "You don't need to say a word. You've finally convinced Ambassador Maromme to let us use the Palazzo Farnese's gallery for the exhibit."

"How did you know?" Freya asked, surprised.

"I can see it in your smile. Now tell me how you did it?"

Before she could answer, Emilio, who'd followed her into the ambassador's office, commented, "When closing deals in Rome, it helps that our beauty here has hair the color of spun silver and eyes so blue that they rival the Tyrrhenian Sea."

"I assure you that it was my persuasive arguments that convinced Ambassador Maromme, not the color of my hair or eyes."

Before Emilio could say anything else, she turned back to the ambassador and explained, "At first he was cool to the idea of honoring the anniversary of the Italian Republic. That's probably because he didn't think of it himself, but during the meeting today I changed his mind."

"But exactly how did you do it? I know how paranoid the French are. They've had that gallery virtually sealed for years."

"I just turned that argument around by pointing out to him that security will be extremely tight during the three-day period."

The ambassador looked skeptical. "You mean, that's all it took to convince him?"

Freya chuckled. "That plus, as you've repeatedly told me, you can always rely on Ambassador Maromme's ego. I think he couldn't resist reminding everyone that the French—not the Italians, the British, or us Americans—own that baroque fresco."

Marshall laughed. "I can just imagine old Maromme's reaction. I'll bet he puffed up his chest and vowed that it was France's duty to share it with the world."

"You do know Ambassador Maromme pretty well, don't you?" she said with a laugh. "Those were almost his exact words."

Marshall lifted his empty coffee cup to her in a toast. "To the best social secretary I've ever had. If you keep pulling off diplomatic coups like this, we may have to change jobs."

Freya looked at the gray-haired man with affection. "There's no chance of that."

"Anyway, you're to be congratulated for coming up with the idea of using the Palazzo Farnese gallery in the first place."

"It was partly selfish," Freya confessed. "When Emilio and I were tossing around ideas on where to hold the festivities, I thought of that ceiling.

I've been dying to see it ever since I came to Rome."

She glanced at her assistant. "By the way, have we heard from the British yet? Have they agreed to send a copy of the Magna Carta? That's the one detail I don't have nailed down."

"While you were gone, the British embassy called. They'll agree if men from Scotland Yard can accompany the document to guard it."

"We're going to have more policemen than diplomats at this festival," Marshall muttered.

She turned to leave, then stopped. "Oh, one last thing. Ambassador Maromme said his social secretary has returned to Paris on a pregnancy leave, and he's afraid the replacement won't be able to handle all the details. Since this whole event was originally your plan, he suggested that I handle most of the arrangements."

Marshall nodded. "Why not? You're the best in Rome. But I'd better warn you, you're going to be busy. The anniversary celebration is in one month, and in addition, when I was talking to our man at the State Department today, he said to expect a group of visiting congressmen. Don't ask me why, but they've suddenly discovered a desperate need to study the Italian wine industry. They'll be here Saturday, so you'd better plan some sort of party."

Marshall picked up a sheet of paper and handed it to her. "Here's a list of who's coming from the States."

Back in Freya's office, Emilio scowled at the list. "Don't your politicians have anything better

15

to do than to pester us? It seems like every week we entertain a different group."

"It's called travel at taxpayer's expense. Unfortunately it's a well-established practice of our elected officials," Freya answered, pulling out a thick book filled with the names and addresses of prominent members of Italian society. She handed it to Emilio. "You start going through this to find anyone connected with the wine industry. Meanwhile I'll make some calls and see what American bigwigs are in Rome. Since that party's in six days, I want to have a tentative guest list on the ambassador's desk tomorrow morning."

"Tomorrow morning," Emilio grumbled. "I thought I might coax you into going out to dinner with me tonight. I've found the most charming Venetian-style *trattoria*. Say you'll come. *Prego*. You know that American expression, 'All work and no play.'"

Freya glanced at Emilio, and a frown creased her forehead. He was an excellent assistant, but his aura of arrogant machismo left her cold. She had no interest in getting involved with him. On the other hand, since they had to work together, she didn't want to offend him. Instead of turning him down directly, she merely shrugged and said, "I'm afraid that tonight, that's just the way it has to be. I'll call Conrad and ask him to fix us dinner so we can eat here."

Late the next afternoon, Freya was addressing the last of the invitations when Emilio returned

16

from an errand. As he entered the office he waved a newspaper.

"You're famous. You made page one."

Freya frowned. "What are you talking about? I haven't done anything to make a splash in the newspaper."

Emilio read aloud, quoting the French ambassador. "It was at the persuasive urging of Freya Davidson, social secretary to the American ambassador, Marshall Whittiker, that France has generously agreed to open the famous Palazzo Farnese gallery in our embassy for this great celebration of Italian independence and republican liberty."

Freya took the paper from Emilio and quickly scanned the article. "I wonder why he mentioned my name. The rest of the interview makes it sound like this whole idea was Ambassador Maromme's. He doesn't even mention Ambassador Whittiker again."

"He just wants a—what do you Americans call it?—oh, yes, a scapegoat, in case someone tosses in a couple of Molotov cocktails for a surprise."

"He doesn't need to worry. Security's going to be so tight, even a cricket couldn't get in without an invitation."

She finished the address on the last envelope with a flourish. "And speaking of invitations, I want you to take these out and mail them. They're for the party Saturday night honoring our visiting congressmen. Then, why don't you call it a day? We've got a lot to do tomorrow."

Emilio grinned knowingly at her. "Are you let-

17

ting me off early because you've got a *caldois-simo* date tonight? I'd like to meet the man that can make you say yes. I've sure had no luck! How about taking pity on me?"

Freya ignored his question. "I don't have a date, hot or otherwise. What I do have is a meeting with the chef to discuss the menu for the buffet Saturday night, and I don't need you for that."

Emilio's mouth hardened. As he turned to leave, she heard him mutter, "So you don't need me! *Dio dolce*, you will!"

For an instant after the door slammed, she wondered what he'd meant, then pushed the question out of her mind as she gathered up the list of menu ideas she'd jotted down.

Freya not only worked in the chancellery, she also lived there, and Saturday evening, she entered the main ballroom early to check on the buffet. She was leaning over a tureen full of steaming Bolognese sauce when Emilio entered the other side of the room.

He let out a low whistle when he saw the way her seafoam-green silk gown clung to every curve. "You are *molto bella*. Could it be the celibate life you've been leading that's keeping you in such wonderful shape?"

Freya lifted the lid off the pesto sauce and sampled Conrad, the chef's, handiwork. "What keeps me in shape is the exercises I do every morning. At my boarding school in Cortina I had two gymnastic specialities, floor exercise and—"

18

"I wouldn't mind exercising on the floor with you."

"— and the balance beam," Freya continued, as if he hadn't even spoken. "I also studied karate, and if you don't want a demonstration you'd better go check to see how soon the pasta will be ready. The guests should be arriving in less than fifteen minutes."

She was sampling the shrimp-and-artichoke sauce when Ambassador Marshall Whittiker entered to check over the arrangements she'd made. There was a small frown as he glanced over the buffet table. "Don't we usually start these dinners with some antipasto?"

"Usually, but this time I tried something different. We're serving a spaghetti bacchanal with homemade pasta, plain plus *verde* and *rosa,* topped with your choice of sauces." She waved her hand over the loaded table. "Conrad fixed everything from pescatora to sauce marinara. Add crisp Italian bread and *gelato di fragola* for dessert, and you have a feast worthy of Bacchus, himself."

Ambassador Whittiker licked his lips in anticipation. "I don't suppose you added my favorite homemade strawberry ice cream, did you?"

"I always give strawberry ice cream to anyone who's kind enough to make me his social secretary in one of the most glamorous cities in the world."

"Not kind enough, Freya," the ambassador corrected. "Smart enough."

Then his smile faded. "You know how much I

care, and that makes me worry about you. Take the advice of someone who's seen a lot of summers. You need to find a young man. Rome is a city made for love. You shouldn't have to watch the moon rise over the Forum alone."

Before she could say anything, Emilio entered, pushing a cart loaded with the three kinds of pasta. Just as she finished arranging them on the warmers, the first guests arrived, and after that there was no time to think about what the ambassador had said.

But perhaps the ambassador's caring words had sharpened her feelings, for Freya sensed the stranger before she saw him. An eerie feeling that someone was watching her scampered up her spine as she checked the strawberry ice cream. She felt a warm flush as she sensed his glance sweeping over her bare back.

The center of the ballroom was filled with a swirl of dancers, yet when she turned around, Freya had no trouble finding him. He was leaning against the far wall. Her breath caught as their gazes entwined.

It was his eyes that held her mesmerized, like a moth before a very enticing flame. Eyes dark, like the most intimate hours of the night. Eyes mysterious, like the depth of a secluded forest pool. Eyes that reached out to her, touched her, held her immobile as he started across the ballroom toward her. Inevitable—the word sprang to her consciousness as he neared. For some unexplained reason she knew it was inevitable that he came; inevitable that she waited patiently for him to come to her.

He said nothing as he stopped, tantalizingly close. Their gazes tangled as he reached for her hand, then slowly brought it to his lips. The stranger brushed warm lips against her skin, then turned her hand over to place a kiss on the sensitive flesh of her wrist.

Shoulders, unusually broad for an Italian, strained the seams of his tuxedo. His skin was golden from the Mediterranean sun. Yet it was his mouth that captured her gaze when he finally raised his head. It was a mouth with a firm, strong upper lip, balanced by a full, sensual lower one.

His voice, when he finally spoke, held just enough of an Italian accent to add charm to its depth. "It is my rule to dance only with the most beautiful woman in the room." His eyes swept down over the plunging décolletage of her green gown, then back up once again, to hold her gaze enthralled as he murmured, "Shall we dance?"

The sound of his voice, the warmth of his touch still enclosing her hand, ignited a blaze within her that made it hard to breathe. Yet when he tugged gently on her hand to lead her onto the dance floor, she didn't move. Instead she quietly insisted, "I have a rule too. I don't dance with strangers."

"A wise precaution but unnecessary where I am concerned. My name is Count Antonio Raimondi, and after we dance, we won't be strangers."

Hearing his name and his title, Freya's eyes

21

narrowed, but when he tugged again, she didn't hesitate to move into his arms.

Before the romantic music mixed with his intoxicating presence could weave too powerful a spell, Freya commented, "Now I'm not dancing with a stranger, but you are."

His arm tightened around her waist, drawing her deeper into his embrace. "I know who you are. You're Freya Davidson, social secretary to Ambassador Whittiker."

Freya drew back a tiny bit so that she could look up into his eyes. "But how? I didn't—"

His deep chuckle stopped her. "When I see a woman who intrigues me, I don't hesitate to find out who she is."

Freya didn't know whether to be pleased or embarrassed by his forthright honesty. There were questions she knew she should ask, but she shocked herself by saying, "When I see a man who intrigues me, I want to know more about him. Do you live in Rome?"

Then she stammered, "Excuse me. I shouldn't have said that. I mean, I don't know what possessed me to . . ."

Dancers surrounded them, but when Antonio pulled her to a stop, she felt as if they were alone in the room. It was a wonderful, yet confusing, feeling. To hide the jumble of emotions warring within her, Freya refused to look up until strong fingers tilted her chin and she had no other choice.

The perplexed note she heard in his voice let her know that he was as confused as she over the magic sparking between them. "What possessed you, *cara mia,* is the same strange spell that lets me see no one else in the room besides you," he confessed. "I think you must be some kind of fairy princess to bewitch me so completely."

"And you must be a sorcerer," she whispered.

Antonio's dark head bent toward her, and Freya knew a kiss was but a heartbeat away when a loud drumroll shattered the moment. With great effort she turned toward the dais where Ambassador Whittiker was standing in front of a microphone and tried to focus on his words of greeting to the visiting congressmen.

As all the introductions rolled on, Freya stirred restlessly, waiting for the speeches to be over so that the music would begin again. Finally Ambassador Whittiker signaled the end of the formalities by urging everyone to get a glass of champagne—California champagne, he stressed—so they could toast the joint effort Italy and the United States had agreed to undertake to breed more disease-resistant grapes.

With a happy smile on her face Freya turned back toward Antonio. "I can think of better reasons to drink champagne, can't you, Count Raimon . . . ?"

The words died. Antonio wasn't there. Somehow he'd slipped away and she hadn't even known he'd gone. After scanning the ballroom Freya checked the courtyard. Then, with increasing unease, she walked from room to darkened room in the back part of the chancellery, flipping on lights, looking, but finding no one. Back in the

23

ballroom, she searched again, but without a word of good-bye, Antonio had vanished.

For an instant she wondered if she'd dreamed it all as she stood staring sightlessly at the dancers who once again filled the dance floor. Only Ambassador Whittiker's voice pulled her out of her abstracted musing.

"Freya, are you all right? You seem miles away."

She turned to see his concerned face. "No, I'm all right, just a little confused."

"Confused about what? Maybe about falling in love?" he said, teasing gently. "I saw you dancing with that dashing Italian. I didn't recognize him. Who was he?"

A deep frown furrowed Freya's forehead. The words came out slowly, almost reluctantly. "He claimed he was Count Antonio Raimondi."

On hearing the doubt in her voice, a matching frown appeared on the ambassador's brow. "What do you mean, 'claimed'?"

Freya chewed on her lower lip a moment as if deciding what to say, then admitted, "Ambassador Whittiker, I made out the guest list and the invitations. Sir, there was no Count Antonio Raimondi invited. I don't know how he got in, or why he came—and now he's disappeared."

CHAPTER TWO

Ambassador Marshall Whittiker glanced around to see if anyone could overhear their conversation. To be certain he lowered his voice. "Are you sure he's gone? Have you searched everywhere?"

He saw the truth in Freya's troubled eyes even before she answered, "Yes, I even checked with the marine guards. No one remembers letting him in. No one saw him leave. If I hadn't danced with him, I'd suspect he was a figment of my overactive imagination. He's just the type of glamorous Latin I'd dream up."

The ambassador's mouth tightened, and he didn't respond to her small joke. "The man slips into this building through all our tight security without an invitation, then disappears before he can be questioned. I don't like this, I don't like this at all!"

Freya, remembering the strangely wonderful magic she'd experienced in Antonio's arms, tried to reassure herself, "There has to be some logical explanation as to how he got in when his name wasn't on our list."

"Oh, I can think of a dozen explanations," the

ambassador snapped, tapping his foot impatiently. "Some fool congressman could have invited him while they were tramping through some vineyard, or maybe he's attached to the Italian embassy." A brief smile flickered as the older man glanced down at her. "Or maybe he saw your picture and couldn't resist a romantic meeting."

Then, as quickly as it came, the smile faded. "But with that reception coming up, we can't take any chances. Not when this part of the world is literally crawling with every kind of terrorist group. Radical left, radical right, anarchists, and everything in between, take your pick. They all mean trouble with a capital *T!*"

The orchestra began a new song, and as the music swirled around them Freya could almost feel Antonio touching her as he had while they danced. It couldn't have felt so good, so right, if he presented a danger. It just couldn't!

Bravely she lifted her chin. "I admit there is some mystery surrounding Antonio's appearance and disappearance, but unless my instincts are very wrong, I don't believe he's a terrorist." Her voice hardened. "He just can't be!"

The ambassador patted her shoulder with fatherly concern. "My dear, it wouldn't be the first time a woman was deceived by broad shoulders and a smoldering glance. I saw the two of you dancing, and it was obvious that you were completely besotted by the man. And to be honest, he looked equally entranced, but I repeat, we can't take any chances. Did he give you any clue about

26

his intentions while you were dancing? He must have said something to you."

Freya's smile softened at the memory. "Well, he did say that he had a rule that he would only dance with the most beautiful woman in the room."

That pulled a chuckle from the ambassador. "I have to admit that your count has excellent taste, but that still doesn't alter the fact that we need to get to the bottom of this. It may turn out to have an innocent explanation, but I want to be sure."

Marshall paused, obviously considering a plan. After a moment he instructed, "All right, here's how we're going to handle our mysterious intruder. I'm going to run a check on him through Interpol, and when you see him again, I want you to—"

"What do you mean, when I see him?" Freya asked, surprised at how appealing the thought was.

"You will." There was no doubt in the ambassador's voice as he continued, "From the look on his face when he held you, I'd say he's hooked and hooked good, which means he won't be able to stay away. When he contacts you, I want you to ah . . . ah use any means you have at your disposal to pump him for information. I want to know if Antonio Raimondi is his real name. I want to know what he's doing in Rome. I want to know how he slipped past the guards to get into the chancellery tonight, and I want to know why he disappeared so abruptly."

Freya raised an amused eyebrow. "Why, Ambassador Whittiker, do you mean that you want me to use my womanly wiles to worm the truth out of our mysterious stranger? I didn't think playing Mata Hari was part of my job."

The ambassador sputtered indignantly. "I'm not suggesting anything of the kind! You are the embassy's social secretary, and that makes you a diplomat, so use those 'diplomatic skills' to find out who and what this man is."

Then the twinkle returned to his eyes. "Besides what I've read, Mata Hari made a pretty lousy spy." He winked. "I expect you to do better with your first spying assignment."

"And just who are you supposed to be spying on, *mia bellezza?*" Emilio asked, speaking from over Marshall's shoulder.

"Emilio, I wish you'd stop sneaking up on people!" the ambassador said, fuming. "I swear, I've never known anyone who moved more like a cat."

The younger man grinned cockily. "It must be the soft Italian leather of my shoes. There is no finer in the world, as well you know. But back to business, as you Americans would say. Just who is my darling boss supposed to spy on? I'm her assistant. I, of course, want to help."

Marshall quickly responded, "You've seen too many James Bond movies. I was merely making a joke. Freya is a great social secretary, but that hardly qualifies her to be a secret agent. We'll leave that to the CIA."

Emilio refused to be distracted. "I thought possibly you were interested in that handsome man I saw dancing with Freya." A trace of jealousy roughened the edges of his voice as he probed. "I didn't recognize him, and I know most of Roman society. Who was he, anyway?"

The ambassador shrugged casually. "Just some guest who was lucky enough to share a dance with Freya."

She realized that the ambassador wasn't going to say any more until they were alone, so she instructed, "Emilio, we can talk about my dancing partners later. Right now, would you please go and see if Conrad is ready to bring out the cappuccino before the guests start leaving."

Emilio resented her dismissal, and he sarcastically tipped an imaginary hat in her direction. "Whatever you say, beautiful boss-lady. My goal is always to please you."

After he stomped off, Freya turned to Marshall. "Do you suspect Emilio, or are you being tight-lipped about this matter just on principle?"

"Just protecting the old image, my dear. When you've been in Rome as long as I have, you'll learn that the Italians love to talk. Your Count Raimondi could possibly turn out to be a threat to our plans, but on the other hand, if he's on the up-and-up, I don't want all of Rome knowing that we suspected him. Emilio is loyal. He's been at the embassy for ages. But for now we'll keep this just between you and me."

Marshall started to move away, then stopped. "I'll let you know when I hear anything from the Interpol computers in Paris. If he's a real count, I'm sure they'll have a record of it. You let me know if our mysterious count reappears in your life . . . as I have no doubt he will. Now I must go bid our 'treasured' guests good-bye."

Under his breath he muttered, "Congressmen! It'd sure make my life easier if they'd just stay in Washington!" Then he glanced back at Freya, and his smile warmed. "By the way, it's been a great party, Freya. The pasta buffet was a definite hit! We'll have to use that idea again."

Later that night Freya pushed open the French doors leading to the balcony of her second-story bedroom and walked out. The serenely glowing moon seemed to mock her confusion. As she leaned against the railing the memories of the evening bombarded her. In her thoughts she contrasted Emilio's arrogant swagger to Antonio's gentle seduction. She remembered the feeling of Antonio's touch as he held her in his arms. She relived the sense of inevitability as he'd crossed the floor to her, and it battled the ambassador's suspicions concerning his unexpected appearance.

Would she see him again? If she did, how could she spy on him? But how could she not? The reception at the Palazzo Farnese was the most important assignment she'd ever had, yet when she thought of Antonio and remembered the feel of his strong arms, she forgot about the assignment.

They'd only had a few brief moments together, yet in those moments he'd reached something within her no other man had. One moment she was alone and lonely, and then he'd appeared and suddenly she felt wanted. And that felt very good indeed.

Yet for all of Antonio's appeal to her senses, the doubts remained. Who was he? Why had he come? Why had he gone? Her fingers curled around the railing until they ached, and an unwanted thought intruded. Did he single her out for some reason other than his attraction to her?

Freya shook her head, trying to clear her thoughts. The ambassador was right. Many women, to their regret, had fallen for a pair of broad shoulders and a darkly sensual glance. She hadn't risen to her position by behaving like that kind of idiot! Her shoulders squared. If the mysterious Count Raimondi reappeared, she'd unravel his mystery. There was no question about that. Being a love sick fool was not her style!

Still, for all her resolve as she turned to go back into her bedroom, the warm night air caressed her bare shoulders, reminding her of the way Antonio's hand had felt as he'd pulled her into his arms. And as she lay down on the bed and closed her eyes, she didn't see the menacing glance of someone she couldn't trust. Instead she saw his dark eyes turn into hot pools of wanting when he looked at her, attracting her as easily as a flame enticed a helpless moth. Even as she tried to deny it she knew that he might burn her heart, but not ever seeing him again might leave a chill within her that nothing could thaw.

As she threw back the covers she muttered, "I was right, the man must be a sorcerer! One dance and I'm starting to talk to myself!"

As she fluffed up her pillow she wondered why she was getting so upset when she might never see him again.

For the remainder of the night her logic battled her senses. She'd doze, then wake with uncertainty. She'd doze, then wake with the memory of his touch. She'd doze, then wake, trembling in fear that some terrorist bomb might destroy not only Carracci's magnificent fresco and the three great documents she was responsible for bringing to Rome, but many lives as well. At last, exhausted, she let the doubts slip away and dreamed of broad shoulders, of tawny gold skin, of dark eyes seeing no one but her.

She slept no better the next night. By Monday morning her eyes felt heavy from the lost sleep. Emilio took one look and brought her a huge mug of steaming coffee. "It looks like you can use this. Obviously you didn't get much sleep over the weekend," he observed with a smile as she took her first sleepy sip. "And I know why. You should have listened to me and accepted my invitation. Then you wouldn't have lain awake for hours regretting your refusal. However, there's always tonight. What time do you want me to—"

She raised a hand to silence him. "Emilio, I don't have time for your nonsense. We have too much to do today. And first on the agenda is to call Ambassador Maromme and ask if we can see him this morning."

Emilio raised a surprised eyebrow. "We? You've never included me in any of your meetings with him before. Ah, but of course, no doubt

32

it was easier to use those *molto bella* eyes on him while you were alone."

Freya sighed impatiently. "As I recall, when we were deciding where to hold the reception, you said you'd never seen the Farnese gallery, so I want you at the meeting. You need to see the layout of the chamber so you can help me decide how the reception should be laid out."

"What about security? Do you want me to handle that? I'm tired of just planning menus and compiling invitation lists," he complained.

Freya laughed, "Poor Emilio. I'm sorry you're tired of menus, but I hardly think the social office is qualified to set up the security for something this important. Besides, Ambassador Whittiker told me he is assigning someone from the intelligence unit to coordinate that with the other embassies. While I'm calling Ambassador Maromme why don't you check with the social secretary over at the British embassy. Tell her we need their guest list as soon as possible."

She dismissed him with a wave of her hand, then reached for the telephone. After her successful call she sat staring out the window. She had endless things to do, but she just couldn't concentrate. When Emilio came back into the room thirty minutes later, she hadn't moved, she hadn't accomplished one thing, but she was smiling.

An hour later the chauffeur brought the embassy limousine around. When Emilio slid onto the leather seat next to her, he muttered, "I've worked for you Americans for years, but one thing I will never understand is your love affair with huge cars. The price of this one car alone could feed a lot of hungry people."

Freya shrugged. "We're on embassy business, so the ambassador thought we should arrive in style."

"You miss my point."

"No, I don't. It's just that I don't want to argue about it. Every culture has traits to dislike. For example, you're always reminding me of the greatness of Ancient Rome. Granted, there is much to be proud of, but they also enjoyed the gladiatorial games."

"You never let me win an argument," Emilio muttered. "But one day, *bellina mia*, I will win."

When the tour was finished and before Emilio could comment, the French ambassador suddenly snapped his fingers. *"Pardon*, Mademoiselle Davidson, the pictures you must see I left in my office. Your indulgence, *s'il vous plaît*. I won't keep you waiting but a moment."

As he left the gallery Freya's glance was once more drawn to the ceiling. She sighed with deep satisfaction. "I don't think I could ever tire of looking at great art. Isn't Carracci's masterpiece everything you thought?"

"Yes, it is. It's a brilliant recreation of something that once was real. The tragedy is that this world had to be recreated at all." His fist clenched. "Rome should have endured as it was."

Freya wondered about his strong reaction, but before she could pursue it, Ambassador

34

Maromme hurried back into the gallery, carrying a set of large photos.

"These came to me with the president's personal letter. This is how our great Code Napoléon shall be displayed," he explained, handing the set of pictures to her.

Freya glanced through them quickly, then handed them to Emilio. "That will be perfect. The Magna Carta and the Declaration of Independence are single pieces of parchment that makes them easy to frame and display, but the Code Napoléon is a book."

He took the pictures back from Emilio and pointed. "The first display will be a shadow box containing one of the original copies signed by the emperor himself. This will be followed by a series of framed letters to the commission he'd established to codify the law. Each is in the emperor's own hand and shows where he made changes in articles the commission proposed. You can see why we are concerned about security. These are as irreplaceable as the gallery itself."

Freya opened her mouth but was surprised when Emilio spoke first. "Don't worry, Ambassador, I will do everything in my power to make things go exactly as we intend."

Back at her office, she forced her thoughts to stay on her work, but it wasn't easy. Dusk was just falling as she strolled outside. For a moment she just stood, enjoying the beauty of the scarlet and hot-pink azaleas filling the front loggia. As she gazed at the flowers she felt a little of the tension caused by the day wash out of her. There had been a hundred phone calls, but none from the man who'd filled her dreams. Each time she jumped for the phone, eager to hear the special voice. Each time she was disappointed, and with each disappointment the tension wound tighter.

Freya shrugged her shoulders, trying to ease the tightness, but it didn't help. Finally she reached her hand across and began rubbing the knotted muscles. With a gasp she suddenly stopped when she felt a warm grasp close over hers.

"Here, let me do that," Antonio whispered in her ear. "Ever since Saturday night I've been dreaming of finding an excuse to touch you again."

His other hand went to her shoulder, and as his strong fingers began the gentle massage all her tension dissolved, leaving her so relaxed that she wanted nothing more than to lean back against his broad chest and close her eyes to savor every precious sensation his touch stirred within her.

Instead another more compelling urge won. Wanting to see his face again, as if to etch it more deeply into her memory, she twisted her head around and gazed at him over the shoulder he was rubbing. "After you disappeared the other night I was afraid I might never see you again."

The soothing warmth of his fingers, flowing through the thin silk of her blouse, reached deep within her, warming her, enticing her to forget everything but his touch. Before his sorcerer's magic could rob her of all thought, she forced out the questions she had to ask. "Why did you go without saying good-bye, Antonio?"

His fingers tensed, stopping their soothing motions. Slowly he turned her to face him. No smile greeted her.

"I had to go, Freya. I can't tell you why right now, but I want you to know that I didn't want to go. You must understand, I had no other choice. I had to leave you but I'm here now. Isn't that enough?"

Confused by his evasive answer, Freya shook her head. "I don't know. Can you blame me for being a little confused?"

"The confusion must be catching," Antonio admitted, his hands tightening a moment on her shoulders. "I didn't plan to see you today. I was afraid Saturday night was just a fantasy I'd created in my mind. I was afraid that if I saw you again, you'd tell me you hadn't felt the same magic. Yet without being aware of where I was driving, suddenly I found myself in front of the palazzo where we'd met. Then there you were, coming outside, and no power could have stopped me from coming to you, from touching you."

Freya reached a fingertip to smooth the furrows of concern from his forehead. "There was no reason to worry, Antonio."

His blazing smile warmed her heart. "Nothing like this has ever happened to me. The last two nights my dreams were filled with images of you. And today I had a dozen important things to do, yet I couldn't keep you from stealing into my

37

thoughts. I'm sure my boss thought my mind wasn't on the job—and he was right."

"I know the feeling," Freya admitted with a smile. "I have to confess that I've had more productive days at work myself. I couldn't stop thinking about our dance."

"Maybe we're both crazy," he said, laughing happily, "but if we are, it sure feels good!"

Her arms slipped around his waist as she murmured, "Hmmm, it sure does!"

Their happy laughter floated over the still loggia, and they were content for a moment just to look at each other, to hold each other. Finally Antonio sighed. "I think I could go on looking at you forever, but if I do that, we'll both starve." His fingers moved with the lightest caress over her shoulders. "Say you'll have dinner with me."

His words made her breathless, yet a nagging fear blunted her happiness. "If I say yes," she whispered, "do you promise that you won't disappear like you did Saturday?"

Antonio's eyes darkened to the deepest obsidian as he vowed, "The only way I'll leave you tonight is if you tell me to go. Please trust me. Leaving you the other night was one of the hardest things I've ever had to do in my life, and I couldn't bear to do it again." His grip tightened. "Trust me, Freya. I swear that's one promise I won't break."

The husky longing of his voice ignited the embers of desire within her. The ambassador's words of warning clamored to be heard, but Antonio's smile and the heat she saw burning in his eyes as he gazed down at her made her deaf to anything but her own wants. Somewhere deep inside she knew that it was stupid to feel for a man shrouded in a mystery, a man the ambassador suspected, a man who merely might be using her, but the doubts had no power to compete with the strange magic that sparked every time they touched.

"That's one promise I'm going to make you keep," she said, making a vow of her own as her blood warmed at the thought of the hours ahead.

Almost reluctantly Antonio removed his hands from her shoulders, and just as reluctantly Freya let her hands fall from his waist. Then, with a formal bow, he held out his arm. "Come, beautiful lady, let me show you my Rome."

As she slipped her arm through his, one of Ambassador Whittiker's orders popped into her head. She felt almost guilty as she followed instructions by asking, "Does that mean that Rome is your home?"

"In a way," he answered vaguely, leading her out of the columned courtyard.

"What kind of answer is that?" she demanded, pulling to a stop. "How can Rome be your home 'in a way'? It either is or it isn't."

Amusement glinted in his dark eyes as he glanced down at her. "You're as inquisitive as you are beautiful. It's an intriguing combination."

"You still haven't answered my question. Is Rome your home or not?"

"Ah, and persistent, too, I see. Well, to answer

your question, it is . . . and it isn't," he said teasingly, obviously enjoying dueling with her.

"Antonio, you've made me very curious, and I detest being curious. Remember, curiosity killed the cat."

As he laughed, his white teeth flashed against his golden skin. "Well, we can't have that, can we? I adore cats. In fact, you remind me of one." He ran his fingers through her long silvery hair. "Yes, in fact, you remind me of a Persian kitten, tiny and spirited and at the same time delightfully soft and silky."

"If you don't want to see this kitten's claws, tell me if Rome is your home," she insisted, refusing to be detoured by his compliments even though she secretly adored being compared to a kitten.

He winked. "Now, there's an interesting idea. I wouldn't mind being clawed by you at all, but only in the heat of passion."

"Antonio!"

"All right, my impatient beauty. Yes, I live in Rome. It's one of several places, scattered about the world, where I have property. But it's not home. No, my home is a secluded villa in the forest near Vicenza. That's a small city just north of Venice." His eyes grew misty. "I'd like to take you there someday. Somehow I know you would love it as much as I do."

The nostalgic thread in his voice, when he spoke of his home, tugged at her heart. If only she knew what he was feeling.

When she remained silent, he commented, "All right, now that you've discovered my deepest, darkest secret, tell me yours. Where is your home? And don't say in that building right behind us."

The happy sparkle died in her eyes. "It's as much of a home as I have."

"I mean, where are you from? I know you weren't born in Italy."

It was Freya's turn to become vague. "Where am I from? Interesting question. I'd guess you could say I'm from everywhere and nowhere."

Antonio chuckled. "Trying to be a lady of mystery, are you? But I see the game you're playing, little one. You're paying me back for my teasing, but I'm not going to fall for your game, because I have another plan in mind."

He rubbed his hands together, obviously delighted with the scheme developing in his mind. "I know a way to find the truth. First we shall stroll through the streets of Rome until you are sated with its beauty. Then I shall feed you a feast only the finest Italian chef could create as we sit overlooking the moonlit Forum. Naturally there'll be lots of Chianti to help wash down the pasta. By that time your will should be so weak, I should have no trouble getting you to answer any question I want."

Freya shook her head as she pretended to pout. "And I thought you Italians were supposed to be romantic. I'm crushed. You describe plans for a romantic evening, and what do you want to do when my will's been weakened with beauty, food, and wine? You want to ask me questions

41

about where I was born! How terribly disappointing!"

The heat blazing in his eyes reached out to her, firing an answering blaze within her. "My bewitching Freya, I promise that tonight you won't be disappointed in any way. Nor shall I. The hours till morning are deliciously long, and there will be many things to share and experience before the dawn's sun blesses our seven hills."

He stroked one fingertip down her cheek, then in the softest caress, the touch moved over her lips as a promise of delights to come. When he spoke, the words came out almost as if against his will. "I know there are questions I should ask. There is much I want to know about you. Yet when I look at you, when I touch you, everything flies from my mind except the need to hold you tighter, to lose myself in your fair beauty." His smile seemed touched with a hint of regret. "I confess, I need no feast or wine to weaken my will. You destroy all my resistance with only a glance."

"Do you want to resist me?" she murmured, enjoying the heat of desire she saw in his eyes.

"I don't think I could, even if I wanted to. And right now I don't want to," he paused, then added softly, "Even though perhaps I should."

His voice had dropped so low, she wasn't sure she heard him correctly, but she didn't want to spoil the moment by asking him to repeat what he'd said. At that moment mere words weren't important. What was important was knowing

that he felt the strange allure drawing them together as strongly as she did.

But some buried seed of caution refused to let
her admit that he held the same irresistible
power over her, a power that tempted her to
throw all caution into the Tiber. So her smile was
touched with a challenge. "I admit that dancing
with you was entrancing. I admit that you
haunted my dreams. And when I look into your
eyes, the rest of the world seems to fade away.
But with my Puritan blood I think it's going to
take the romantic evening you described before
all my resistance is gone."

The roguish spark in Antonio's eyes met her
challenge. "Puritan blood or no, tonight your resistance will melt like ice under the Italian sun, I
promise you. I will make it happen."

The spark cooled as his eyes grew serious.
"This is meant to be, Freya. You are my destiny,
and soon you will know it too."

"Maybe we met in another life," she murmured, hardly aware that she'd spoken.

"Maybe we loved in another life," he countered, twining his fingers through hers. "Maybe
that's how I know. Maybe that's how I knew the
instant I saw you."

His words left her breathless. Everything was
happening too fast. They'd only just met. They
hadn't even kissed. And there were too many
unanswered questions, too many doubts to let
him steal her heart so easily.

"Antonio, I don't know . . . I mean, before

43

Saturday night I didn't even know you. . . . It's just too—"

He laid a stilling finger against her lips. "Shhh, little one, I know I am rushing you, but I couldn't help letting you know how I feel."

Freya swallowed. "Antonio, please understand, I just have to be sure. I just can't—"

"I know," he said, interrupting her. "You can't feel without thinking. I don't blame you, it's in your blood. I've known a lot of Americans. You're all alike." He tapped her gently on the forehead. "You depend on your logic, while we Italians rely on our emotions. You let your mind speak instead of your heart. Things have to be proven to you that we Italians know by instinct, so I'll give you time." He smiled a smile that fluttered her heartbeat. "But time won't change what will be between us. That you shall see, my bewitching lady."

CHAPTER THREE

Freya gazed up at him, troubled by his words.
She wanted to believe him, she wanted to believe
in the wonderous destiny he described for them.
It would be so easy because she'd sensed the
same compelling magic at the moment she'd
turned and seen him across the crowded ballroom. Yet deep within her the doubts persisted.
She searched his dark eyes, trying to find answers, but the doubts wouldn't fade.

Maybe he was right. Maybe she was being too
analytical, but she just couldn't make herself believe that falling in love could be so simple. She
hardly knew him. And while he attracted her as
no other man had, that wasn't enough. She
wanted to see beyond his sensual mouth and his
hypnotic eyes, which made thinking almost impossible. No, for love to happen for her she had to
see his soul.

When she remained silent, Antonio drew her
gently against him. *"Cara mia,* let your heart
speak. Let yourself feel as I feel."

"Antonio, I don't think—"

"For tonight don't think."

She smiled a sad smile as she admitted, "I'm too American not to."

He sighed deeply, then, as gently as he'd drawn her to him, he let her go. Strong fingers lifted her chin so that she couldn't look away. "You are stubborn my little one, but that will only make the winning sweeter. And make no mistake, I shall win!"

She eased the tension crackling between them with a saucy toss of her head as she challenged him. "Perhaps. Perhaps not."

Antonio's roar of laughter startled the pigeons nesting above them in the ornately carved surrounding columns.

"Shame on you," she said, teasingly. "All those sweet birds were bedded down for the night, and you woke them up."

"Those birds are pigeons, and they are not sweet. They're messy." Suddenly he laughed again. "How in the world did we get from speculating about being lovers in a previous life to talking about pigeons? I do believe you are deliberately trying to distract me, but it won't work. The assault on your willpower shall begin on schedule, and that means a moonlit stroll through Rome on our way to dine by the Forum."

"You can't dine by the Forum," she said. "It's surrounded by streets."

Antonio threw up his hands in mock disgust. "You're determined not to let me win any points tonight, aren't you? All right, let me rephrase my plan of attack. We shall have a romantic moonlit stroll on our way to dine *overlooking* the Forum."

Freya linked her arm with his. "You said the winning would be sweeter if the victory wasn't too easy. I'm just trying to make the game more tantalizing."

Antonio's eyes glowed with an inner fire as he threatened, "I'd be careful if I were you, *cara mia*. If you make this evening any more 'tantalizing' than it already is, we'll skip the stroll in the moonlight, we'll skip the dinner, and I'll show you that I can break your will to resist me right here and now."

Freya felt her heart throb at his delicious warning, but she was enjoying the duel too much not to prolong it. "All right, I'll behave for now. I don't want to pick up tomorrow's newspaper and see the headline, AMERICAN SOCIAL SECRETARY CAUGHT IN SCANDALOUS POSE WITH NOTED ITALIAN COUNT. I'd probably be fired, and I'd have to leave Rome, and then"—she sighed deeply in pretended regret—"I never would get to dine overlooking the Forum."

Antonio grinned rakishly, but his eyes told her that he was speaking from the heart. "Since, my bewitching lady, the idea of you leaving Rome is a most unappealing thought, I shall delay the assault until we find a much more private place."

"I see just one more problem with your plan. The Forum's miles from here. By the time we stroll there, we'll be too tired to eat"—she tilted her head provocatively to one side—"or to do anything else."

"There you go again, being logical instead of romantic," he said, gently scolding, "but as much

47

as I hate to admit it, you do have a point." He snapped his fingers. "I know, we'll take our stroll after dinner, and I know just where I want to take you."

"Somewhere private?" she murmured.

Antonio raised one eyebrow and smiled slowly as his gaze raked over her face, then down to stroke over her figure like a caress. "Why don't you wait and see, my curious little kitten? As they say, the element of surprise is critical to the success of any attack. And this is one attack I want to be successful. So, before you can think of any more problems with my plan, let's go."

Freya's blue eyes widened with delight when he stopped beside a bright red Alfa Romeo. Running her hand across the sleek hood of the sports car, she sighed. "I've always loved these cars. I had one while I was in school in the north but had to sell it when I joined the embassy staff."

As Antonio helped her into the car he asked, "If you loved it, why did you sell it? That, my levelheaded American, is not very logical," he said, teasing.

When he was settled behind the wheel, she explained, "It's called 'Buy American.' Ambassador Whittiker didn't think it looked right for his social secretary to be seen zipping around Rome in an Italian sports car." She wrinkled up her nose in distaste. "The embassy supplies me with a Ford, which has about as much zip as a sleepy turtle!"

He reached a hand across and trailed his fingers through her long silvery hair. "If you're very, very good, I'll let you go zipping around in my sports car."

"Hmmmmm"—she ran her tongue suggestively over her lower lip—"I admit that's an enticing incentive!" Then her moist lips curved into a slow smile as she stepped into the driver's seat.

The restaurant he took her to was tucked away on the second floor of a medieval palazzo located on a low rise west of the Forum. As the waiter led them out onto the balcony where tables lit only by candlelight were scattered, Freya gasped. By then the moon was rising high, and its radiant light glittered over the ruins below like a shower of stars. She'd seen the sight many times, even toured it twice since she'd come to Rome, but she'd never had this view of its stark beauty.

"Julius Caesar, Marcus Antonius, Cicero," she whispered almost reverently. "I can almost see their ghosts walking there."

Antonio's arm slipped around her waist, and he hugged her against him. "I know. That's the feeling I always get when I come here." Then a touch of bitterness seared his voice. "The Forum, the ruins of Rome, you would think we Italians would have learned, but there are those who still wish to destroy our country, to make new ruins to add to the old."

Before she could say anything, he shook off the depressing thoughts. "Forget my ramblings, *cara mia.* Tonight I want nothing to blunt the happiness I feel when I look at you. Come, our table is ready."

When they were seated, and after the waiter

had filled their crystal wineglasses with the fragrant Chianti, Antonio lifted his in toast. "To our future."

Freya clinked her glass against his but did not take a sip. "Before we drink to the future, don't you think we should discuss the present? I don't even know what you do for a living. For all I know, you might be an international jewel thief after my Great-aunt Emma's pearls."

He lifted his eyebrow speculatively. "All this beauty and pearls too. The lady has everything! Are they very valuable?"

"Only for sentimental reasons." She tapped one finger against the rim of her wineglass. "You're evading my questions again. Does an Italian count live on inherited money, or do you have to work for a living like the rest of us mere mortals?"

He smiled that secretive smile of his, which made her wonder what was really going on in his head. "I inherited some money. Now, shall we order or shall we let the chef decide what food is best for the weakening of a beautiful woman's will?"

"Do you know you are an exasperating man?" she demanded, realizing that he hadn't really told her anything about himself.

He winked. "So I've been told."

Before she could respond, Antonio raised his voice and called over the waiter to order.

While he and the waiter engaged in a long debate, obviously trying to plan a perfect dinner, Freya leaned back in her chair and gazed out over the ruins of the Forum. Antonio was right. The beauty of Rome did sate her senses. The city enchanted her. As Marshall had said, it was a city made for lovers. At the thought she felt her skin warm, and her gaze was drawn back to Antonio.

A city made for love. A man obviously made for love. Would she have any power to resist such a powerful combination? Did she even want to resist what she knew he would soon offer? She remembered his words of desire, and she couldn't still her response. To be in his arms, to feel the texture of his golden flesh beneath her fingertips, to submit to his most intimate caress, to love the hours of the night away—just the thought sent a bolt of longing to the innermost part of her, and she trembled.

"*Cara mia*, what is wrong?" Antonio asked with concern as his hand reached out to close protectively over hers. "The night is warm, yet you shiver. Did you see the ghosts of our past walking again?"

Freya forced a smile. "It must be your forceful nature that makes me tremble."

Antonio's gaze searched hers, then he smiled. It was a smile of a man who knows that he has triumphed. "You are not a very good liar, little one. Even in the flickering light of the candle I can see the truth shining in those gorgeous blue eyes of yours. At this moment you are letting your heart rule your head. You are remembering my words and realizing that they are true."

How could he read her thoughts so easily? It was as if he could look into her soul and see the fire burning there, a fire lit by his presence. Freya wasn't sure she liked that or not, for it left her too vulnerable for comfort.

"I'm right, am I not?" he insisted, his fingers tightening about hers.

Her laugh was shaky as she struggled for control. "Perhaps. Perhaps not."

She was saved from any further probing by the arrival of the first course, and she was glad for the interruption. When the waiter placed the steaming plate of crepes swimming in a creamy shrimp sauce, Freya shoved the doubts away and concentrated on enjoying each moment as it came.

As she speared one of the tiny bay shrimp she licked her lips. "Maybe you are a mind reader, Antonio. At least when it comes to things I like to eat," she added quickly when she saw the sparks flare in his eyes. "This is my favorite appetizer."

"I'm glad you're pleased, but I have to admit that this wasn't my first choice. I wanted to feed you oysters, lots and lots of oysters, but unfortunately they weren't on the menu tonight."

"I can't imagine why you'd want me to eat oysters," she said while silently admitting to herself that no aphrodisiac could be as stimulating as the way his smile glittered in the candlelight. "They're disgusting, slimy things."

He grinned. "It was their other 'properties' I was thinking about. After all, knowing how stubborn you are, I need all the help I can get to make this evening end as I wish . . . as you wish it to end also, even if you refuse to admit it."

It alarmed her how just the thought of what he

suggested jumbled her heartbeat and fired her blood. No man had ever held such power over her senses. It was wonderously frightening. To cover her confusion she retreated back to a discussion of the moonlit ruins before them.

Slowly her heartbeat slowed as they talked of Rome's past instead of the hours that lay ahead.

When the spaghetti carbonara arrived, Antonio twirled the long strands of pasta around his fork. As he savored the first bite he commented, "When I was in America, I never could get used to your idea that the pasta was the entrée. Here it is but the prelude for what will come."

She cocked her head as she looked at him, surprised that he'd never mentioned being in America before. "Did you just come to the States as a tourist?"

He hesitated, as if thinking how to answer, then admitted, "No, the visit was connected with my work."

"I thought you said you lived off inherited money?"

"Correction. I said I inherited some money, not that I lived off it."

"You're being vague again," she protested, and continued, undaunted. "Just where did you visit in America and what did you do when you got there?"

"That's easy." He grinned. "I went to Washington, D.C., and when I got there, I studied."

"You mean you were an exchange student?"

"Not exactly."

"Where did you study? At Georgetown University?" she asked, determined to slash through the aura of mystery with which he was surrounding himself.

Antonio smiled, equally as determined not to let her succeed. "No, not at Georgetown. I suppose you might say I studied at a sort of private school."

Freya took a fortifying sip of Chianti to keep from losing her temper. "You were not *exactly* an exchange student! It was *sort of* a private school! Won't you ever make a direct statement?"

"Of course I will, *cara mia*. Here is a direct statement. The veal scaloppine has arrived. The lemon butter sauce the chef creates here for his veal is memorable! I hope you'll enjoy it as much as I do, because I want this evening to be a night you'll never forget.

He was right, the sauce was exquisite, but what filled her thoughts as the veal disappeared and the chocolate mousse arrived was his evasive answers. Was he just playing a game, or was there a reason for his evasiveness? All of her instincts screamed that the ambassador was wrong to distrust him, but instincts weren't proof. Also, something Emilio had said surfaced and brought a frown. He wasn't the only one who knew most of the important people in Rome. She'd been there three years. Why hadn't her path crossed with Antonio's before?

She leaned her elbow on the table and studied him as he finished the last of his mousse with obvious relish. When he glanced up and noticed her inspection, he asked, "Someone once told me that I was a fascinating man, but you seem absolutely rapt. Does that mean your willpower is already gone and I've won the assault even without the moonlight stroll?"

"Not exactly," she said teasingly, mimicking one of his favorite phrases. "I was just wondering why we've never met before. I've arranged a lot of parties, and since Americans always seem to be impressed with titles, Count Antonio, surely you'd have been on one of the embassy's guest lists before if—"

"If I'd been in Rome, which I haven't," he said, finishing her sentence.

"Will I get a direct answer if I ask where you've been?" Freya asked.

"You can try." He smiled, making no promise.

"All right, where have you been these last three years I've been in Rome?"

His teeth flashed in the candlelight. "Obviously not where I should have been, or I wouldn't have just met you. Think of it, three years of my life wasted. Three years of not holding you, of not kissing you." He paused as his voice dropped to a more intimate level. "Three years of not making love to you."

As he spoke, she realized that the past had been as lonely for her. The days were filled with work she enjoyed, often the evenings were filled with parties, and yet she ended each night alone. She looked at him and spoke the truth. "It's been a long three years. Where have you been?"

She half expected him to say "Here and there" or "Everywhere and nowhere." Instead he

55

fooled her by answering, "For the last three years I've done a lot of traveling through the Middle East, Asia, and South America, but when I wasn't living out of suitcases, I was in Paris. I only returned to Rome the day of your embassy party."

Warning bells should have pealed in her head, but instead she sighed. "I wish you'd returned sooner."

"So do I," he murmured, his hand clenching. "I want to curse the fate that brought you to Rome at the time it sent me away. Yet how can I do that when that same fate has finally brought you to me? As I said, the waiting will only make our time together sweeter. And now I do believe that I've waited long enough!"

When he turned to signal the waiter for the check, Freya felt a shiver snake through her. She'd never met a man who made her feel as sensually responsive as Antonio did. He made no attempt to hide his desire. And with only words he had awakened an answering flame within her. If his words alone held such power, what would his kiss do? The thought thrilled. The thought disturbed.

After he'd tossed a thick pad of lire on the tray, he looked back at her and frowned. His hand quickly reached across the table to enclose hers. "Little one, what is the matter?" he asked, his voice deep with concern. "Your eyes were soft and smiling but a moment ago. Now I see a storm within them. Have I said something or done something wrong?"

She wondered if she should let him see the

doubt in her heart. Finally the words came out hesitantly. "I guess I was wondering how much of a Don Juan you are. Does only the conquest have meaning to you, or is there any future beyond tonight?"

She desperately wanted words of reassurance. Instead he shoved his chair back and stood up. "Come, little one," he said, never letting go of her hand, "it's time for our stroll in the moonlight. I have something I want to show you and something I want to ask you."

She should have said no. She should have called a cab and rushed back to the safety of the chancellery, but what she did was leave her hand nestled snuggly in his and rise to stand beside him. At that instant, as they gazed at each other, nothing seemed more important than being together, than strolling through Rome, than letting all questions drift away on the warm evening breeze. As he'd begged, she let her heart speak instead of her head . . . and it felt wonderful.

It didn't matter where they were going. She was completely content, maybe for one of the few times in her life, and it was because she was beside him. Finally Antonio's steps slowed as they neared one last corner. "*Cara mia*, we are here."

Freya blinked, as if slowly waking. She looked around at the anonymous buildings, each boasting of a different business. "We're where? This could be a corner in Brooklyn, except that the buildings are older."

His hand deserted hers but only so that his arm

57

would be free to slip around her waist. As he drew her to him he murmured, "Don't you know where we are? Don't you know what's around the next corner?"

Silently she shook her head, too bemused by his presence, by the promise of the evening, of the tantalizing possibilities of the future, to notice much of anything.

His arm tightened around her waist. "You asked if there was a future for us. Let me show it to you."

When they rounded the corner, Freya's step faltered as she whispered, "Have you read my mind again, Antonio? How did you know that the Trevi Fountain is one of my favorite spots in all of Rome?"

He turned her in his arms until she had to look at him. "I didn't know, *cara mia,* but it means so much to me, I wanted to share it with you."

Neither spoke as they gazed at the spectacular fountain. She'd been here often, taking official visitors to see the most famous fountain in Rome, yet tonight everything seemed different. With Antonio at her side every sense sprang to life. Her eyes saw details about the figure of Neptune and his ornate shell chariot she'd never noticed before. The horses plunging and bucking in front of him as the Tritons tried to control them seemed more lively and realistic. Even the gurgle of the water cascading over the carved rocks into the traquil pool below was a sound she knew she'd never forget.

Finally she felt Antonio press something into

the palm of her hand. When she glanced down, she saw that it was a gold coin.

"You know the legend. Throw it in, then if you ever leave either Rome—or me—you shall have to return."

"But, Antonio," she said, protesting, and noticing how the gold shone richly in the moonlight, "this is too valuable a coin to throw away. Don't you have a lira?"

"You're not throwing it away. You're making an offering to the spirits of the fountain, to Neptune, to Rome, to our future. The gold will make the magic of this place just that much stronger."

She knew it was foolish to believe in magic or legends. No doubt thousands of people had thrown their coins into the Trevi Fountain and never returned to Rome at all. Still, suddenly the thought of the symbolic gesture seemed very appealing.

She glanced down at the gold coin gleaming in her palm, then looked back up at Antonio. "Are you sure you want me to use this?"

"*Si, cara mia,* I do. But we must do this properly so we don't offend the spirits. I want them very much on our side! So turn around, hold the coin in your right hand, and toss it over your shoulder."

As the gold coin splashed into the water he took her into his arms.

CHAPTER FOUR

For a long moment Antonio gazed down at her. Desire was turning his eyes into dark, glowing pools, yet he made no move to possess her. When he spoke, his voice was husky. "I didn't think it was possible, Freya, for you to be any more beautiful than that first instant I saw you, but I was wrong. This is how I shall always remember you, with the moonlight turning your hair to silver and your eyes smoky with longing as you wait for my kiss."

There were other people around, tourists and strolling lovers, but for Freya, at that moment, only the sound of Antonio's voice had any meaning. Somewhere deep inside a warning tried to sound, but again it was her heart that spoke, not her mind, as she wound her arms about his powerful neck, then snuggled closer against him. "I'm tired of waiting, too, Antonio," she whispered, urging his mouth down to possess hers.

The spirits of the Trevi Fountain must have been pleased with her gift of gold because they turned their first kiss into the most magically wonderful kiss of her life. Warm, firm, his lips moved slowly over hers, evoking every possible sensation.

The kiss spun on and on, each touch drawing her closer to him, each touch caressing away a bit more of her will. With endless patience Antonio stoked the fire within her, until she was the first to press herself hungrily against him, letting her lips part and running her tongue over the warm valley guarding the moist intimacy of his mouth. Beneath her breasts she felt his chest expand in a satisfied sigh as he offered what she begged for.

Freya felt almost dizzy when he reluctantly let the kiss slip away. For delightfully long moments he just held her tightly against him while he struggled for control.

"I knew I should have . . ." Roughened by the passion of their kiss, he had to clear his throat before beginning again. "I knew I should have waited to kiss you in a more private place."

Without his lips fogging her senses, sanity returned. "Maybe it was better this way," she whispered. "Being swept away by the moment sounds romantic, but it could lead to regrets in the morning."

He shook his head, trying to understand her doubts. "I could never regret a second spent with you, *cara mia!* And in your soul you feel the same about me, even if that stubborn will of yours won't let you admit it yet."

With a sigh, not of passion but of regret, he eased her away from him. "I have an idea. Let's take a bottle of champagne and climb to the top of the Palatine Hill, where Rome first became a

61

city, and watch the sun rise. At night it's a place of mystery, of history, and"—he paused as his eyes sparkled mischievously—"of many secluded places where lovers can be alone."

The thought intoxicated her far more than any champagne; still she hesitated, wanting desperately to be with him, to feel the power of his complete possession, yet sensing that it was too soon.

"I have an idea too," she countered quickly, before she could change her mind. "How about a cappuccino at a small café I know near the Spanish Steps?" She licked her lips at the delicious memory. "They serve a Cappuccino Royale with huge scoops of whipped cream that I can't resist."

He turned so that his broad back blocked anyone else's view. "So you can resist me but not whipped cream? I'll have to remember that, little one."

He drew one fingertip across her lips, then before she could stop him, he unbuttoned the first button of her silk blouse so that his caress could move down to trace suggestively over the warm valley between her breasts. "I love whipped cream, too—and not just in Cappuccino Royale. But for now I shall give you your wish. I'll collect my wish . . . later."

Hand in hand they turned away from the Trevi Fountain, but at the corner Freya couldn't resist one last look at the place that had blessed their first kiss. As she glanced back at the figure of

Neptune standing in the moonlight, it almost seemed as if the god smiled in approval.

Even before they could see it, they could hear the activity taking place up and down the Spanish Steps. The noise of the flower vendors shouting to attract customers vied with artists hawking their paintings and food vendors selling from their carts.

Antonio pulled her to a stop. "Are you sure you want to spend what time we have left among that noisy rabble? I know you love whipped cream but—"

Her understanding smile stopped him. "You don't need to ask. I agree," she commented, knowing exactly what he was thinking. "The café would be so noisy, we could hardly talk."

"Let alone do anything else," he quipped, grinning.

Freya ignored his suggestion as she made one of her own. "Instead of cappuccino, why don't we walk by the Tiber and watch the boats sail by?"

Antonio squeezed her hand. "I like the way the lady thinks."

As they turned toward the river he observed, "Sometimes, like now, I almost hate Rome."

His statement surprised her. "Why? It's an enchanting city, full of history and art."

"It's also full of people! Kissing you, holding your hand makes me think how much more perfect this evening would be at my villa." He stopped walking and closed his eyes. "If we were at my home, we could dismiss the servants, drink all the cappuccino we wanted by the fireplace,

63

and never be disturbed." His eyes opened slowly, and he seemed far away. "I really love it there. The villa has been in my family for generations. It's part of my blood."

Then, as if embarrassed by the intensity of what he'd said, Antonio forced a playful chuckle. "I should have thought of my villa sooner. It's so isolated that I could have kidnapped you and locked you away there so you would never leave me, and I could have saved that gold coin. I wouldn't have needed Trevi Fountain at all."

"Don't be too sure. I'm pretty skilled at escaping. After all, aren't we going to take a walk by the very public Tiber River instead of sipping champagne in some secluded spot on the Palatine?"

Antonio's arm swept around her waist, and he pulled her to him. "As you Americans say, you may have won round one, but the final bell hasn't rung yet. Something tells me that we have several more rounds to go, and I don't intend to lose. You'll be on the mat before you know it, and that's one knock-down you won't mind at all."

His hard swift kiss sealed his vow. And like the boxer in his allusion, when he released her, her knees felt too wobbly to fight much longer. If she wasn't careful, round two would be his—and very soon!

For an hour they meandered along the winding river. Finally Antonio stopped. Gently he kissed her hair, not in passion but almost in thanks. "I can't tell you what this evening has meant to me. I've never met a woman like you.

I've never felt about a woman as I do about you. You captivate my senses until even in my dreams I see nothing but your face." His touch lifted up her face. "And it's such a beautiful face. Freya if only you . . ."

Unexpectedly his eyes opened in surprise as he repeated, "Freya! Of course, how could I have been so stupid! Freya, the Norse goddess of love and beauty. No wonder you can so easily bewitch me!"

At the mention of the connection to her name Freya's eyes misted with pain. As he rambled on, comparing the Norse goddess to Venus and Aphrodite, she looked away and gazed out over the river, not wanting him to see the sad tears.

She hardly heard him as he continued, "The only reason I know about the Norse Freya is that when I was younger, I loved reading about mythology. How in the world did you ever get such an unusual name? Although I must admit it fits you."

Suddenly his arms tightened around her as he realized that something was wrong. Strong fingers forced her to look at him. "Freya, what's wrong? There are tears in your eyes. What did I say to make you cry?"

She swallowed back a sob. "It's nothing you said. It's the past that hurts. I thought I was over it, but what you said just brought back all the bad memories."

"I don't understand. What memories?"

His hands tightened painfully around her upper arms. "Memories of another man?" he demanded, a surprising amount of jealousy scarring his voice.

After she nodded, she flinched, hearing his explosive Italian oath.

"It's not what you think, Antonio. I do have sad memories of a man, but that man wasn't my lover. He was my father."

Relaxing, Antonio threw a comforting arm across her shoulders. "Come, little one. We've kissed; now I think it's time we talk," he suggested, leading her to a bench beside the river. "If either of us had had any sense, we'd have done that in the first place. There's much we must learn about each other."

Freya's painful story slowly came out as she explained, "My father's a brilliant man. He's one of the best petroleum engineers in the world, and he has an uncanny knack for finding offshore oil reserves. That's why Sweden hired him when the first strikes started being made in the North Sea."

Antonio's glance wondered over her long silvery hair, hair so typically found in Scandinavia. "I think I'm beginning to understand."

She paused to brush back a tear. "It's an old story. A lonely engineer meets a beautiful Swedish girl named Ingrid, and they marry. Only this story didn't have a happy ending. My mother died the day I was born."

Antonio gathered her against him as he tried to absorb some of her pain. He rocked her almost as if she were a child as she haltingly continued. "He named me Freya, for the goddess of love, in remembrance of the love and beauty he lost that day. I've seen pictures of my mother. I could be her twin." Hot tears dampened the front of his shirt as she swore, "He doesn't hate me, I know he doesn't! It's just that seeing me brings back too many painful memories, and he still can't handle that."

"So he doesn't see you very often," Antonio guessed.

"He used his traveling as an excuse to put me in one expensive boarding school after another. The last was in Cortina." A trace of bitterness added a sharp edge to her voice. "Why should I complain? I always had more clothes than I could wear and more money than I could spend. I suppose his guilt saw to that. I studied in the finest schools all over the world. I learned to speak five languages." Fresh tears scalded her eyes as she confessed. "He gave me everything I needed, everything but the one thing I really wanted—a loving, secure home."

Antonio held her snug in his arms until the last racking shudder left her body. Finally, when she lifted her head from the comforting cushion of his shoulder and looked up at him, her eyes were bright with tears.

There was a note of desperation in her voice as she begged, "Antonio, I don't want to be alone tonight. I want to spend the hours till the dawn with you. I want to be wanted. Hold me, make love to me. Please."

She wound her arms around his neck, urgently pressed herself deeper into his embrace, and then reached up to place a hungry kiss against his lips. For an instant his lips softened under hers, then hardened again. When he didn't respond as she expected, she drew away, puzzled.

She saw the desire blazing in his eyes, but it was a fire he had firmly under control as he sadly shook his head. "*Cara mia,* I want that more than anything you can imagine. You know I planned for this evening to end with you in my arms. Right now I want you so much, I ache with the longing. I want to kiss you. I want to slowly strip each piece of clothing from your body to discover all of your beauty. I want you to lie beneath me, to feel the power of my possession. Yet I don't think tonight is the time to make you mine."

"But, Antonio—"

"No, little one, I must be strong for both of us. You're too hurt, too vulnerable right now. If I made love to you tonight, I'd be taking advantage of that weakness. And for you the morning might bring regrets."

She tried to muster up a smile. "I thought you wanted me weak?"

"I do. I want you weak from desire. I want you weak from my kisses, from my caresses. I want you so weak with wanting me that you can deny me nothing. But when you come to my bed, I want you completely free to return every precious ounce of passion I will pour into your body! And right now I don't think you could give me that."

"Don't you understand, Antonio? Tonight I want to be weak for once in my life. I'm tired of being alone. I'm tired of not being wanted. Antonio, I'm not using you to forget."

She read the doubt in his eyes. She also read the desire. One hand slipped from behind his neck so she could touch his face. As she stroked his lips she whispered, "Tonight you begged me to feel and not to think. That's what I'm doing. All my life I've thought, and all it has brought me is pain. Now I want to feel. I want to belong to you. I sensed that need the first instant I saw you. I knew for sure when you kissed me by the Trevi Fountain."

"But in the morning . . ."

"There will be no regrets in the morning." She took a deep breath, knowing, as she did so, the effect it would have on him as her breasts brushed against his chest.

For a moment he closed his eyes. When they opened again, she saw that the fire had turned into an inferno. *"Cara mia,* I'm trying to be strong, but I only have much strength."

Like the lightest of kisses, her fingertip stroked over his lips as their gazes locked, caressed, spoke without words. Finally his lips parted, and her finger slipped into his mouth.

"Be weak, Antonio," she whispered as the velvety rasp of his tongue tasted her flesh. "You said the only way you'd leave me tonight is if I asked you to. Have you changed your mind?" she asked, gently drawing her hand away.

"God help me, but I haven't! I know I should say no—but I can't. Freya, the Norse goddess of beauty and love, tonight I almost believe in rein-

69

carnation." Strong, warm hands cupped her face as he murmured, "No wonder you can conquer years of training with only a touch."

His kiss was full of passion, yet gentle. The power of his kiss drugged her senses, and as his tongue slipped between her open lips and his hand found her breast through the sheer silk of her blouse, she knew dawn would come too soon.

The warmth of his mouth, the moist thrust of his tongue, the scandalous feelings evoked when hers rose to meet his in the ancient dance of desire left her as weak as he could have wished. The kiss spun on and on, heating blood already hot, stoking desire already kindled into a blaze. In the dark, with the silent Tiber as their only witness, hands sought and found spots of pleasure bringing the ache of need into a raging force. She arched against him, needing to feel more, much more, of him. His response needed no words as she felt the power of his desire rise hard and full to thrust against her.

Reaching for his face again, as if to memorize every rugged plane, she let her fingertips trace over his lightly bruised lips. "Don't ask me to stop, Antonio."

He sighed deeply as his gaze raked over her lips, then fell to where the sheer silk brushed provocatively over her breasts. "I know I should . . . but I can't. When I look at you, all I can do is wish that there was some magical way to get back to my car. It's blocks away."

"Blocks away," she echoed regretfully as she looked around at the lights flickering around them on the river walk, then at the tour boats passing. "How depressing! I wish it weren't so public here."

Antonio rose, grabbing her hand. "Tonight you belong only to me. Come, little one," he said, pulling her to her feet, "let's find some place private."

The night air surrounded them like a cloak as they started back for his car, but it was not that warmth that stirred the fires in their blood. Both knew what lay ahead, so each touch of a hand, each casual brush of a thigh stirred senses already tingling with anticipation. And yet they didn't hurry, knowing that there were hours and hours left to love.

When they reached his car Antonio gently pulled her into his arms. His kiss was soft, tentative, telling her that if she had any doubts, he wouldn't use passion to force her into his bed. But at the moment Freya had no doubts.

He'd begged her to feel and not to think. In his arms she had no other choice. It didn't matter about his mysterious disappearance. It didn't matter about his evasive answers. It didn't matter that sanity might return with dawn's light. Nothing mattered but belonging to him, if even for just this one night. Her lips willingly opening beneath his told him her answer.

Antonio's arm, thrown across her shoulders, snuggled her against him as he started the car. At a stoplight the temptation proved too much, and Freya couldn't resist the urge to taste his kiss again. As the touch of her hand guided his mouth toward her, he whispered, "I thought you were going to behave."

"I am. I'm behaving just as I want," she murmured a second before their lips touched.

Only the angrily blowing horn of the car behind them shattered the spell. "Impatient Italian drivers! Can't they see we're busy?" she said, drawing away.

"That's not the only thing Italians are impatient about." Antonio grinned, sliding his hand up the sheer silk of her hose until it rested, warmly, suggestively, high on her thigh.

"Hmmm, I see what you mean." An inspiration popped into Freya's head, and she smiled. "I wonder just how impatient you can get!" she said, a moment before she started blowing in his ear.

Cara mia, I'm going to wreck the car if you . . . ahhhh." His scolding sank into a satisfied sigh as her tongue darted into the sensitive interior of his ear. Then, when she gently took the lobe between her teeth, he swerved the car to the curb and yanked on the brake.

He dragged her almost roughly into his arms. He demanded. She gave. Neither was breathing evenly when the pleasure of lips caressing lips, of tongue touching tongue, finally eased the throbbing passion just enough so that he could start the car again.

As they drove, Freya closed her eyes, content for the moment to rest her head on his shoulder. When she felt the car slow and heard the splashing water, she looked up. Her eyes widened when she saw Bernini's Fountain of the Four Rivers in the middle of the Piazza Navona. "You don't mean you live here? This is my favorite piazza in all of Rome."

"It seemed the perfect place. For years I've traveled all over the world, so why not live near the fountain honoring the rivers of the world."

"I love Bernini's work." She smiled happily. "His nude of—"

Antonio grabbed her and silenced her words with a kiss. When he finally pulled away, he vowed, "It's not Bernini's nude I'm interested in right now. I don't want to wait any longer to make you belong to me—body and soul."

Without another word he led her into the baroque palazzo located behind the fountain. His home was filled with antiques that normally would have fascinated Freya, but not this night. She saw nothing but Antonio as he reluctantly let go of her hand and turned toward the fireplace.

"Isn't it a little warm for a fire?" she asked as he struck a match.

His smile slowly widened as his gaze swept over her. "Everything about tonight must be perfect. I want the windows open so we can hear the fountain when I make you mine. I want the firelight dancing over your body as I lay you before it."

As he walked toward her she saw the sparks in his eyes begin to burn hotter than the flame in the fireplace. "As I said, I've waited a lifetime for you. Freya, I'm tired of waiting."

Somewhere deep inside she knew that the fantasy must end . . . but not yet. No man had kindled the passion in her soul like Antonio had in a few short hours. In his arms she felt wanted and desired, and that was too good to resist.

No hesitation stopped her from coming to him. And no blush touched her cheeks as Antonio's hands reached for her. One button, two buttons, then the rest fell to his questing fingers. When he stripped the blouse from her body, she heard his quick intake of breath as he gazed at the swell of her breasts straining the sheer lace beneath.

One hand gently cupped her breasts as his other reached to release them from their lacy prison. When he bent to kiss them, Freya gasped, closing her eyes at the pleasure. Her hands sought the front of his shirt, ruthlessly shoving buttons aside, needing to feel his flesh with the same urgency that possessed him.

Beneath the open windows, the water splashing over rocks Bernini had carved added music to their desire. Like that water, endlessly flowing, their passion had the power to suspend time. Neither knew how long they kissed. Neither were really aware how bit by bit each piece of clothing fell to the floor. And then there was no clothing left between them.

He couldn't hide the need to possess her. He didn't try as he came proudly to her; then, lifting her high in his arms, he carried her to the plush Oriental rug, glowing like a jewel before the fire. After laying her down he rocked back on his heels a moment, content just to look at her. In the flickering light of the fire his skin darkened to the richest gold. The same light turned her fair hair to silver. Gold and silver, linked from the beginning through all of time. How could she question that destiny? She didn't, as she opened her arms and legs to welcome him.

The kisses, the caresses, the fire he had built within her needed no further stoking to make her burn with desire. At his first powerful touch her body rose to meet him, welcoming his possession, needing him to satisfy the raging passions that turned her already heated blood into a red-hot inferno.

Freya had never experienced the sensations he created with each touch . . . and she wanted more! Again and again he drove deep into her willing body, bringing shudders of pleasure, yet they were not enough as every part of her soul wanted him to plunge deeper, to force her to belong to him as she had to no other man.

No matter what he did, she couldn't get enough. His kiss plundered her parted lips, yet she wanted more. His caress found her bare breast, yet only the touch could not satisfy her hunger. Like the smoke rising from the fireplace, their passion spiraled upward, each climax only a prelude to the next pleasure—a pleasure even more delicious than the one before. Needing to feel all of his power, Freya wrapped her legs around Antonio's waist, trapping him, forcing him to move deeper within her. And still it didn't end.

Each gave pleasure to the other, and each took pleasure, as if both wanted to prolong the magical moment forever. Time and time again he filled her body, relieving the throbbing ache within her for a moment, only to pull away until her moans and the clutching of her hands and legs brought him back to her. As if to bind her to him forever, he refused to let it end as his kisses, his intimate caresses, brought such exquisite pleasure that finally she lay beneath him, helpless to the needs he'd fired within her. Then to repay the beauty he gave, her kisses would possess him, her hands would seek, caressing him until a new surge of desire burned within him and he was as helpless as she.

CHAPTER FIVE

Freya's fantasy didn't end with the first pale rays of the dawn. After a night of exquisite loving during which Antonio had repeatedly taken her to magical realms of passion, they had fallen asleep in front of the now smoldering fire. With his shoulder for her pillow, Antonio cradled her in his arms, keeping her safe and secure against what little that was left of the night.

At the first rosy rays of the new day she stirred, then, with the sigh of a completely sated woman, let sleep reclaim her again. Dreams, often her enemy, came easily and beautifully. She was in a field full of flowers; the sun warmed her face as the softest of breezes caressed her skin. She stretched like a contented kitten as the breeze, scented with a hint of roses, touched her lips, her throat, before moving lightly over her bare breasts.

It was that sensation that penetrated through her curtain of sleep. A foggy question tried to form. What was she doing in a field of flowers with no blouse on? How delightfully decadent, she decided groggily as the breeze moved over the sensitive flesh of her stomach, then lower.

She couldn't keep a moan from escaping as the delicious pleasure flowed on and on.

Her lips parted as her breathing raced, and that was too much for Antonio as he bent to claim the warm intimacy of her mouth. Automatically Freya's arms wound around his neck, trapping his body against hers. When the kiss finally ended, her eyes fluttered open to find him holding one long-stemmed red rose.

"I dreamed you were the warm breeze, caressing my skin," she whispered, settling herself more intimately beneath him.

"And I dreamed I was a Roman god who'd found some wild wood nymph sleeping in the forest. I couldn't resist taking what was offered."

Freya smiled as her glance stole over his darkly romantic features. His black hair easily could have been tossed by the winds of Olympus; his broad brow spoke of wisdom; his dark eyes commanded with the power equal to any Jupiter could have possessed; and his sensuous mouth reminded her that the gods made love more often than they hurled thunderbolts.

She sighed contentedly. "It's not hard to visualize you as a Roman god." She stirred beneath him, reveling in the renewed proof of his desire. "And what mortal woman could resist the temptation to make a god hers, if only for a night?"

Over the next two hours Antonio proved again and again that Jupiter wasn't the only Roman who knew how to please a woman. And they actually bettered the gods in one way. As far as Freya knew, there was no jealous Juno to be wary of as time after time they rested only long enough to let desire build to a new delicious level before sampling the sweet nectar again. Finally, as the sun appeared full and hot over the Piazza Navona, sleep reached to snare both of them one last time.

But the interlude in time didn't last. Finally reality intruded in the shrill blast of the telephone, which shattered the paradise they'd found on the floor in front of his fireplace.

Reluctantly Antonio rolled away from her to grab the offending receiver.

His mumbled *"Si,* I understand. *Si,* I know what is important. *Si,* I will be there in an hour!" finally roused her, pulling her awake to the reality of another workday.

She hadn't been at her desk more than an hour when Emilio entered carrying three dozen red roses.

She looked up in surprise. "I see you've decided on a new tactic. But I'm still not sure that courting me with flowers will get me to—"

"These aren't from me," he snapped, dropping them on her desk as if they burned his hands. "They were just delivered, and it takes little imagination to guess who they're from. I knew that man was trouble the first moment I saw him dancing with you."

Freya ignored him as she picked up the card. On it Antonio had written, "To my favorite wood nymph in memory of the hours I shall never forget."

She lifted the bundle of roses from the tissue and sniffed the sweet fragrance. It brought back all the wondrous sensations of the dawn and of Antonio. Without being aware of it, her blue eyes softened in a dreamy trance.

Emilio stared at her in disgust. "I could make you look like that if you'd let me. But when I offer, all I get is another 'not tonight' or 'I don't think so.' " As the door slammed, she heard him mutter, *Dio mio,* someday I promise you won't say no to anything I demand!"

Freya frowned a moment, but then shrugged thoughts of Emilio away. She had too much to do to worry about him.

After putting the roses into a crystal vase she started sketching out some rough ideas for the three-day reception. When an intriguing idea occurred to her, she reached for the telephone to see if the ambassador was free. Before she had time to dial his number, he knocked on her door.

When Marshall entered and saw the flowers, he chuckled. "What's all this? It looks like someone bought out the flower shop."

Freya smiled. "They're from my mysterious count."

"I assume my speculation was correct and he tried to see you," the ambassador asked, studying her reaction closely.

Before she could answer, he smiled. "No, you don't even need to tell me. One look at the stars blazing in your eyes and I can see that he has."

When he saw her blush, he chuckled again. "Ah, to be young again!" Then he grew more serious. "Just how did this meeting occur? Was it an accident or did he plan it, do you think?"

Freya cleared her throat uneasily, wishing that he hadn't voiced his suspicions. "Antonio was waiting for me when I left last night." She paused, hating to go on, but she did. "He said he hadn't planned to see me but couldn't resist. He just sort of found himself in front of the chancellery, and then I came out and he was waiting for me." Freya noticed Ambassador Whittiker's frown and hurried to explain. "Antonio is just a man who finds me attractive, that's all."

The ambassador's frown eased, and he smiled. "I have to admit that that's not the first time that's happened around here. He has excellent taste."

Freya blushed as she said insistently, "You see, there's nothing dangerous or mysterious about Antonio."

"There's not?" Emilio demanded, barging into her office in time to hear Freya's last statement. "That's not what Interpol has to say. Sir, the answer to your inquiry just arrived," he explained, handing a folded piece of paper to the ambassador. "They've just finished decoding it."

Ambassador Whittiker frowned as he read the message, then he glanced skeptically at Freya. "According to this, your count Antonio Raimondi doesn't exist. Interpol has no record of him. According to their records, he's never been issued a passport. He's never paid taxes." Freya's heart started to pound as he continued reading from the report. "He's never owned a car, and their

81

sources in Vicenza have never heard of him or the Raimondi family."

"That's crazy! They have to be wrong," Freya argued desperately. "He told me he'd traveled a lot. He said in the last three years he'd been in the Middle East, Asia, and South America. In fact, he said he'd just returned from France. He must have a passport! And I rode in his car. He has a red Alfa Romeo."

"The Middle East, Asia, and South America are all areas where you find a lot of terrorist activity. Maybe he was there, learning to build better bombs." Emilio commented with a mild sneer in his voice. "You won't accept a dinner date with me, but you are more than willing to receive flowers from a terrorist."

"Now let's not jump to conclusions," the ambassador said trying to soothe Freya. "There could be a perfectly innocent explanation." He turned to her. "What did he say he did for a living? Maybe that would explain all the travel."

She shifted uneasily, remembering all of Antonio's vague answers. "He didn't exactly say what he did."

"Did you ask him?"

Freya nodded unhappily. "Yes, I tried to follow your instructions, but it wasn't easy to get information from him. We, ah . . . we had other things to discuss."

"I'll bet you did," Emilio agreed with a knowing smirk. "I saw how he looked at you. I saw how you looked at him. I'm surprised you did any 'talking' at all."

Freya ignored his innuendo as she protested. "Ambassador Whittiker, I refuse to believe that Antonio is involved in anything nefarious. My instincts tell me—"

"Do your instincts tell you why he's obviously using an assumed name?" Emilio observed, pointing to the paper in the ambassador's hand. "I can think of only one reason why he'd do that."

"You don't know that it's an assumed name," Freya argued, grasping at anything to explain the information Interpol had sent. "The computer might have made a mistake. Or maybe whoever called up the information misspelled his name. It wouldn't be the first time a mistake like that has happened."

"I don't like this. I don't like this at all!" Marshall said, repeating his earlier observation. "Interpol isn't the only agency that's been busy. One of our intelligence officers heard from one of his informers on the street that at least one group of terrorists is expressing a disturbing amount of interest in our plans."

He threw his hands in the air. "All I wanted to do was honor Italy, and by doing so, it looks like we've set up the perfect target. Hell, it appeals to everybody, from the religious fanatics, who want to make an example by destroying one of Italy's most famous pieces of 'decadent' art, to the extreme left, who'd just love to blow up the documents of republican liberty."

"And don't forget the anarchists, who are against all forms of government," Emilio offered with a smile. "Sometimes, especially around tax time, I think they're right. No government. No taxes. That would certainly make my life easier."

"Emilio, this is a serious matter," Marshall said, rebuking him. "Maybe I'm being overly cautious, but I'm concerned. Call it gut instinct, but I think something's afoot, as Sherlock Holmes would say."

Almost unwillingly he glanced back at Freya. "There are just too many coincidences. This count—if he *is* a count—appears from nowhere, obviously to seek you out at the embassy party, then he makes sure you meet again. There may be a perfectly logical explanation for all of that. It's obvious that he's attracted to you, but we have to be sure there's nothing else behind it. You possess a lot of valuable information, especially about our plans for this Italian celebration. Did he pump you for information about anything in particular?"

Suddenly Freya brightened. "I just realized that we didn't talk about my job here or the Farnese gallery being opened to display the documents at all. That should prove that he's not after some inside information!"

"Maybe. Maybe not," Emilio argued. "The reception is still several weeks off. He's got time to pull the information out of you piece by piece, so slowly that you don't even realize all you're telling him. Once someone figures out how to penetrate the security and when to time the explosion so that it will do the most damage, it doesn't take long to build a bomb."

The words of protest were on her lips, but before she could open her mouth, Emilio turned to the ambassador. "Sir, is it possible that Interpol refused to send us any information on this man because they already have him under investigation and don't want you Americans to interfere?"

"It's possible," the ambassador said slowly. "It's also possible that . . ."

He paused, scratching his chin a moment, and then, when he finished the sentence, Freya was sure he'd changed what he was going to say "It's also possible that the CIA might have some information for us on Freya's mysterious count." He turned abruptly. "I think I'll put a call through to our friends in Washington."

Emilio's sharp glance made her uneasy as he commented, "With plans as important as we have, I'm getting more and more curious about this mysterious stranger myself. So, if you don't mind, sir, I'd like to ask some questions on my own. Interpol isn't the only one with sources."

The ambassador nodded. "I don't suppose that could do any harm." His eyes returned to Freya, and he wasn't smiling. "Before I call Washington, I need to speak to Freya alone."

After Emilio had left, the ambassador looked at Freya a long moment before speaking. When he did, it was with obvious reluctance. "My dear, you know I care deeply for you. You are like the daughter I never had, so what I'm going to ask is not easy for me."

Freya twisted her hands nervously in her lap. "Go ahead, ask away. I'm ready. Do you want my resignation?"

Marshall blinked, hardly believing her words, then hurriedly reassured her. "Certainly not! I don't know what I would do without you. It is going to take some time to get that information back from the CIA. Anyway, I'm afraid I'll have to ask you to keep seeing your mysterious count if the opportunity arises. If he is deliberately keeping an eye on you for some reason, then we need a spy in our corner to watch him."

Warm memories of the night before flowed easily in her mind. "It will be my pleasure," she answered in total honesty.

The ambassador didn't smile. "My dear, I want you to be careful. For all we know, this man might be dangerous."

"Isn't that why we had everyone on staff take those classes in karate?" she teased. "I can protect myself."

"There are other types of danger than just physical danger. I've never seen the look that was in your eyes this morning. I don't want you falling for some dashing Italian who's only out for a fling with a beautiful woman, or worse."

She smiled fondly at him. It was nice to know that she had someone in her life to give her "fatherly" advice. Too bad it wasn't her real father. But she pushed that thought from her head. "I'll be careful, I promise. As you pointed out, I hardly know the man. How could I be falling for him?"

But even as the words came out, memories of Antonio's eyes when he looked at her, the flash of his smile, the way his skin glowed golden in the firelight exploded in her mind, and she knew she'd lied. She was falling for him, falling harder and faster than for any man she'd even known. It should have frightened her, but strangely it didn't.

The ambassador rose to take his leave. "Just remember one thing, my dear, your first duty lies here," he said as he reached the door.

Abruptly, before she could say anything else, he turned and yanked open the door. When he did, Emilio almost fell into the room.

The ambassador's eyes hardened. "I don't like people who listen at doors!" he thundered.

"Sir, I would never do that. It's just that an emergency has arisen and I needed to talk to Freya."

With that information the steel in his back weakened. "Okay, if that's all it is, I will let you two handle the social emergency."

After the ambassador left, Freya turned to Emilio. "All right, what's the emergency that made it necessary for you to lurk outside my door?"

Sputtering, Emilio said, "You know I would only interrupt if it was an emergency, and this definitely is one. That crazy social secretary over at the British embassy has gone completely insane this time. She has decided, without consulting anyone, that the British embassy shall handle the food for all three days of the anniversary celebration." He paused as a fastidious shudder rippled through him. "And to honor Italy, they want to serve all Italian food. Can you imagine that very traditional British chef trying to fix Spaghetti alla Bolognese? No doubt it would come out like soggy Yorkshire pudding. It would be a deliberate insult to my country!"

Freya had indeed eaten at the British embassy, and Emilio was right. Letting that chef attempt Italian food would probably cause an international incident. Italy had been an ally for forty years. She'd hate to see that end over plates of overcooked pasta.

Reaching for the phone, she instructed, "I'll take care of Lady Redding-Holmes. You get on the phone to Washington. I want you to start collecting names of congressmen and cabinet officials who proudly claim Italian descent. I think the ambassador will agree that they should be invited for this festival."

There was a sudden glint in Emilio's eyes as he asked, "Are you sure you want to do that?"

"Why not?"

He started ticking off points on his finger. "Those irreplaceable documents will be there. A lot of high-ranking Italian governmental officials will be there, plus a number of diplomats. Isn't adding important American leaders to the event just increasing the temptation for someone to take action? Remember that tragic mess in Iran. These days, important Americans are favorite targets of most terrorist groups."

A frown of worry creased her forehead. "Maybe you're right, but I'm still going to invite them. To be honest, I don't think the temptation could get any greater. I almost wish that Ambassador Whittiker had decided to honor Italy with a nice safe parade instead of coming up with this brilliant, but undoubtedly dangerous, idea."

He shrugged, turning to leave "What's your American expression, 'It's their funeral'?"

Freya raised her voice. "Before you go, I have one thing to say. If you were listening at my door —don't! I'll tell you what you need to know."

Emilio swung back to look at her. "Before you dismiss me, I have one question. Why did the ambassador need to speak to you alone? That leads me to think that something is going on I don't know about."

Freya tapped her fingers impatiently on her desk. "I thought I just told you, I'll tell you what you need to know. Now please go. You have work to do, and I need to call Lady Redding-Holmes before their chef starts cooking the fettuccine."

After an exasperating thirty minutes on the phone with Lady Redding-Holmes, the two agreed to meet over tea at the British embassy to discuss the matter. A few hours later Freya walked out of the British embassy, victorious but exhausted.

She paused a moment on the steps to let her eyes adjust to the bright light of the late-afternoon sun. She didn't see Antonio waiting across the street, but he saw her.

Apparently he'd just come out of a tailor's shop when he'd spotted her. Freya shaded her eyes when he called to her, then smiled a welcome as he hurried across the street to join her.

As he neared, his happy smile told her that he was as delighted as she at the chance meeting.

When he reached her side, he vowed, "I knew fate was pleased we'd met. With millions of people in Rome the one woman I want to see more than anyone appears before my eyes."

He gazed down at her, and the passion she remembered so vividly from the dawn ignited again in his dark eyes. "The day's almost over. Do you have to go back to work?"

She hesitated, then let her feelings speak. "I should, but—"

"But you're not going to, are you?" He chuckled, knowing that he'd won. "Come on," he urged, tugging on her hand, "I know just where I want to take you."

"Where are we going?"

He winked. "Somewhere we won't be disturbed."

At that most appealing thought she gave up all resistance, and after phoning Emilio to tell him that she wouldn't be back in the office that day, she followed Antonio to his car. As she settled into the leather seat an unwelcome question from her discussion with the ambassador surfaced. She glanced at him out of the corner of her eye, hesitated, then forced herself to ask, "Is this your car, Antonio?"

There was a wary glint in his eyes as he turned to look at her. "What a strange question. Of course it's my car. Did you think I stole it?"

"No, but you might have borrowed it," she said reluctantly, remembering the disturbing report Interpol had sent.

He turned the key in the ignition. "It would

have to be a pretty good friend to loan out a car like this." He patted the dash as he pulled away from the curb. "No, this beauty is all mine. I needed a powerful car, so I decided I might as well buy one with some dash."

"Why do you need a powerful car?" she persisted, almost unwillingly. "Is it for your work?"

"Right now it's for taking the most beautiful woman I've ever met out for a surprise adventure." One hand left the steering wheel. As he reached across to stroke a fingertip over her lips he murmured, "It seems like a long time since this morning."

"I know," she agreed as she trapped his hand against her cheek. "I awoke to find you beside me with that rose. And even though I saw you, touched you, smelled the rose, it didn't seem quite real."

"I know what you mean. The beauty and love I discovered last night was like a perfect dream." He flashed a heartfelt smile at her.

Slowly she shook her head. "It sounds like we're both living in a fantasy world, and fantasies, no matter how beautiful, never last."

"Then we'll have to make reality as beautiful! And we'll do that starting this afternoon. I know just the perfect place."

CHAPTER SIX

As Antonio turned into the Piazza Navona where his apartment was located, vivid images of a fire, of golden skin, of his powerful possession raged in Freya's mind, and she felt her breathing quicken. Embarrassed by the intoxicating power of the memories heating her blood, she tried to joke the feelings away by teasing. "So this is your place of fantasy? Your apartment? But maybe you're right. Last night, as I recall, lying before the crackling fire, it was rather a bewitching place."

She opened the door and started to get out, but his hand stopped her. "You're too impatient, my bewitching lady. This isn't the place I have in mind to make fantasy and reality become one." He squeezed her hand. "You stay here. I need to run in and gather a few things from my apartment, then we'll be off."

Hating the thought of being parted from him even for a moment, she asked, "Can't I help?"

His eyes were serious as he gazed down at her. "You tempt me to forget my plans. You tempt me to take you in my arms right now and carry you to your bed before my fireplace. And if I let you come with me, that's exactly what would happen.

I would have no power to stop myself from taking you. Yet right now another fantasy is even more compelling, so wait by the fountain, my little one. I won't be long."

Together they walked hand in hand to Bernini's masterpiece. As she sank down on the stone wall surrounding the fountain, he pointed to one of the figures, whose head was shrouded in a cloak, and said teasingly, "While I'm gone, see if you can think of some interesting ways to convince the Nile River god to continue hiding his face. I hear the reason he's hiding is that he's easily shocked." Antonio winked. "So be creative. I'll be your willing victim for anything shocking you want to try."

When he left, Freya gazed at the nude, veiled figure Antonio had pointed out. She knew from her studies that Bernini had veiled the figure representing the Nile, because, during his age, the source of this great river was a mystery. But as she looked at it the figure took on a different symbolic meaning. Heavily muscled and nude, the figure evoked powerful images of Antonio, nude before the fireplace. With his arm outstretched, he evoked the memory of Antonio reaching for her, moments before his plunging possession completed his conquest.

Still, for all the wonderful memories the figure created in her mind, she couldn't tear her eyes away from the veil shrouding its face. Mysterious, unknown, that also was Antonio. Like the figure, she sensed that he was hiding something. Yet her instincts insisted that the feelings he stirred couldn't be so wonderful if the mystery had the power to hurt or destroy.

Suddenly her uneasy musing was interrupted when Antonio curled a possessive hand over her shoulder. When she turned to look at him and he saw no smile, he asked, "I leave you with smiles. I come back to find a frown. What's wrong?"

Slowly, hesitantly, some of her fears slipped out. "It's just that the Nile River god reminds me of you. You appear, you disappear, and I can't help but feel that you're hiding something from me, just like he is."

Almost angrily, Antonio dragged her to her feet. "Am I hiding how I feel about you?" he demanded. "Am I hiding how much I want you? I desperately need a clear head, yet since you've come into my life, bewitching all my thoughts, I can't think when I'm near you. I can only feel. I have no power but to let my instincts lead me where in my heart I know I must go."

Suddenly, as quickly as his anger had flared, it cooled, and he released his painful grip on her shoulders. "Little one, forgive me. It's just that I can't bear for you to have any doubts about what I know so clearly."

He smiled the smile that always smothered any doubts. "I promise if there is a mystery, it shall be solved with time. Remember, today is a day for fantasy, so put away your questions and just feel as I am feeling."

His fingers slowly stroked down her bare arms until he captured both her hands in his. "Please, bewitching lady, come with me. My surprise is ready."

How could she say no when every molecule within her begged her to say yes?

As she returned his smile, she admitted, "I never could resist a surprise!"

His rich laugh echoed across the Piazza Navona. "You'll see it soon, and I promise the wait will be worth it!"

"It had better be, because leaving your fireplace behind is something I'm finding very hard to do."

"Actually, in a way my fireplace inspired this idea," he added mysteriously. "So let's go. I am as impatient as you."

There seemed little to say as he drove north out of the city. She was satisfied just to be with him, to let him create a world of fantasy where she could forget the pressures of the upcoming reception, of all the decisions left to be made, of all the dangers that might—or might not—lay ahead.

Outside the city, the road began to climb, heading up into the surrounding hills. Antonio stretched an arm out to touch her shoulder. Tugging gently, he urged her to slide across the seat and cuddle next to him as she had the night before.

He glanced down at where her head nestled on his shoulder. "The last car I had had bucket seats. I'm sure glad this one doesn't. I love how you can slide right over and nestle your body close to me."

She raised a skeptical eyebrow as her gaze swept over his darkly compelling features. "Do you mean you've only just discovered this advantage? I would have thought it might have occurred to you before. That is, unless you've just escaped from a monastery."

He glanced at her, and his hand reached to stroke over her silvery hair. "You still don't understand, do you? I won't lie. There have been other women in my life."

"I'll bet *lots* of other women," she added, knowing it was true even before he admitted it.

His teeth flashed in a confident grin as he shrugged. "As I said, I won't lie. Yes, many women have shared my bed. I'm not a saint and have no wish to be one." Then his grin faded as his hand reached to touch her again, "But no woman has ever affected me as you do, Freya, goddess of love. You've crept into my heart, filling it until I can't even recall the name or face of any other woman I've known."

For an instant she saw the same confusion she felt dulling his eyes as he confessed, "I feel like my whole world's turned over. Nothing seems quite the same. I don't think it ever will be again." He glanced at her. "I wish I knew how you do this to me. I think you're dangerous."

Then, as suddenly as the cloud of doubt came, it lifted. "But," he said with a chuckle, "I've always loved danger. It makes life more interesting!"

"I think you're the one who's dangerous," she muttered. "Usually I'm very sensible but not with you. What sane woman would get into a car without even knowing where she's being taken?"

As he turned from the highway onto a narrow dirt road, he said, "You know where you're being taken. You're being taken to a place of fantasy."

For a second his hands tightened on the steering wheel as the car continued to climb. "Unfortunately reality will intrude soon enough. For tonight, at least, I want to pretend that there is no other world but the one I find in your arms." His dark eyes searched hers as he asked, "Can you give me that, *cara mia?*"

The desire caressing his words robbed her of any will to resist. She wanted this night as much as he. Like him, she wanted his embrace to become her world. She wanted to feel his hands strip the clothes from her body. She wanted to feel his caress heat her blood until, unable to stand the exquisite torment another instant, she'd beg to be taken again and again in every way, as she had the night before. She closed her eyes as her breathing pounded. Yes, more than anything, she wanted to lie beneath him and feel again his power drive her to the edge of sweet, passionate madness.

"*Cara mia,* answer me. Say you'll give me this night?" Antonio repeated.

Her eyes opened, and no shame jumbled her words as she confessed her weakness. "You know I want this as much as you. So for tonight, Antonio, I am yours. Ask anything." A hot blush seared her face as she confessed, "I'll deny you nothing."

"Nothing?" he whispered, his dark eyes beginning to glow with the thoughts her confession fired.

Somewhere deep inside she feared, like all fantasies, that this one must end, and if it must, she wanted all the memories of him she could possess to fill the empty nights that probably lay ahead, so she repeated, letting no doubt or shame stop the words, "For tonight ask what you will of me, Antonio. I will say no to nothing."

His fingers curled tightly around hers, and their eyes met a brief moment before he had to return his gaze to the narrow road curving ahead of them.

On either side of the road the gnarled branches of an ancient grove of olive trees shielded her view of what lay ahead, but she didn't care. Freya leaned her head back against his shoulder and closed her eyes, reveling in the warmth of his hand encircling hers. The heat flowing from him into her held such promise of the hours to come that she silently begged him to hurry.

Finally the bumping stopped, but before Freya could open her eyes to see where they were, Antonio gathered her into his arms. And as his kiss possessed her she willingly parted her lips to receive the thrust of his questing tongue. Long, delicious moments later, Antonio drew away. As he deserted her she tried to follow, but he gently pushed her back against the leather of the seat.

He traced loving fingers across her lips. "There'll be hours and hours for you to return my kiss. I promise you that. Right now I want you to promise something else."

Without thinking she whispered, "Anything."

"Anything? Hmmm, this evening is looking better and better!"

Embarrassed by the weakness she seemed to have no power to control, Freya straightened up in the seat. "I suppose you want me to promise to be good?" she teased, trying to lighten the intensity of the mood.

He grinned. "If you are, neither of us will have much fun. No, I want you to promise to sit here and wait while I get everything ready."

Freya looked around but could see nothing but olive trees. "We're in the middle of an olive grove. Is this what you call a place of fantasy? Besides, what's there to get ready?"

"You'll see." His smile flashed against his golden tan. "Now stay in the car. I'll come back to get you in a moment."

Freya watched him take a wicker basket from the trunk of the car. He pulled something white from it. As he looked at it, then at her, his eyes glittered like the blackest onyx. "I almost forgot. I want you to put this on while I'm gone," he requested, tossing it into her lap. "When I saw this in the store window, I couldn't resist."

Then he turned and walked away. Her eyes never left his broad back until he disappeared into the trees. "There he goes, disappearing again. He just has to be mysterious, doesn't he?" she muttered.

Then she relaxed. So far, all promises he'd made had brought her nothing but pleasure, pleasure like she'd never known before. She glanced down at the garment in her lap and smiled. She held it up, suspecting what it was before she even saw it. She was right. Of the sheerest silk, the one-shouldered gown was modeled on the togas worn by the Roman gods and goddesses.

Freya felt decidedly decadent as she slipped out of the car and started to undress. When the last garment fell to the ground, she spread her arms wide, as if embracing the day. To be outside, to be naked, to feel the late-afternoon breeze caress her bare skin were sensations she'd never experienced before. With no one to see her but the birds, she stretched, relishing the feel of the sun and the wind on her naked body. Then, almost reluctantly, she pulled on the gown Antonio had given her.

When she turned back, Antonio had reappeared. She gazed in his eyes and knew he'd seen her brief affair with the sun and the breeze. Without a word he held out his hand. Without a word she went willingly to him.

Silently, hand in hand, they walked through the grove of olive trees. Then, suddenly, the trees parted to let her see the clearing to which he was leading her.

Her eyes widened, hardly believing what she saw. Like something out of a beautiful dream, in the clearing there was a crystal pool reflecting the ruins of a small Roman temple. Spread beneath the boughs of laurel trees was a simple feast of crusty Italian bread, fruit, cheese, and a jug of wine. And on the blanket one scarlet rose waited for her.

"Oh, Antonio," she whispered. "I don't believe this is real."

His arm swept around her, and he pulled her hard against him. "It is real, and tonight it will belong to us. No one will disturb us."

"How can you be sure?" She gazed up at him, knowing from what she saw in his eyes, what she felt as her body moved against his, that soon the ground would be her bed. She shivered in anticipation. "I'd hate to be in the middle of some bacchanalian rite and have a busload of camera-toting tourists arrive."

"The only person who's going to see that enticing body of yours is me," he promised. His arm swept in a wide arc. "This land belongs to a friend of mine. When I told him I'd found the perfect wood nymph to share it with me, he said he'd see that we weren't disturbed."

His hand glided slowly down her body. His caress stopped a moment to savor the thrust of her nipple against his palm before continuing down to the curve of her hip. As he drew her even more intimately against him, he smiled. "You do remind me of a wood nymph, you know. No wonder the gods longed to possess them. You don't plan to run as Daphne did, do you?"

"No, I don't plan to run. I have no desire to be turned into a tree," she murmured, alluding to the myth. "Apollo was always my favorite among the gods. I always thought she was a fool to resist him."

Antonio's eyes blazed. When he spoke, his voice rasped with need. "I'd planned"—he paused to clear his throat—"I'd planned for us to eat and watch the sun set, then make love in the moonlight. I'd planned to slowly seduce you with the beauty of this place, with the food, the wine . . . then finally the rose."

He paused as if struggling for control, but he lost to desire, a desire that burned just as hotly within her. "But when I look at you, when I touch you, I can't wait. I want you, Freya. I want you now!"

She wound her arms around his neck. With long, sensuous strokes she rubbed her body up and down against his, letting him know that the same fire raged within her. He needed no words to understand her message.

With strong arms he lifted her high against his chest and carried her toward the blanket. The night before, his seduction had been deliriously slow, arousing her until she was helpless to resist, even if she'd wanted to. But now the need in both burned too hotly for that. The moment her back touched the blanket, his hands were on her, shoving the silk aside, desperately seeking the flesh beneath. And she worked as feverishly to find his.

Buttons flew from his shirt in her quest, but she knew that he didn't mind when she heard his sigh as her hands slipped beneath the fabric to twine in the dark hair curling across his chest. Hard muscles rippled beneath her fingertips, but the warmth of his chest wasn't enough, and her hands stroked lower, needing to find the source of pleasure that soon would be hers.

His sigh turned to a groan when she touched him, and he couldn't wait any longer. Instead of undressing her so that he could see her naked beneath him, his hands roughly shoved the silk up above her waist so that his fingers could explore the sweet, moist well that soon would be his.

Freya's eyes had been shut, but as he plunged his fingers into her they flew open to meet the passion burning in his. He felt her writhe under his stroking, begging the touch to go deeper. But even at that moment, when she knew that he must ache with need, he prolonged the desire. Touching her, teasing her, then retreating. Kissing her deeply, then pulling back. Rubbing his chest against hers, then taking the exquisite torment away, leaving only the evening breeze to caress her bare breasts.

Finally she couldn't endure not having him inside her a moment longer. Her hands, as eager as his had been, reached for his zipper. Her touch shattered the last of his patience. After kicking his garments away, Antonio came to her . . . and she was ready.

No more kisses, no more caresses, no more waiting, he took her where she lay. Their bodies entwined so perfectly together, it was as if each had been created especially for the other. Throbbing with hungry need, he filled her completely as she, in turn, wrapped around him like a wondrously tight silken glove.

His first powerful thrust into her body brought a ripple of release for both, but neither was satisfied as again and again the rhythm of their passion brought them to the realm where only sensation exists.

Over and over, refusing to let the pleasure end, her hips rose to meet him, accepting the delicious invasion of her body, wanting nothing more than for it to go on forever. With each stroke of pleasure the desire flamed hotter within her. Instead of satisfying, it only made her crave more, only made her want to give more. Wrapping her legs more tightly around Antonio, she urged him to roll over until he lay beneath her. His eyes, black with desire, met hers, and he smiled.

Then, rising up, feeling him thrust even deeper within her, Freya began to move above him, using her body to whirl the passion within him, until a low moan escaped his lips. As he watched her the black in his eyes, already hot, began to glow like burning coals, and his hands came up, brushing her long hair aside so he could capture her breasts. And then it was her turn as he rolled her taut nipples beneath his fingers, bringing a moan to her parted lips.

Slowly Freya's eyes closed, wanting only to feel. Instinctively her back arched, and she began to slide against him again, back and forth, needing to feel more of his hands on her flesh, needing to drive his possession even farther into her.

Fighting against letting the pleasure end, Antonio's hands tightened around her waist, trying

104

to slow the movements that were rapidly destroying any control. "Freya, I can't take much more if you—"

Quickly bending, her kiss silenced him. Through his parted lips her tongue sought and found his. Rhythm echoed rhythm as each new thrust of his body into her brought her tongue hard against his. Finally Antonio couldn't take any more. Rolling her beneath him again, the frenzy of desire built as hands touched and caressed, turning hot blood into fire, a fire that didn't end until a racking shudder captured both at the same beautiful instant.

The daylight faded into moonlight by the time Antonio finally lifted his head from the satiny pillow of her tousled hair. Slowly he bent and placed a gentle kiss against her sweet lips. It was a kiss of thanks for pleasure given, not a kiss of passion, and it brought tears to Freya's eyes.

As one tear slid down her cheek he brushed it tenderly away. "I want nothing but to fill your life with happiness, and yet I have made you cry. Ah, my bewitching Freya, what's wrong? Wasn't it as beautiful for you as it was for me?"

Her arms twined around his powerful neck. "Antonio, there can be tears of joy as well as sorrow."

His cocky grin returned. "I'm glad I pleased you."

She returned his smile. *"Pleased* is hardly an adequate word for what I felt."

Deep within her she felt him swell with renewed desire. His smile widened. "So you aren't satisfied with the word *pleased*. Well, I guess if that word's inadequate, we must try again and see if we can come up with a better description of your feelings."

She wiggled her hips provocatively beneath him. "I can't think of anything I'd like more."

Lying beneath him, she felt his power grow, and he possessed her time after time. As she rolled over in his arms until she was on top again, the moon rose high. The silvery light shone down to bless them, and it seemed to contain magical properties to arouse their passion yet one more time. Only when exhaustion claimed them did they finally sleep, still holding each other, still one.

Much later Freya's eyes slowly opened. The moon, already on its downward trip, shining through the leaves of the laurel tree, bathed the scene with a breathtaking silvery glow. Her arms still around him, Antonio's head rested heavy on her shoulder, yet she didn't mind the weight, for it reminded her of the wondrous hours just past.

As if wanting to store every memory, she turned her head to look around once more at the place of fantasy he'd brought her to. In the soft moonlight the columns of the ruined temple seemed almost new. Yet it was the pool that lured her. The sweeping branches of the huge laurel tree shaded most of the area, but through one bare patch the moon slipped down to be captured in the crystal waters of the pool. Glittering, beckoning, the reflected moon lured her to share its magical light.

In a way she was reluctant to leave him, yet bathing in that pool enticed her to desert the warmth of his arms. Easing herself slowly away, she heard him mumble a protest as his arms tightened for a moment, then sleep reclaimed him and he let her go.

All the illusions to fantasy seemed to seep into her soul as she cast off her gown, then slipped naked into the warm water. Never before had she swum in the nude, and somehow it made her feel like the wood nymph Antonio saw when he looked at her. The water flowed around her like a silken cloak as she paddled contentedly around. At the center of the pool, where the moon seemed to reside, she reached out a hand to capture it for herself, but the ripples the motion made let it slip away.

She sighed at the loss until Antonio's laugh shattered the mystical moment. She raised her head from the water and looked at him, standing tall, muscled, bronzed, and splendidly naked at the edge of the pool.

"You are in Italy, Freya. Not even the Norse goddess of love can capture the moon here. It belongs to our Diana."

He stepped into the water and started to wade toward her. "But if I cannot give you the moon, my bewitching lady, I can give you myself. Come and see how easy I'm prey to your powers."

The pool was small, and she had no desire to escape as he came toward her. They met in the middle where the moon blessed the moment, and she wrapped her legs around him, blessed

107

the moment he gave himself to her, blessed the moment she returned pleasure for pleasure.

Diana, the virgin goddess, would not have been pleased, but they were—time and time again.

CHAPTER SEVEN

After carrying Freya out of the water Antonio tenderly dried her off, then, cradling her in his arms, they slept again under the stars. The first threads of the dawn were painting the waters of the pool in tones of rose when they finally stirred awake.

When Freya felt the lightest whisper of a kiss against her cheek, her eyes slowly opened and she smiled, seeing Antonio bending over her.

Resting on one elbow, he stroked a fingertip under her eyes. "Maybe I should have let you sleep. I know you're tired, but I couldn't resist seeing how your eyes looked after a night of love."

"After two nights without much sleep they probably look bloodshot," she said teasingly.

"You couldn't be more wrong, *cara mia*. They're more beautiful than ever. I see so much in those wondrous eyes of yours. The blue glitters, reflecting the spark of the passion we shared, yet there is also a smoky quality that speaks of a completely satisfied woman."

Freya stretched like a contented cat. "You should know how satisfied I am, Antonio. You were the one who gave me that gift." She smiled at the memory of just how many times he had given her that gift of pleasure, then added, "Or I guess I should say 'gifts.'"

She spoke the truth. "Antonio, I've never spent nights like you've given me."

"Neither have I," he confessed. "I ask, and you give yourself completely. You deny nothing of yourself when I touch you. How can I not be inspired to love you, then love you again and again, in every way I can?"

Freya blushed, remembering all the places where their passion had led them through the hours of the night. No man had ever been able to sweep all her inhibitions away with a kiss, a caress. She should be afraid of the power Antonio held over her will, but she wasn't. She'd wanted to give what she had, and again, as before, the dawn brought no regrets.

She twisted her head around, to gaze once more at the place of fantasy he'd brought her to. The pool, the ruins, even the symbolic laurel tree, it all seemed out of a dream. Her eyes returned to his face and she smiled. "It must be this place that inspired us. When I'm with you, the rest of the world seems to disappear."

"I know exactly what you mean." He sighed deeply. No smile returned hers. "I wish it would stay that way, but it won't." He picked up the white gown. "Here, it hurts my heart to say this, but you'd better put this on. Your bare flesh will tempt me to love the day away, and we both have work to return to."

110

Freya stood up and slipped the silk gown over her head. As the soft folds settled around her she said, "Speaking of work, you never did tell me what you do."

Antonio moved away from her and didn't seem to hear what she said as he pulled on his slacks, then bent to pick up one of the loaves of crusty bread. He held it toward her and offered, "For some strange reason we failed to eat last night. Would you care to taste the cheese and fruit now?"

She nodded. "It sounds wonderful. I have to admit that I'm hungry. Must be because of all that exercise I had last night!"

Antonio grinned. "Could be? I have to admit that I've never enjoyed *exercising* more!"

For long moments she munched contentedly as her gaze wandered over the small glade, as if trying to memorize every blade of grass, every flower, every ripple in the shallow pool. Finally her glance returned to the ruins of the small temple, and she frowned.

She turned back to Antonio. "How come I've never seen this temple or even heard of it? Ruins have always fascinated me. I thought I'd visited every one in the area, but obviously I missed this one."

Antonio picked up a ripe pear and handed it to her, then explained, "Like all our archaeological sights, this one is registered with the Antiquity Commission, but since it's on private land, few know of it."

She bit into the pear as she glanced back at the

faint Latin words carved into the frieze. "Who is it dedicated to? I can read five languages, but unfortunately Latin is not one of them."

When he hesitated, she glanced at him. "What's wrong? Don't tell me we desecrated a pool sacred to the vestal virgins? After what we did last night that would get us in trouble for sure with the gods! Do I need to worry about dodging any thunderbolts?" she teased, throwing her arms over her head as if for protection.

Antonio laughed at her pretended fright. "It's not as bad as that." He looked at the temple, then shrugged. "I hesitated to tell you because I didn't want to ruin this spot for you. I'd like to say that it's a temple to Venus, the goddess of love, which after last night would be very appropriate, but unfortunately it's not. It's a temple dedicated to Pluto, god of the Underworld." He grimaced. "He's not one of my favorites."

He looked at her in surprise when she smiled. "Maybe I will start believing in destiny. I should have known that's who it would be. But you're wrong about one thing. I think it's very appropriate. If it wasn't for Pluto, I wouldn't be the social secretary for the embassy, and we wouldn't have met."

"I have to admit that I wondered how you ended up working for the embassy. A lot of diplomats spend their careers without ever landing such a unique and powerful assignment."

"Why work years when tears will do?" she said jokingly.

When she saw his confusion, she started to tell

him what had happened. She smiled at the memory. "It was luck, just pure luck, that I landed at the embassy. When I finished my last year at the boarding school in Cortina, I decided to stay. There was so much I hadn't seen, and since—as I told you—I had no home to go to, I decided to stay in Italy for a while. After visiting Venice I headed for Rome."

Her eyes grew misty again, but this time it was not from unhappy memories. "I'll never forget that special day. As you've probably guessed, Bernini's work has always fascinated me, so one of the first things I did after arriving in Rome was visit the Galleria Borghese. I was standing looking at his magnificent sculpture of Pluto's abduction of Persephone when I couldn't stop the tears. The scene was so real. I could see her terror as the god carried her passed Cerberus into Hades. I could see his fingers pressed into her flesh, already telling of her fate."

Suddenly those same tears came again as she stared off into space, conjuring up in her mind the two figures. "The sculpture seemed so alive, so poignant. Persephone fought, but you knew she was doomed."

Her voice faded as Antonio gathered her in his arms to comfort her before he used a corner of the tablecloth to dry her tears. She managed a watery chuckle. "That's just what the ambassador did."

"It is?" he demanded in mock severity. "Do you mean to tell me that right in the middle of the Galleria Borghese the American ambassador

113

grabbed you in a passionate embrace like I'm doing? That could have caused a sweet scandal! And I thought he was such a gentleman."

She started to giggle as he continued his teasing. "I'll bet old Pluto inspired him to try the same thing. I'll bet he decided to kidnap you and carry you off so he could enjoy your 'favors' just like our infamous god. I'm shocked! The Italian police should know about this! And your American State Department. I'll call the newspapers. The world should know of this scandalous behavior!"

"Will you stop?" she protested, choking with merriment at the thought of Marshall Whittiker harboring any such lecherous ideas. When she finally regained control, she hurried to explain. "It wasn't like that at all. I just meant, when I looked at that statue and started to cry, Marshall pulled out a handkerchief and dried my eyes just like you did."

"That's all?" Antonio asked, obviously skeptical.

"Well, no, actually that's just how we met. His appointment as ambassador was fairly recent, and naturally he'd been very busy settling in, so he hadn't gotten to see much of Rome. When he found out we both shared a love of Renaissance and baroque art, we started exploring the city together."

Freya smiled wistfully. "He is a widower with no children, and at the time I think he was as lonely as I was. Anyway, gradually our friendship developed. When his social secretary requested a return to the States, he asked me to take her place."

"So you didn't plan to meet Ambassador Whittiker at the Galleria Borghese that day? It was just an accident. Right?"

She twisted her head around so that she could look at him, disturbed by the tone of his question. "Yes, it was an accident. I explained how it happened, so why do you ask?"

Antonio kissed her on the tip of her nose. "No special reason. I was just thinking how fate seemed to have decided to take control of our destinies. From that first afternoon you met Ambassador Whittiker, I think it was planning what would be for us. Otherwise, why—"

Suddenly his words clipped off. "Otherwise, why?" she inquired when he remained silent.

When he spoke, she was fairly sure he'd changed what he was going to say. "Otherwise, why all this involvement with Roman gods and goddesses. You meet the ambassador in front of Pluto. We dine for the first time overlooking the temples of the Forum. We love the night away in front of another temple. You even get the Farnese opened with its famous fresco of *Loves of the Gods,* to honor my country."

He raised her hand to his lips. "All of Italy will thank you for that. But I can't help but wonder how you managed it. The French have had that gallery closed to outsiders for years."

Antonio settled her back against his bare chest as he cut off a piece of cheese and handed it to her with a fresh crust of bread. "How did you do it, *cara mia?* Of course, you could talk me into anything." A hint of possessive jealousy touched his words. "I hope you didn't use those same enticing techniques on Ambassador Maromme."

Freya nestled deeper into his embrace. Then she chuckled, remembering the scene in the Farnese. "With an ego the size of his there was no need to appeal to his senses." She nibbled on the cheese as she told him with delight how she'd convinced the French to open the gallery for the celebration.

"How did you ever think of using the Farnese?" Antonio asked with curiosity when her story wound down. "Most people don't even know about that fresco or the fact the French own one of our national treasures."

Freya sighed lazily, content to watch the sun rise and talk to the man who with each passing second filled more and more of her thoughts.

"I guess there's one good thing to say about exclusive boarding schools: You always learn a lot about art history. It's part of being 'cultured,' I suppose. Anyway, I particularly loved the Italian Renaissance and baroque periods. The pictures of Carracci's work were so fabulous when I came to Rome that I wanted to see the real fresco. Then I found out the French had it locked up. When Ambassador Whittiker came up with this idea and Emilio and I were tossing around ideas where to hold the ceremonies, I immediately thought of the Farnese."

His embrace tightened around her. "Who's Emilio?" he demanded.

She tilted her chin to look at him. "No one to be jealous of, I assure you. He's just my assistant. And I have to admit that he's excellent at his job, even if I can't say much for his personality."

Antonio's grip relaxed, and he dropped a quick kiss against her silvery hair. "Sorry, bewitching lady, but I can't stop feeling jealous of the other men around you. From the first moment I saw you, I couldn't stand the thought of another man touching you or making love to you. Forgive me?"

She twisted in his embrace until she could wind her arms around his neck. Her kiss, softly possessing his mouth, told him there was nothing to forgive. Instead of resenting his possessiveness, she delighted in it. Never before had anyone cared enough to desire her totally for himself, and she adored that feeling of being wanted.

For an instant Antonio let the kiss deepen, then slowly he drew away. When he looked at her, she saw the fire burning there, but it was a fire he obviously intended to keep banked. "Freya, what you do to me! I know so little about you. I want to spend a few hours talking, getting to know more about you, not loving again, but you tempt me to forget all my plans."

He eased her away until she was resting against his chest again. "I think we'd be safer concentrating on your job, because if you kiss me again, you won't make it back to the embassy at all today, so let me ask another question. *Cara mia*, I admit I'm fascinated at the coup you pulled off. You're not only the most enchanting creature I've ever known, you're obviously also one of the brightest. How did you ever convince the French that it wouldn't be too dangerous to open their gallery? I know there have been threats."

She wiggled deeper into his embrace, delighted with the fact that he admired more than the unusual color of her hair or her blue eyes. Happily she explained, "At first they adamantly refused, but when I pointed out to Ambassador Maromme how much security would be available, he finally agreed."

"Are the French bringing in special agents from the Sûreté to handle the security?"

Suddenly she realized that they were talking about the one subject she'd told the ambassador he hadn't mentioned before. Her eyes narrowed slightly as she pulled out of his arms so she could look at him. "Antonio, how did you know I was responsible for talking Ambassador Maromme into opening the Farnese?"

He laughed. "I didn't know it was supposed to be a secret. I can read a newspaper, Freya. If you recall, the information was in the paper the day of the embassy party."

She conceded that he had a point, but she wouldn't retreat. "That still doesn't explain why are you so concerned with our security arrangements."

His broad shoulders moved up and down in a characteristic shrug. "I'm just curious, that's all, *cara mia*. I know how nervous the French are about protecting that gallery. I just wanted to know how you convinced them it was safe to open it now."

"I'm not sure it is safe," she admitted with a frown.

Then, reluctantly, a fear that had always existed within her, but one which she refused to admit, escaped. "I'm not sure you are, either."

The hurt dulled Antonio's eyes. *"Cara mia,* how can you spend a night of love in my arms, then think I might be a danger to you? Trust your instincts. They are my guide in this, and I know they won't fail." His fist clenched as he vowed, "I know they won't!"

Her troubled thoughts didn't let her wonder why he swore with such vehemence. "I want to trust my instincts, Antonio, more than anything I've ever wanted in my life."

"Then do so, as I must."

He tried to trap her fingers beneath his, but she pulled her hand away. One touch and she knew she was lost. She'd buried the doubts, refusing to question for fear that the dream would end, but now that they'd crept back into her mind, she couldn't ignore them any longer.

She hugged her arms around herself, as if unconsciously trying to protect herself from the blow that might come. Bravely she met his appraising glance. "Antonio, it's just that there are so many unsolved mysteries."

"The only mystery I see is why fate waited so long to bring you into my life. It makes me sad to think of the nights of loving forever lost to us. But now that destiny has entwined our lives, my arms will never be empty again."

Her heart thrilled at his words. Nights of loving like the one just past. Feeling wanted and safe in his arms. Never to be lonely again. The thoughts seduced her, but for once Freya did not give into them.

"Antonio, how did you get into the chancellery the night of the party? Your name wasn't on the invitation list."

"Cara mia"—he laughed—"is that the mystery that's been puzzling you? Such imagination! How can my appearance at your side be mysterious? Your chancellery and embassy is extremely well guarded. I'm sure there are alarms, to say nothing of those young policemen that are on duty everywhere."

"They're not policemen," she automatically corrected. "They're marines."

Antonio smiled. "You see, that's even more impressive. How could I possibly get in if I wasn't supposed to be there? Someone asked me to attend and got me in. It's as simple as that. So, you see, there's no mystery, my beautiful one."

Freya laughed with relief. Her suspicions really were absurd. She could just imagine him sneaking across the rooftop like some cat burglar in his tuxedo!

"I knew there had to be an explanation. I guess that planning for this celebration is making everyone jumpy. There's so much at stake. I don't want to be the one responsible for losing the Declaration of Independence. We don't have a Siberia, but they probably wouldn't hesitate to exile me to the Aleutian Islands if anything happens to it. I'm sorry. I don't know what madness made me suspect you."

He leaned nearer and ran a hand possessively over her breast. Through the sheer silk of her gown it responded to the touch. When he felt the nipple harden beneath his palm, he chuckled. "If we didn't have to return to Rome, I'd make you apologize over and over again for harboring even the tiniest suspicion of me."

Her hand closed over his, trapping it against her breast. "One of the things they taught us at boarding school was that we must apologize for our mistakes. I know there's not time now to do it properly, but I can think of several interesting ways to do it later."

A spark fired in Antonio's dark eyes. "I can think of some interesting ways to make you apologize, too, and I can hardly wait, bewitching lady."

With a sad sigh he drew his hand away. "The thought of leaving you even for a moment makes me ache inside, but I have no choice. Unfortunately there is a world outside this magical place, and we must return to it. I know you have work to do at the embassy, and there are matters I must attend to as well."

He slipped into his shirt, then laughed when he noticed that all the buttons were gone. "How am I going to explain to my tailor where the buttons went? I hate to lie, so I think I'll tell him I was attacked by an amorous Persian kitten." His hand

121

reached to stroke through her long hair. "I have to admit that I loved the way you pounced."

Freya felt a blush warm her cheeks as she remembered the passionate need that drove her to rip the shirt from his body. "It looks like I have another item to add to my apology list. At this rate I may never get any sleep!"

She couldn't stop the irresistable urge to yawn at the thought. From behind her hand she muttered, "And obviously, since I need sleep, give me your shirt and I'll fix it."

His hand slipped beneath the hem of her gown and slid up her bare thigh. "I'd rather have your apology. I'm thinking of more creative ways to accept with each passing moment."

Even though his touch stirred delighted sensations within her, she protested. "Antonio, I thought you said we had to get back to Rome."

Slowly he withdrew his hand. "Unfortunately we do."

When they returned to his car, she quickly redressed in her staid suit. Handing the silk gown to Antonio, she smiled. "Keep it for when we can find another place of moonlight and fantasy."

The worst of the morning rush-hour traffic was over by the time they drove into the city itself. Freya glanced at her watch, hardly believing that it could be after ten o'clock. They'd awakened at dawn, and yet the hours with Antonio had flown by so fast, she hadn't realized it had gotten so late.

As they neared the chancellery Antonio's hand left the steering wheel to twine in her hair. "I have much to do today, Freya. I don't know when I will be free to see you."

Freya smiled wearily. "And I don't even want to think of the pile of work on my desk. I still haven't decided what I want to serve for the finale. It has to be something spectacular." She hesitated, then ventured, "Will you be free for dinner? At boarding school we were taught never to delay making our apologies."

"The more I hear about this boarding school, the more I approve," he said, teasing.

Then the light behind his smile died. A somber cast steeled his eyes, turning them almost charcoal gray. "Coming back into Rome makes me realize that reality is a harsh place. There's much I must do today, and I know I'll resent every minute we're apart." His hand returned to the wheel, and as he gripped it she saw his knuckles turn white with strain. "If only we could have stayed by that pool forever!"

She sighed, both with joy and unhappiness. "Antonio, last night was a beautiful dream, but we both knew it couldn't last."

"I know," he admitted as he pulled the car to a stop on the curving drive in front of the chancellery. "I don't like it, but I know you're right."

Before she could answer, one of the marines guarding the front entrance opened the car door and, with a snappy salute, greeted her. "Welcome back, Miss Davidson. The ambassador requested that you join him as soon as you returned."

As she climbed out, Antonio tossed her a kiss. "I'll call you when I can."

As she walked through the loggia toward the entrance she encountered Emilio pacing up and down among the columns. When he saw her, he snapped, "Well, it's about time you showed up. I've covered for you about as long as I can. The ambassador is waiting for us. From what he said, the State Department is insistently asking what special plans we've made to honor Italy." His eyes narrowed. "You do have some special plans thought up, don't you? Or have you been too busy chasing about Rome with that pseudo Italian count you met to worry about doing your job properly?"

Freya swallowed, but she refused to let Emilio see how close to the truth his words were. All of her thoughts, when they should have been on the celebration, had been on Antonio instead. She bit her lower lip and lied, because she honestly didn't have an idea in her head. "Let me get my notebook from my office, then I'll tell you both about the fantastic scheme I've come up with."

CHAPTER EIGHT

Freya ran up the marble stairs and hurried into her office. As she shut the door she gave herself a hard mental shake, telling herself that she was acting like a moonstruck teenager and that it had to stop, stop now! She possessed one of the most exciting, challenging, and coveted jobs anyone could ask for, and she was letting one man—a man she hardly knew, if she was honest with herself—dominate all her thoughts. She'd better remember her job! That was reality, not some interlude by a pool.

Unconsciously she squared her shoulders and turned toward her desk. As she reached for her notebook her eye was caught by a picture in the *National Geographic* she'd been reading. It was an article about Kansas, and the picture showed a field of golden wheat rippling in the breeze.

As she looked at the picture ideas suddenly bombarded her. Kansas wheat, grain to feed the world. Wheat turned into golden loaves of bread. With bread you needed butter, butter from Wisconsin. As the plan started clicking faster and faster in her mind, without being aware of it she started humming the tune to "Oh, What a Beautiful Morning."

Freya paused a minute to twist her long hair into a serviceable chignon. As her fingers twined in her hair she remembered Antonio's touch. In the harsh light of the morning, standing in the middle of her office the night before almost seemed like a dream. Every time she was with Antonio he seemed able to weave a spell of unreality around her, clouding her thoughts, drugging her senses, until he became all that mattered.

Freya shook her head. How did he do it? Why did she let him? No man had ever held such power over her, and she had no will to resist. She sighed. Maybe he was right. Maybe destiny had brought them together. Maybe that's why deep in her heart she believed that what was happening was meant to be.

Suddenly she grabbed her notebook and turned toward the door, determined to banish Antonio from her thoughts, at least for the moment. Destiny, fate, whims of the gods, she was letting the dreams seduce her again, and she had too much to do to dream the day away, as she had the night.

As she left her office she found Emilio impatiently pacing outside. "Emilio, what's wrong with you? I've never seen you this uptight," Freya said.

He continued pacing. "I think I have good reason to be upset. This celebration is the most important assignment I've ever had, and you don't seem willing to sit down and work out the details. There are plans to make, and I don't even know the schedule you've worked out for that final day or what you want me to do."

Freya frowned at him, surprised at his outburst. Emilio was an excellent assistant but a bit lazy. He rarely pushed himself to do anything extra, and here he was demanding that she give him work to do. Then she relaxed. After all, this event was planned to honor his country, so naturally he wanted everything to be perfect.

He stopped pacing and spun to face her. "Well, do I have to plan all this myself or do you—"

"Emilio, calm down. Believe it or not, I have everything under control. I know you want the best for your country at this special time, and to use one of my grandmother's favorite expressions, I've come up with one lollapalooza of an idea! It's going to mean a lot of coordination from this office, and"—she paused, grimacing at the thought of their temperamental chef, Conrad— "and a lot of extra work in the kitchen, but the result will be a feast to end the festivities that no one will ever forget."

Emilio's eyes glittered with excitement as he rubbed his hands together. "A feast, that's perfect. I was afraid you might plan one of those open-house-type things you Americans are so fond of. You know, where people come and go at will. This way all the dignitaries will be there all at the same time."

Freya smiled at his enthusiasm. "The Farnese Gallery, those unique documents, all the important people who'll attend, I think a celebration honoring forty years of Italian liberty deserves no less."

A little of Emilio's eagerness faded. "Forty years of liberty still hasn't brought us the power your country possesses. Once we Italians ruled the world. Now we can't even dominate the Common Market."

Remembering the ruins of the night before, which had once been a proud Roman temple, she sympathized with his feelings. "Times change, Emilio," she said softly. "The past is gone."

Some of the fire returned to his eyes. "Yes, it is, isn't it! If I had champagne, I'd make a toast to a better future for my country, a future I want to make far different from what has been."

She laughed. "I'd say that's an excellent toast and one I'll drink to later, but it's just as well that we don't have any champagne right now. We have too much to do to be sipping away the morning." She reached for the telephone. "I'll call and see if the ambassador is free."

When he answered the phone and heard her voice, Marshall sighed in relief. "Well, there you are. I was beginning to wonder if you'd been kidnapped! But since you're safe and sound, I would like you to come to my office. Those idiots at the State Department have been burning up the telephone wires demanding to know what we have planned. You'd think this embassy had never hosted a party before," he muttered in disgust.

Emilio held the door open for her as they entered the ambassador's plush office. Then he threw himself into a chair by the ambassador's desk. He didn't notice the ambassador's disapproving scowl as he sputtered, "The boss, here, says she has a plan, but—"

He stopped when Marshall held up his hand. "Young man, will you be careful! That chair has survived from the sixteenth century. I don't want it destroyed by your impetuous behavior."

Freya turned to see Emilio's eyes begin to burn in anger. Quickly she moved to calm the situation. "If Emilio is acting impetuously, it's my fault. He's impatient with me. Like you, he's concerned about the plans for the festival." She seated herself in a gilt chair on the other side of Marshall's desk. "After all, it is his country we're honoring, so here's the idea I've come up with." She didn't add that the idea was conceived only twenty minutes ago in her office!

"I hope it's spectacular," Marshall observed. "The French have that damned gallery of theirs to show off. I don't want them upstaging our effort."

Freya sat back confidently in her chair. "They won't top this. What better way to honor Italy than to present the best America has to offer?"

"My dear, I'm afraid I don't understand. Of course, we'll do our best, we always do."

"No, I'm afraid you don't understand. What I want to do is bring the finest foods each of the fifty states has to offer to serve for the banquet." Her eyes shone with excitement. "Think of it, lobsters from Maine, terrapin from Florida, king crab from Alaska, the choicest beef from Colorado, wheat from Kansas for the bread, fresh pineapple from Hawaii, the richest butter and cheese from Wisconsin, fresh salmon from the rivers of Washington." She spread her hands wide. "What country in the world could present such a feast!"

The ambassador licked his lips. "Hmmm, I can almost taste it. And don't forget my favorite. I want some pheasants brought from Nebraska. Some quail would be nice too," he mused, licking his lips again.

Then he turned his attention back to her. "Freya, it's brilliant. Each and every part of the United States will play a role in Italy's fortieth anniversary celebration."

Freya turned to her assistant. "What do you think of the idea, Emilio? You were the one who was worried that I couldn't come up with something special."

"I agree with the ambassador. It's a fantastic idea, and I suspect the headaches that go along with it will be fantastic too. Coordinating deliveries of fresh food from your fifty states should really be a challenge." He cleared his throat uneasily. "Have you discussed this with the chef?"

Freya winced. "No, I haven't. Fifty dishes to prepare, I can hear his screams now." She made a move to stand up. "If there's nothing else, I guess I'd better go face the music in the kitchen."

Marshall motioned her to sit down. "You haven't mentioned anything about a finale. We need something really sensational to crown a feast like that. Any ideas?"

Freya glanced at Emilio, but all she got for her effort was a shrug. "I suppose we should have some sort of pastry. I'll think about it and let you know. Now if there's—"

"I'm afraid there is something else, and I would prefer to discuss it with you alone. So, Emilio, if you don't mind, please leave us."

When the door closed behind Emilio, the ambassador inquired, "I am quite concerned about you, my dear. You left the chancellery yesterday afternoon and did not return. I suppose you were with Count Raimondi."

When she nodded, he added, "Now, I know I asked you to keep tabs on this man, but frankly I did not expect it to go this far."

"Neither did I," Freya admitted. "When I'm with Antonio, things just happen which I don't seem to have any control over."

Marshall stared distractedly out of the leaded glass of his window. "I remember that feeling very well. I first saw my future wife, Amelia, on the Boston Common. She was feeding popcorn to the pigeons and offered to share her bag with me." He smiled fondly at the memory. "We were never apart after that."

With effort he pulled his attention back from the past. His voice was stern. "However, your situation is a little different. My wife didn't slip in and out of embassy parties uninvited, and there was no doubt who she actually was. We cannot say the same about your count, if he really is a count."

Freya shifted uneasily on the embroidered seat. "I suppose that means no word has come from Washington."

"All I got for my trouble was a curt inquiry, demanding to know why we were checking on this man. I think sometimes those guys at the CIA are too suspicious for their own good—or ours!"

"What are you going to do? Just drop the matter?" Freya asked, failing to keep the note of hope from her voice.

"I can't do that, my dear, and you know it. I wired back that it was none of their damned business why I needed to know and insisted that they send any information as soon as they could. Tell me, how did you get together last night? Did he call you?"

"No, actually it was an accident. We ran into each other outside the British embassy. Remind me to tell you sometime about our narrow escape from soggy pasta."

Her quip didn't produce a smile. "You say it was an accident. I wonder. Could he have planned to run into you?"

She squirmed uneasily on her chair, hating to admit the truth, yet not lying. "I don't think so, but I suppose it is possible that it wasn't an accident."

The ambassador was sensitive to her disquiet, but that didn't stop him. "My dear, I hate to put you through this, but with all that's resting on this celebration, we have to be sure. So I'll have to ask you: Have you found out anything else about our mysterious stranger?"

Freya lowered her gaze, not wanting to see the suspicions in Marshall's eyes. In a hesitant voice she admitted, "I found out that Antonio knew I was the one responsible for getting the Farnese opened."

"That's hardly damning. That information was in the newspaper. Did he try to pump you about anything else?"

"We did discuss how I got this job. And"—she paused, unwilling to go on, but knowing that she must—"and he did inquire about our security arrangements for the celebration."

"Damn!" The word exploded from Marshall.

Before he could say anything else, she rushed on. "But he convinced me that there was nothing mysterious about his presence at the party. As Antonio pointed out, how could he get past our marines guarding the entrances? Someone brought him, but he wouldn't tell me who it was."

"I'd like to have that information," the ambassador said. "I double-checked with the guards, and I'm convinced that our security is adequate. So for now we'll believe him."

His questions about Antonio made her uneasy, so she changed the topic back to the feast. After nervously rambling on, she realized that the ambassador was barely listening.

"Hmmm, crates of food. Yes, that should work perfectly," he mumbled.

She stared at him in confusion. "What should work perfectly?"

His attention snapped back. "Your idea for the feast should work perfectly, that's what, my dear."

She knew more lay under his words than just that, but when she opened her mouth to ask, he hurried on. "And don't worry, my dear, if Conrad protests too much. Just remind him that I can always have him transferred to some remote embassy in equatorial Africa."

Then he sobered. "Check with me this afternoon. We may have word then on your count. I can tell from your eyes that you'd like all doubt removed."

Fifteen minutes later Freya took a quick step back as Conrad, the embassy's chef, brandished a huge cleaver at her. "You expect me and my staff to do what?" he demanded, after she'd explained about her idea. "You are quite insane, I assure you. Fifty dishes! It's impossible!"

An hour of arguing, of appealing to both his ego and his patriotism, of finally threatening to ask the chef at the French embassy to prepare the banquet if he refused produced both a reluctant agreement from Conrad and a throbbing headache for her.

She was about to ask the chef if he had any aspirin when Emilio charged through the swinging door.

"I thought I'd find you here. I've come up with a fantastic idea for the finale to our dinner. Why

134

don't we bake a huge cake in the shape of the Victor Emmanuel II monument?"

Freya conjured up the image of the enormous tiered and columned monument in her mind. Ornately built of white marble with a sweeping staircase in front, she privately thought that it was a bit gaudy, but on the other hand, she instantly saw how the building could be copied to make a spectacular dessert.

"Emilio, that's a wonderful idea and very appropriate, too, since Victor Emmanuel II was responsible for unifying the separate Italian states into one nation."

"That's what I thought," he agreed with a smug smile. "Conrad can add sugar statues in place of—"

"No, Conrad cannot!" the chef snapped, joining their conversation for the first time. "Planning, baking, then decorating something that looks like that very complex monument would take days, and I don't have days to spare, not if you expect me to create fifty unique dishes."

Before Freya could start insisting, Emilio interrupted. "I think I've come up with an idea that should please everyone. Why don't we just hire an outside caterer to do the cake? The embassy has used them before. Wouldn't that solve everything?"

Conrad nodded. "As long as I approve of the caterer, I have no objection."

With a huge sigh of relief that she'd escaped another battle, Freya smiled and said, "Good, then it's settled." She turned to her assistant.

135

"Emilio, you find two or three caterers. Have them each bake a sample of their best cake and we'll decide who gets the contract."

He smiled in satisfaction. "I can't tell you how pleased I am that you like my idea for the finale. Already I have a caterer in mind who will make the evening end just as we wish. I will go and call her right now and tell her to start her oven."

CHAPTER NINE

Ambassador Whittiker was eager to see Freya when she arrived at his office, letting her enter ahead of several other staff members who were waiting. As she opened his door he smiled. "I'm glad to see you survived the encounter with Conrad. I half expected to hear his bellows from here."

"You almost did. To say the least, he wasn't happy with my idea. You have to admit, it will mean a lot of extra work for him."

Marshall shrugged. "That's what he's paid to do. How did you convince him? Did you have to threaten exile to some primitive isle?"

"Hardly." Freya spread her hands as she explained. "Handling his type is easy. When he balked, I merely suggested that if he couldn't manage to prepare fifty different dishes, I was sure the chef at the French embassy could."

"My dear, I congratulate you. This is going to be one evening none of us will ever forget."

"Oh, I almost forgot. We've come up with an idea for the finale. What would you think of a huge cake baked in the shape of the Victor Emmanuel II monument to finish the evening?"

Marshall clapped his hands. "I think it's brilliant! I knew you'd come up with something unusual, yet suitably perfect."

"Well, actually, it was Emilio's idea, so I can't take credit, but—"

A sharp rap on the door silenced her. "I hate to interrupt this, my dear. I don't know when I've been more excited about a celebration, but this must be important. I instructed my secretary that we were not to be disturbed unless it was an emergency."

He hesitated before giving her hand a reassuring pat. "Maybe it's news about your Count Raimondi."

Freya lifted her chin. "I hope it is. I want this uncertainty cleared up. I honestly believe that Antonio is who and what he claims to be, an Italian count who's only interest is in a petite blond he met at an embassy party."

From Marshall's expression she knew that he was far from as sure about Antonio as she was.

The tone of his voice was comforting. "My dear, for your sake I pray you're right. I've never seen any man affect you this way, and frankly it worries me."

In her heart she had to admit that she worried also about the power Antonio possessed over her. Maybe it was her own needs and desires that were finally ruling her mind, but either way she didn't want Marshall to see her weakness.

The rap came again, this time more insistently. "Unless you want your door knocked down, I think you'd better tell that visitor to come in," she suggested more calmly than she felt. "It doesn't sound like he's going away."

There was still confused doubt in his eyes when Marshall raised his voice and instructed, "Come in."

The third secretary in charge of decoding entered with a snappy salute. "Sir, that communiqué you've been waiting for from the C—" He glanced at Freya, then changed the wording. ". . . from Washington just arrived." He presented a piece of paper with a flourish in the ambassador's direction. "I felt it was my duty to bring it to your attention immediately."

Marshall held out his hand to accept the document. His casual manner changed as he read the communiqué. When he finished, his gaze reluctantly flew to Freya, then to the third secretary standing rigidly before his desk at attention. Marshall's order snapped crisply. "Thank you, young man. You're dismissed."

When the third secretary had left the office, Marshall reread the report, obviously to make sure he hadn't erred, then once again his glance returned to his social secretary, only this time it was accompanied with a frown.

"My dear, I'm sorry to be the one to say this, but it appears that it's time for the chickens to come home to roost."

He paused, then finally finished by extending the piece of paper across the desk to her. "Freya, I'm sorry."

His expression told her more than she wanted to know. She didn't want to see what was printed on the paper. She didn't want to see what damning evidence the CIA had found about Antonio, and yet she had to know. Her fingers trembled as she reached to take the offered paper, and she didn't draw them back.

Words, words, and more words, but only a few jumped out to strike her. Her name. Antonio's name, and then the last, which hit like a physical blow. "He's an agent!" she whispered.

Her anguished glance reached across the desk to find sympathy in the ambassador's expression. He cleared his throat uneasily. "Freya, as I said, I'm sorry. But I'm afraid this communiqué explains everything—your Count Raimondi's appearance, his sudden disappearance . . . and, I hate to add, his insistent courting of you."

How could she deny the truth of his words? It was all there. All the damning reality. With an angry twist she wadded the offending paper into a tight ball and threw it in the direction of the ambassador's leather wastebasket. As it missed and bounced on the priceless Aubusson carpet, she muttered, "You're right. That communiqué explains everything! Everything except how I could have been such a complete fool!"

Even with the paper destroyed, the horrible word *agent* burned in her mind, twisting like a searing knife within her. Marshall tried to console her, but none of his words could help as the tears stung her eyes. Without even answering him she shoved back her chair.

Over and over again the same thoughts

pounded. Damn the CIA. Damn Antonio. Damn everyone!

Marshall's outer office was full of people, but Freya saw no one as the hot tears scalded her eyes. She frantically fled from that damning word on the decoded cable. *Agent.* Antonio had deliberately used her. And she had been fool enough to let him! His betrayal seared with blinding pain, yet what hurt even more was the knowledge that she'd encouraged him!

With burning shame she remembered how she'd almost begged him to make love to her. How he must have laughed! Her fist clenched as one ugly truth after another slapped her. All that romantic trash about destiny and fate bringing them together. Fate had nothing to do with it. He'd planned it! The cable left no room for doubt on that score. He'd planned everything. And her falling willingly into his bed was a bonus no hot-blooded Italian would refuse. Remembering the confessions she'd made lying naked in his arms, she knew that he'd even used that to further his plan.

The ambassador had tried to warn her. Emilio had tried to warn her. Even her conscience had tried to warn her. But she'd listened to nothing but her heart, and now that heart was breaking . . . and she deserved it!

Blindly she ran up the marble stairs. She didn't even see Emilio until he grabbed her arm. "Freya, what's wrong? You're crying. Was Conrad that angry over your idea for the feast? I knew you should have let me handle him. We Italians are used to temperament. His screaming doesn't bother me."

She yanked her arm away. "Emilio, will you leave me alone! It isn't the chef."

She tried to move past him, but he barred her way, grasping her by the shoulders. "If it isn't the chef that's making those beautiful blue eyes of yours swim with pain, then it must be that damned count of yours. I tried to warn you."

"Well, you were right!" she muttered, refusing to look at him. "That should make you happy."

"What would make me happy, my beautiful Freya, is if you'd dine with me tonight. I can make any woman forget that other men even exist."

With effort she wrenched herself out of his grasp. After brushing the tears away with the back of her hand, she faced him. "Emilio, will you give it up? I am not going to tumble for your line, not now, not ever! Right now I've had it with all men, you included. Now get out of my way!"

After slamming the door to her bedroom she threw herself on the bed, wanting to give into the anger tearing at her. Surprisingly no more tears would come.

Instead of dwelling on Antonio's betrayal, images of a moonlit pool filled her thoughts. Instead of remembering how he'd used her and why, memories of firelight on golden skin came, turning the anger into desire.

"Damn him!" she muttered, slamming her fist

into the pillow. "He *is* a sorcerer if he can do this to me!"

Disgusted with herself and her weakness, Freya sat up. There was only one thing to do. She had to see him. She had to throw the lies back in his face. She had to let him know that she knew the truth of his deceit. Only then did she have a chance to exorcise him from her heart and find some peace.

It took several layers of makeup to hide the signs of her tears, and a few deep, steadying breaths before she was ready to face him. Suspecting that Antonio would be waiting outside for her as he had that first night, Freya signed out with the marine on duty at the front entrance, and after forcing her pounding heart to slow to normal, she walked out into the late-afternoon sunlight. It took several moments for her eyes to adjust to the bright light, and when they did, she saw a man step out of the shadows cast by the setting sun. For an instant her breath caught, wanting yet not wanting it to be Antonio. Then her shoulders sagged as she recognized Emilio.

"I knew you'd change your mind and have dinner with me," he said, coming toward her. "No woman can resist me for long. Come, let's go drown your problems in a plate of fettuccine alfredo. I'll make you forget that that pseudo-count ever existed."

She knew that in his own way Emilio was trying to cheer her up, but she'd had enough of smooth Italian lines. "Emilio, trust me, I wouldn't

143

be good company tonight. Besides, I'm waiting for someone."

Emilio stepped closer, but she backed away as he said insistently, "Freya, you're an idiot. When I found you crying, I thought you'd finally seen the truth about that man."

"I have," she muttered, consciously letting her anger build anew.

"Then why won't you—"

"No, Emilio, I won't have dinner with you." Turning back toward the chancellery, she admitted, "I've lost my appetite."

Time crawled as she waited. A dozen times she went to the windows overlooking the front of the chancellery, but Antonio was never there. She tried to work on the menu for the festival, but he crept into her thoughts, and the paper blurred beneath her eyes as his image returned again and again. Pacing the floor, she told herself over and over that she wanted to see him, to hurl his deception at him, yet somewhere deep within she knew that wasn't why she wanted to see him at all. Damn it! Why couldn't she stay angry!

Finally, in frustration, she shoved back her desk chair and headed back to her bedroom. If work wouldn't keep him out of her thoughts, maybe she could exhaust herself into not thinking, into not feeling, into not wanting.

The black-and-red-striped leotard she'd competed in during her gymnastic days felt like an old friend as Freya slipped it on. She turned the dial on her radio to a rock station, then glanced around the room to find something to use as a warm-up bar. Nothing seemed suitable. Then, through the double glass doors, the balcony railing caught her eye. After flipping off the alarm guarding the doors she opened them and walked outside. The railing worked perfectly as, bending and stretching, she forced muscles, taut with tension, to relax.

Slowly Freya let the music claim her. Moving off the balcony, she began to dance to the pounding rhythm. Remembered moves from her training for floor exercise and on the balance beam returned as her body swayed, twisted, whirled to the music. Faster and faster, as if trying to drive demons from her body, Freya danced.

Then suddenly she froze. She heard something and saw a flash move across the roof outside in the darkness. A jagged tremor of fear shot through her. Something was wrong. The marine guards were everywhere, but somehow she sensed that someone was out there, someone who shouldn't be.

Moving quickly, she snapped off the overhead light, hoping to see better into the darkness. Terrifying scenes of other embassies under attack flashed through her mind. Still she hesitated, reaching for the phone. Had she seen something or not? She didn't want to panic the staff with a false alarm, but—

It all happened so fast, she didn't have a chance, as the dark figure dropped onto her balcony. Freya whirled to run, but he moved too fast for her. Grabbing her from behind, he yanked her back against him as a hand clamped over her

145

mouth, muffling her scream. Frantic, her heart pounding with fear, she struggled against her attacker.

"Freya, stop it. I'm not going to hurt you."

In her terror the voice didn't register as she twisted, trying to escape the powerful arms binding her.

"Freya, it's me. It's Antonio."

"Antonio!" she gasped, the truth finally ripping through the fear.

For a moment she sagged in his arms in relief, then twisted to face him. "You almost frightened me to death. I was sure we were being attacked by terrorists. What are you doing here?"

Her eyes widened in horror. "Antonio, the guards might have shot you!"

That horrible possibility smashed her anger at his betrayal, and her arms swept around him as if reassuring herself that he really was safe.

He smiled down at her. "That's just the type of greeting I was hoping to get from my bewitching lady. Now, how about something a little more intimate?"

Her lips opened with a protest, but his kiss stole away her words, and it was a sweet theft, one which, at that instant, she had no desire to prevent.

Only when he swept her up in his arms, then turned toward the bed, did sanity return. "Antonio, no! Put me down! I'm not going to let you do this to me again."

Puzzled, he set her on her feet. "Freya, all I

want to do is make love to you." He grinned. "As I recall, that's something you enjoy."

She backed away from him, then hurried to turn the light back on as if it would protect her from the dangers of his presence. Feeling safer in the lighted room, she lifted her chin defiantly and faced him. "That was before I knew who you were."

Obviously confused, Antonio shook his head. "I don't understand. I told you who I was that first night."

"Maybe I should have asked what you are, not who you are," she snapped.

His smile faded. "Ah, so you've found out. When?"

"Word came in from the CIA this afternoon." She angrily paced through the room. "Tell me, Antonio, does Interpol have a special school to train their agents how to seduce women? Is that your speciality, bedding women and then getting them to talk, because I have to admit that you're a master at it. It must have been disappointing that I offered so little challenge."

His dark eyes glowed. "Freya, you've never disappointed me. You never could."

For a second she wavered. It sounded like he spoke the truth, but she'd believed him before. She shrouded her heart in ice to protect it as she said accusingly, "Interpol discovered that I was responsible for getting the Farnese opened, and because they suspected me, they sent a handsome count to find out if I was innocently involved or if my motives were more sinister. You

147

used me. That's why you came to the party. That's why you asked me to dance. That's why you seduced me. Don't try to deny it!"

"Freya, I don't deny that that is why I slipped into the party. I was under orders. I don't deny that that's why I asked you to dance. Too much was at stake with this celebration. We had to know the truth about you." His voice raised as he pleaded, "But you have to believe the rest of what happened between us had nothing to do with my job."

She stopped pacing and whirled to face him. "I'll bet!"

His hands reached toward her. "You have to believe me. From the moment I saw you, you stole into my soul."

It was Antonio's turn to start pacing. "When I'm with you, I can't think. I can only feel," he confessed. "Freya, look at me right now. I've trained for years to be an agent, to let nothing and no one come between me and the job I have to do. Yet what happens? I come tonight because I have something urgent to discuss with you, and instead of talking, all I can think about is making love to you."

Some of the ice encasing her heart began to melt as she heard the throb of passion mixed with confusion in his voice. It was a combination she knew only too well. Still, she couldn't forgive him.

She hardened her voice. "I don't like being used, Antonio."

"If I used you, you did the same with me," he

said countering her. "All those questions about where I was from and about what I did weren't just harmless inquiries. I know that Ambassador Whittiker asked Interpol for information about me. I also know that they refused to comply. So unless my instincts are very wrong, he told you to stay close to me until you could verify my identity."

For a moment her anger blinded her to the truth of his words. Then she realized that they were true. In a very real way she had used him as much as he'd used her. She felt a little sheepish as she confessed, "Well, what did you expect when a stranger mysteriously appears, then disappears?"

She glanced back at the open glass doors, then at him, as the truth finally hit her. "You did break into the embassy the night of the party, didn't you? You broke in just like you did tonight."

Now that the soft lilt had returned to her voice, he relaxed. "Getting into places without an invitation is one of my specialities. Even on a second-floor balcony you shouldn't leave your doors unlocked." He grinned. "You don't know who might drop in."

She hardly heard his jest as an old wound returned to gnaw at her. "Antonio, where did you go that night? Why did you leave me? Do you wonder why that made us suspicious?"

Quickly he came to her side, but he didn't reach for her. "I told you that was the hardest thing I ever had to do, and that wasn't a lie. But I had no choice. I'd been assigned to slip into the party, meet you, then cable a report back to my superior in Paris at precisely eleven o'clock. When those cables don't come in on time, Interpol agents tend to get nervous. I didn't want him alerting the Italian police that one of his agents may have been captured inside the American ambassador's residence."

A husky rasp deepened his voice as he ran a fingertip down her cheek. "Of course, in a way I was captured that night. At least my heart was, and it has no desire to escape from its captor."

He threw up his hands in disgust. "Do you see what I mean? I look at you and I can't keep my mind on business for more than a minute! If I'm not careful, they'll kick me out of the agency and I'd deserve it."

Secretly Freya was delighted that she had such an affect on him, but she didn't let her joy show as she moved away from him. "Maybe I should help you. Interpol needs all the good agents it can get. Tell you what, I'll stay on this side of the room. You go to that side, and then we'll talk. I'll start. Why did you come dropping onto my balcony tonight? I admit that having a lover sneak into my bedroom is romantic, but wouldn't a phone call be easier?"

All lightness dropped from his voice as he explained, "After what happened this afternoon I couldn't risk calling. I thought my cover was secure, but it's been blown."

"What do you mean?" she asked with growing concern.

"This afternoon I was coming to see you when I discovered that I'd picked up a tail."

Unconsciously she moved to his side. "Are you in danger?"

He hesitated. "I don't know. I don't think so. I think somebody just wanted to know what I was up to."

"Who?" she whispered, getting more nervous by the second.

"Probably the same people I came to speak with you about tonight. After I lost my friend, the tail, I decided it was too risky to call you in case your phone was bugged or to see you in public in case we were overheard."

"Antonio, what are you talking about? You're frightening me."

He gathered her protectively into his arms. "I don't mean to, but you have to know the truth. Interpol has picked up strong rumors that the celebration is in danger. Until the official word comes through from Paris, I can't go directly to the ambassador, but I had to come and warn you to be careful. I figured that this was the safest place to talk."

"Interpol isn't the only one who's heard the rumors. I almost wish the ambassador had never thought of this idea, and I wish I'd never thought of using the Farnese."

His embrace tightened around her, drawing her deeper into his arms. "I won't lie. You know how dangerous these radical groups can be. And as much as I hate to admit it, you couldn't have picked a more tempting target for them to hit had you tried."

Antonio squeezed her so hard, she could hardly

151

breathe. "Freya, I don't know what I'd do if anything happened to you. Since you came into my life nothing seems quite the same."

She tilted her head back so she could look at him. "I know the feeling. This afternoon I was hurt. I felt betrayed. I wanted to be furious at you. I tried to stay angry, but memories of our beautiful moments together kept creeping in to blunt the feeling."

That passionate beat she knew so well entered his voice as he murmured, *Cara mia*, I'm very glad you're not angry with me, because it's certainly not anger I feel when I look at you."

"And what do you feel? Respect?" she said jokingly, enjoying the way his eyes were already burning with a fire she knew would soon consume her with its heat.

"I respect your mind, all right." Antonio smiled. "You are a most intelligent lady, but—"

"Good, then we can spend the night discussing philosophy. Do you think that if a tree falls in the forest and no one hears it, that—"

"Freya, be silent," he ordered, so gently that she had no desire not to obey. "I want to spend the night with you but not to talk philosophy. In fact, I don't want to talk at all."

"You don't?" she whispered, relishing in the way his words were already heating her blood. But still she couldn't resist teasing him. "What will we do if we don't talk?"

"Things like this," Antonio answered as he started nibbling on her ear.

"Oh, I see." She sighed happily as his warm

breath blew his message of desire into the sensitive interior. "Anything else?"

"And this," he murmured, reaching to turn off the light before he slipped her leotard off one shoulder so that he could taste her flesh with his kisses.

She stretched like a contented kitten. "Hmmm, that's nice. Anything else you have in mind? Dawn's a long way off."

"How about this?" he suggested, sweeping her up in his arms and turning toward her bed.

This time she had no desire to tell him no as he laid her back against the satin coverlet, then followed her, pushing her body down into the soft mattress with the weight of his.

His kiss plundered her willing lips and stirred the embers within her. Her fingers twined in his dark hair, urging a rougher taking, a taking they both desired. Freya moaned beneath him when his hand found her breast beneath the leotard.

So intent on their rising passion, they didn't even hear the repeated knocks on the door. Then, without warning, the lights flipped on and the ambassador's voice finally cut through their haze of desire.

"I guess I was wrong. We will have to tighten security around here," Marshall observed with an amused chuckle. He walked toward the startled couple with his hand outstretched. "Count Raimondi, it's a pleasure to finally meet you."

153

CHAPTER TEN

With a startled gasp Freya pushed Antonio away. The ambassador's eyes sparkled with merriment as he surveyed the scene on the bed. "My dear, I never would have intruded, had I known your conversation with the count was over and your ah, your . . . well, let's just say, your conversation was over."

The heat raging across her cheeks told Freya that her face rivaled a sunset as she yanked the shoulder of her leotard back in place and sat up. Antonio, with more aplomb that she could muster, rose easily from the bed and moved to shake hands with the ambassador.

Still shaken, Freya stared in disbelief as the two men exchanged polite greetings. "I don't understand. How did you—"

The ambassador chuckled. "How did I know that the man in your bedroom was Count Raimondi? My dear, who else would it be? Certainly not Emilio."

Seeing her confusion, Marshall continued. "Maybe I'd better explain. I was working late in my office when this important communiqué came across my desk. Since it concerned Count

Raimondi, I decided to come up and ask you how to contact him. When I heard voices"—he shrugged—"well, you know the rest."

He smiled kindly at her. "I did knock several times. I certainly had no intention of embarrassing you, my dear. You must know that, but this was of first-class importance."

The ambassador turned to Antonio. "When I first suspected that you were an Interpol agent, I—"

At his words Freya leapt off the bed. "Now wait just a minute," she said, interrupting. "What do you mean when you suspected that he was an agent for Interpol?"

Marshall looked at her. "I thought it was obvious when Interpol refused to send any information on him, it was possible that he was one of their own."

"It wasn't obvious to me!" she muttered, remembering all the agony of doubts and uncertainties she'd endured, not knowing for sure who he was or what he was. Marshall's slight deception hurt. "Why didn't you tell me? You knew I was going through hell."

The ambassador patted her shoulder. "How could I, my dear? What if I was wrong? Besides, I needed you to keep close tabs on this fellow here, just in case he wasn't who I suspected he was." The twinkle returned to his eye. "And you have to admit that you performed that assignment with obvious delight."

Antonio threw back his head and laughed. "I had my own private Mata Hari on my trail, and I didn't even know it. We're quite a pair, bewitching lady. You were suspicious of me. I was suspicious of you."

Suddenly Antonio's dark eyes softened as he gazed at her. "At least I was suspicious until I saw you that first night. The moment you turned and looked at me, my instincts knew that you could never lie or deceive anyone."

"Children, I'm afraid this billing and cooing will have to wait," the ambassador said, admonishing them. "We have important work to do tonight. It's urgent that we speak, and what better place than right here? We shouldn't be interrupted, and there's less chance of being overheard than in my office."

The ambassador's hand swept toward the small satin-covered settee and two wing chairs grouped before her fireplace. "Shall we?"

For a moment after they were settled, the ambassador closed his eyes and rubbed tired fingers across his forehead, as if trying to ease the pain. Then his eyes opened and he glanced at Freya. "My dear, if I ever again come up with an idea as complicated as this celebration, please tell me to forget it. Just the security for this is a nightmare. And I admit that it's all my fault. I just didn't think this through before I proposed it, and of course, now it's too late."

"I know you're worried about using the Farnese Gallery, but there'll be plenty of security," she said, trying to reassure him.

"Yes, but whose? Think about it. We can't even

guard our own Declaration of Independence once it goes on display."

"Why not? Our marines are the finest in the world. They can . . ." The words trailed off as she realized the problem. "No, they can't, can they?"

"You're right, they can't." Marshall agreed with a frown. "You know how touchy the French are. Once it's in the French embassy, it is legally on their native soil, and our guards won't be allowed anywhere near.

"What are we going to do? Antonio says his sources have picked up the same rumors we heard of a possible terrorist strike."

"As I said, it's a security nightmare. With three embassies and four governments involved, the only thing we can do is turn part of our security over to Interpol." The ambassador turned to look at Antonio. "The communiqué I mentioned was Interpol's agreement to accept the assignment." He became much more formal as he announced, "And since you are already assigned to this case, they want you to coordinate all the necessary security measures."

Antonio didn't smile at being handed the choice assignment. "That may be more difficult than we even thought." He glanced past the ambassador to catch Freya's eye, and finally the smile appeared. "That was the second part of what I had to tell you, but somehow we got sidetracked."

"Yes, indeed, I saw how you two got sidetracked!" The ambassador winked. "But back to business. What were you going to tell Freya?"

"Until the official word came from Paris, I couldn't come directly to you with this information, Mr. Ambassador, but I did think I could slip an unofficial warning into Freya's ear," Antonio explained.

The ambassador's ever-present sense of humor easily rose to the surface. "Oh, now I understand what you were doing on Freya's bed. You were slipping a warning into her ear. And here I thought you were just nibbling on it," Marshall said teasingly. "I'll have to remember that line if I ever get interrupted with my paramour." He sighed. "That is, if I ever get another one." The jesting tone faded from his voice. "But enough of my troubles. What is this new information?"

"Again I can speak only of rumors. But about a week ago some of our agents broke up an arms-smuggling ring in Marseilles, a ring linked to at least two terrorists groups. Under questioning, one of the men boasted that we could expect more trouble throughout the Mediterranean because some of their members had infiltrated certain embassies in this area."

"Which embassies?" Marshall demanded.

"We don't know. We're not even sure that Italy is one of the countries where they'd either placed or recruited people for their group." Antonio cleared his throat. "To be honest, we're not even sure this hoodlum knew what he was talking about. He might have been lying to send us off chasing ghosts that don't exist. It's happened before."

Freya only half listened as she studied Antonio while he spoke. Knowing him as a lover, at first it was hard for her to visualize him in the role of an Interpol agent. But now, after hearing him snap out information with such authority, after seeing how his shoulders squared as if ready for action, she wondered how she could have thought that he might be anything else. The analysis might have gone on had not the ambassador's explosive "Damn!" yanked her out of her musing. She glanced quickly at him with concern.

"Just what I love, rumor and vague innuendos! How can we act on those?"

Then Marshall straightened his shoulders as if shaking off the additional problems Antonio had brought. "Well, they're not going to stop us. Italy is going to get its fortieth anniversary celebration, and no real or fabricated terrorist group is going to stop us. Besides, as much as I hate to admit it, it's already too late to stop the plans. So we shall proceed."

His glance swept between Freya and Antonio. "Just before the cable came in from Interpol, I received another. Our copy of the Declaration of Independence, in its specially constructed, hermetically sealed display case, is on the way to Italy by sea. It should arrive in a week or less."

"But why?" Freya frowned. "The celebration is still several weeks off. Why have they sent it so early?"

"According to those idiots—I mean, gentlemen—at the State Department, they wanted the document here early, so it could be displayed at the embassy during a series of receptions they want us to hold for members of the American colony, Italian dignitaries, and, no doubt, more visiting congressmen."

Freya's head sagged into her hands. "I was praying that they'd just fly it in and fly it out before anyone had a chance to touch it."

"So was I," Marshall agreed. "But wait, it gets worse. To give the Declaration of Independence a send-off worthy of its importance, our people in Washington hosted a huge press conference on board the naval carrier that's bringing it over, the *Constitution.* Now anyone who's interested knows what ship it's on."

"I'm not sure that was wise," Antonio ventured.

"Wise?" Marshall's fist crashed into the arm of the settee. "Of course, it wasn't wise! It was idiotic!" Then, with effort, he calmed himself. "But as my wife always used to say, you can't cry over spilled milk. What's done is done. So, Count Raimondi, I'm tossing you your first hot potato. You're in charge of getting that document from the docks, through the streets of Rome, and into this chancellery without it being blown up, burned, or stolen."

Freya had never seen Antonio look more determined as he nodded curtly. "Don't worry. I promise that the document will arrive safely."

"It had better, or heads are going to roll, and mine will be the first to go!"

Marshall rose slowly and stretched. "It's been a long day. I think I'll skip going back to the office and go directly to bed." He smiled impishly in understanding.

Then his glance flickered to the doors opening onto her balcony. As he walked over, closed them, then set the alarm, he suggested, "Count Raimondi, in the future why don't you try using the front door? This derring-do onto and off Freya's balcony could be dangerous. Now that she's found you, I'd hate for her to lose you because you slipped on some loose tile and plunged headfirst into one of the rosebushes below."

They watched him leave. When the door shut, Antonio glanced at her. "He really is quite a remarkable man."

"I wish he had someone to share his life."

Then she noticed the faraway look in his eyes. "Antonio, what's wrong? You seem a million miles away."

He brought his attention back to her. "No, not a million miles, just about five hundred."

"Would you care to explain that rather cryptic statement?" Freya asked. "It's too late for riddles."

Antonio rose to his feet and grabbed her hand, pulling her up beside him. "How much would it take to bribe you, my bewitching lady?"

"Depends on what you want." She swayed nearer. "I suspect that I could be persuaded to do almost anything you wanted—if you used the right technique. Of course, you might have to try

161

several different techniques before you found one that worked."

He grinned. "One thing they taught us in secret agent school is to never give up. If the first technique doesn't work, we've got all night to find one that does."

His embrace swept her hard against him. "Now, let's see," he murmured, brushing her long hair away from her ear. "As I recall, before we were interrupted, I was nibbling on your ear. That seems like a good place to start."

Freya closed her eyes as his warm breath began stoking the fire alive within her. With whispered words of desire blown softly, gentle nips of his teeth tugging at her earlobe, moist thrusts of his tongue driving into the interior, their desire quickly sprang back to life. Yet it was so sweet, neither wanted to hurry.

Antonio drew away, and her eyes fluttered open. "Ready to accept that bribe yet?"

She smiled. "That technique was persuasive, I admit, but I'm not ready to grant you your every wish, at least not just yet."

"You're not? Too bad." He pretended disappointment. "I should have remembered how strong your will is. I suppose I have no choice but to go on to technique number two."

"And what's that?"

"Well, if the ear didn't break you, maybe the throat will," he murmured, starting to nibble again. Freya tilted her head back, letting him have his way as the sensations spiraled deeper and deeper within her at each touch of his lips, at each rasp of his tongue.

A slow, deep moan was her only response as his kiss found the pulse throbbing wildly up the column of her neck. The moan changed to a delighted gasp as his hand finally found her breast. Through the sheer nylon of the leotard, her nipples responded as they thrust hungrily against his questing palms.

She knew the desire that burned hotly in her eyes as he drew away once more to look at her. She wanted him to see her need, wanted him to know that soon she would be his . . . but not quite yet.

"Technique two was even better than one, and three was best of all," she told him in a husky voice. "And my resistance to taking your bribe is definitely tottering, but it's not ready to tumble yet."

"It's not?" He sighed deeply.

Even though he forced his voice to sound full of regret, his eyes didn't lie. He was as delighted as she at the deliciously long building of desire.

Forceful hands came down on her shoulders. "This calls for drastic measures because, both for the ambassador's and my sake, I want you to take this bribe and give me what I want."

His words intrigued her but not half as much as the wild passion she saw blazing in his dark eyes. Give him what he wanted. She strongly suspected that that's exactly what she'd do—and soon. And knowing his power over her when he touched her and kissed her, he'd get anything he wanted from her, and more than once.

"Antonio, I—"

He put a finger across her lips to still the words. "Shhh, *cara mia*, let me convince you how sweet defeat can be."

Using his hands on her shoulders to guide her, he marched her backward across the bedroom, until she felt the edge of the bed touch the back of her knees. Gentle hands forced her down to the mattress, and suddenly she didn't want to resist anymore. Opening her arms in invitation, she whispered, "I'm ready to take that bribe. Ask anything. It's yours."

"Not yet, not before I try technique four. You made me wait to make you mine. Now *you* can wait. Giving in is no longer enough, *cara mia*. I want you to beg to be taken."

Freya's heart began to pound as he continued in that richly sensual accent that affected her almost as much as a caress. "I want the desire so hot within you, you'll think you're back lying naked before my fireplace. I'll be heating your flesh, not the flames."

He paused as his gaze raked over her. It touched her lightly parted lips, then moved slowly downward, lingering over the curve of her breasts before moving on again.

"Freya, turn over," he commanded.

How could she resist when even his voice set her blood on fire? A soft moan escaped her parted lips when she felt his kiss begin to taste of the sensitive flesh behind her knee. As his lips danced from one knee to the other his hands began long caresses, moving in arousing strokes from her ankles upward, over the backs of her thighs, then down again. The heat from his hands and his kiss warmed her. And soon that warmth stole upward until she throbbed more hotly than she ever had before.

On and on it went, until her moans grew louder, and still he wouldn't stop the kisses, the tiny bites, the caresses that were slowly driving her wild. Then, just when she didn't think she could stand the delicious torment a moment longer, his kiss traveled upward, tracing a path of desire along her inner thigh . . . and beyond.

"Oh, Antonio," she said with a moan as his fingers slipped inside her leotard to torment the spot already aching for his touch.

"Antonio . . . please," she cried, writhing under his probing touch, wondering if she could live a second longer without drawing him into her.

"Please what?" he murmured in her ear. "Tell me what you want."

And suddenly she knew. She wanted him as weak with wanting as he'd made her. She wanted him to burn until he begged that they become one, just as she had almost begged.

Her unexpected rolling away caught him by surprise. For a moment his eyes were questioning as she slid from the bed and stood up. Then he smiled when he saw her hands go to her hair to loosen it from its coil. As it tumbled down her back, reaching almost to her waist, she slowly slipped out of the tight leotard. Antonio's breathing was ragged as she stood before him, teasing him with her nudity, yet standing just out of his reach. Then she came to him.

With tantalizing slowness she unbuttoned his shirt, finally stripping it from his body and tossing it aside. As he lay before her she ran her hands up and down over the hardened muscles of his chest, then bending, she found the hard nipple with her mouth. Around and around her tongue caressed him, then her teeth closed gently over him. As she tugged gently, his control snapped and his arms came up to pull her to him, but she evaded him yet again.

Freya smiled serenely as she moved beyond his touch. "We have all night, Antonio."

"So we do," he responded, his breathing slowing as he laced his arms behind his head and relaxed back against the pillows, obviously waiting to see what she'd do next. He didn't have to wait long.

His desire couldn't be hidden as her eyes swept down over his body. As if they possessed a power of their own, her hands reached to touch, to caress, to bare the source of the pleasure that soon would be hers. And his pants quickly followed his shirt to the floor. But still she wouldn't let him pull her onto the bed to lie beneath him.

Instead she knelt beside him on the bed. Using her long hair to caress his body, she teased him. Trailing it over his chest, his stomach, then lower, she pulled a groan from him. Again and again she let the silken strands of her long hair give pleasure, only to pull away again as she watched Antonio's chest rise and fall with ever-increasing speed.

Her hands followed the same path, touching first his face, his lips, then moving slowly over his chest, until finally her fingers touched, then curled around him, causing a bolt of pure desire to surge through him. Antonio's eyes opened, and he looked at her—wanting her and yet hating the magic to end. Then, as her fingers stroked, she saw his fists clench.

"Freya . . . please. I can't . . ."

Her body sliding on top of his silenced the words. Quickly, as if to keep her from escaping again, his arms swept around her, and in one powerful motion he lifted her high, then lowered her onto him until in one bold movement they became one.

Hours later, long after the sun was up, long after exhaustion had triumphed over a passion finally sated, a discreet knock on the door finally roused them. Not wanting the maid to walk in on them as the ambassador had, Freya leapt out of bed and frantically searched for a robe while yelling that she'd open the door in a minute.

Nestled deep within the comfort of her bed, Antonio propped himself up on one elbow. He watched her with amusement as she discarded a sheer black wrapper, choosing instead to don a very staid terry-cloth robe.

"Want me to hide in your closet? Obviously you're concerned about your reputation. Maybe I should slip back onto the balcony."

Freya stopped belting her robe and relaxed,

realizing that she was being rather silly. "Think of my reputation, then. I can see the headlines now: SCANDALOUS INTERLUDE CAUSES INTERNATIONAL INCIDENT. NAKED COUNT SHOT BY MARINES ON SOCIAL SECRETARY'S BALCONY. ALL OF ITALY ENRAGED! The ambassador would probably be recalled, and no doubt I'd be deported. Maybe you'd just better stay where you are."

His eyes flashed. "That's a most inviting idea, I assure you. Hurry back. The bed's getting cold."

"After last night it could probably use some cooling off. It's a wonder that we didn't set it on fire," she said over her shoulder as she hurried toward the door.

Outside, the uniformed maid was holding a heavily loaded silver breakfast tray.

"Are you feeling all right, Miss Davidson?" she asked with concern. "You usually just have an English muffin and a pot of coffee. This looks like enough food for a small army. Maybe that chef, Conrad, got it wrong, but he told me that the ambassador had ordered him to fix all this for you and have it delivered at ten o'clock." The maid studied her closely. "He said you worked real late last night and deserved a rest."

A smile lurked in the corners of Freya's mouth. "That was very thoughtful of the ambassador. I'll have to thank him. I know he's been concerned that I've lost weight lately. He probably ordered all this food to fatten me up."

"Well, this should do it. There's even a pot of hot chocolate along with the coffee." The maid

168

paused, then tried fishing for information. "That must be why there are two cups."

Freya smiled serenely as she lifted the heavy silver tray from the maid's hands. "Yes, I'm sure that's why."

With a stack of pillows at his back, his arms laced behind his head, Antonio looked like a naked sultan when she reentered the room. "The ambassador thought of everything. Even why my breakfast tray needed two cups."

Antonio chuckled, reaching for a buttery croissant as she set the tray on the bed in front of him. "That's why he's the ambassador. He's diplomatic."

"He's also a wonderful friend." Freya snapped her fingers. "Which reminds me of something. Last night you said you wanted me to accept the bribe for both yours and the ambassador's sake, but you never told me what it was you wanted."

Antonio reached over and slipped his hand beneath the terry-cloth robe. When his hand rested warmly on her breast, he murmured, "Told you? I thought I showed you over and over again last night what I wanted. And as I recall, you did a little demonstrating of some wants yourself."

"That's not what I mean, and you know it. I proved, rather convincingly I think, that I'm willing to take a bribe. Now, what is it you want me to do?"

Reluctantly Antonio withdrew his hand. "Something you said about the ambassador last night triggered an idea. Wouldn't you say that

169

this celebration is one of the most important of his career?"

"Sure, but—"

"Let me finish. Since you agree that it's so important, wouldn't it be nice to commemorate this celebration in a very special and unique way? Wouldn't it be nice to give him something he could keep forever, to remind him of the honor he bestowed on my country by conceiving and organizing this celebration?"

Intrigued by his idea, she poured both of them a fresh cup of coffee and agreed. "I know Marshall would love that. What do you have in mind?"

"An oil painting of the ambassador inside the Farnese, surrounded by all the powerful men of the day, and standing before your Declaration of Independence. That's what I have in mind. It could be your special gift to someone who obviously means a lot to you."

Freya's eyes glowed at the idea of how pleased Marshall would be.

Antonio cleared his throat as he tried, unsuccessfully, to look innocent. "I happen to know one of the foremost portrait artists in Italy. This person hasn't touched a brush in years, but for the chance to actually be inside the Farnese, to actually see the work of the great Carracci in person instead of in photographs, I think I could convince this painter to come out of the self-imposed seclusion."

"Your idea sounds wonderful! Where can we find this painter?" she asked.

Antonio looked strangely uneasy as he sipped his coffee and continued. "I know this person. This painter will want to get close to Ambassador Whittiker, to get to know him, to find the man inside the official facade, and to do that they need to meet, talk, and spend some private time together. Maybe the artist could move in to the chancellery while working on the project?"

When she noticed his slightly guilty expression, she dropped the bite of croissant she was about to devour and demanded, "Antonio, just who is this artist of vast repute?"

"I didn't lie, Freya. I assure you, her reputation is well established, if unused lately. You can check that with any art gallery."

"And?" She drew the word out, realizing that there was something he hadn't told her.

He couldn't meet her gaze. "And . . ." He paused. "And this famous reclusive painter is my mother, my widowed mother."

CHAPTER ELEVEN

Freya glanced at Antonio with affection. "The lonely widower meets the widow. Sounds like the title for an operetta, but I like the idea. Are all Italians so romantic? In America most men condemn matchmaking, and here you are promoting it."

No smile answered her gentle teasing. After sliding off the bed and pulling on his slacks, Antonio began pacing the room. "It's a little more involved than simple matchmaking, *cara mia*, although if my mother did find happiness with another man, I would be pleased." He took her hand and led her to the settee before the fireplace. "Perhaps I should explain. My father was quite a bit older than my mother when they married. Maybe that's why she worshiped him more than most wives. Ah, they were so happy, those two, until . . ." His words faltered.

"Until?" Freya gently encouraged him to go on.

Antonio reached for her hand and squeezed it hard. "I'd been with Interpol for five years and was home between assignments. Papa had given Mother a new car, a white Fiat convertible, for her birthday." He closed his eyes, remembering the scene. "I stood outside on the drive and watched them set off on that first drive. I'll never forget how happy they looked as they waved good-bye." He squeezed her hand again. "Papa never made it back from that drive."

Tears sprang to Freya's eyes, knowing the pain he must have felt. "Oh, Antonio, how awful! What happened?"

"They were sideswiped by a truck, and Mother lost control. The accident wasn't her fault, but she's never forgiven herself. That was six years ago. Since then she's just shut herself up in my family's villa, existing but not really living. I've tried a dozen times to get her to come to Paris, to Barcelona, to Athens, wherever I was assigned, but she never would. But this celebration just might lure her back into life."

Freya put her arms around him, as if trying to absorb some of his pain. "Antonio, being trapped by memories of the past imprisons your spirit and eats at your soul. I know. I let my father's rejection sour too many of my days. I hate the thought of your mother living in that kind of prison. Tell me what I can do to help."

"I knew you wouldn't let me down. Of course, all of this will have to be cleared through the ambassador, but here's what I thought we could do. Check my mother's artistic credentials. They really are quite impressive. Then—"

"Antonio," she said, interrupting with a laugh, "that won't be necessary. If you say she's talented, that's enough for me, and I know it will

173

be enough for Ambassador Whittiker. Besides, we both know there's more going on here than commissioning a painting."

He gave her a conspiratorial wink. "With any luck you'll be right. If the ambassador agrees, then have the embassy issue a formal invitation to her to come to Rome, stay here, and begin work on the painting. For my part, I'll probably have to resort to applying a little psychological, patriotic, and historical pressure to get her to agree."

She glanced at him in confusion. "How can anyone apply pressure from history?"

"In the Raimondi family it's not only easy, it's actually inescapable." Antonio twisted to face her. *"Italia dolce io servire,* Sweet Italy I serve," he said, translating. "That's been our family's motto since the Renaissance. Down through the years the Raimondis have fought for our country. They opposed the despotic rule of the d'Medicis. They fought Austria to free Venetia. They were with Garibaldi on his march to Rome. My grandfather died challenging Mussolini's usurpation of power."

"And you're an agent for Interpol."

He shrugged. "I cannot escape history, either. It seemed the best way for me to serve Italy. Even if my mother hesitates, as I know she will, I will remind her that as a Raimondi, completing this painting is something she must do for our country."

An hour later Emilio glanced up as they walked into her office and frowned. *"Dios mio,*

174

what's he doing here?" her assistant demanded. "Isn't it enough that he pesters you at night? Does he have to interrupt our work? We have important things to do today."

"Nothing we have to do could be as important as the mission Count Raimondi has been given."

"If he *is* Count Raimondi!" Emilio challenged.

"He is," Freya insisted. "Confirmation came in last night from Washington. You'll know soon enough, anyway, so I'll tell you now. Count Raimondi is an agent from Interpol."

Emilio's eyes narrowed to two dark slits. "An Interpol agent! What's he doing sneaking around here?"

Antonio looked at the other man, and Freya could tell that he didn't like Emilio any more than Emilio liked him. His voice cracked with icy authority. "Interpol's mandate has been extended to handle cases of terrorism. That's why I'm here."

"He's been put in charge of the security arrangements for the documents and the celebration," Freya explained more fully.

Surprisingly Emilio laughed. "That's interesting news. Now I can take off my bulletproof vest. Surely no one is going to try anything with the almighty Interpol in charge." His smile was a shade insolent. "Next to James Bond, you fellows are supposed to be the best. Someone would have to have a perfect scheme to fool you, wouldn't they, Count Raimondi?"

"I've been with Interpol eleven years in nine different countries, and I haven't been fooled yet.

I've known many who thought they had a perfect scheme, and now they're doing their future planning behind bars."

Emilio didn't seem impressed as he shrugged. "I'll remember that if I ever decide to trade arranging seating charts for visiting congressmen for tossing Molotov cocktails."

Antonio started to say something, then changed his mind. Instead he turned to Freya. "I need to consult with the ambassador on security for the arrival of your Declaration of Independence. Will he be here or at his office in the embassy?"

"He almost never goes over to his office at the embassy, unless he has official business. I'll call the operator and double-check to see where he is and if he's free."

"I'm getting sick of hearing about your precious Declaration of Independence," Emilio commented. "What's the big deal? It's just a piece of old parchment."

Freya's temper flared as she glared at him in disbelief. But, holding her temper in check, she reached for the phone and confirmed that the ambassador was in his private office. When she put the receiver back, she smiled at Antonio. "I'll walk you over. I wouldn't want you to get lost."

"It's down the corridor and to the left. How could he possibly get lost?" Emilio said, protesting. "Besides, I need you here. The caterer is coming any minute with the sample of cake you wanted to try. You have to be here."

"I thought I told you to call several," Freya reminded him.

"Believe me, it wasn't necessary," her assistant argued. "When you taste this caterer's work, you'll think it was baked by an angel."

She started to remind him that when she gave an order, she expected it to be carried out as issued, then decided not to get into a fight in front of Antonio. "We can talk about it later, Emilio. Right now I plan to walk Count Raimondi to the ambassador's office."

When they were in the hall, Antonio's fingers twined with hers. He glanced down at her. "What do you know of Emilio? I can't say I care much for his attitude."

"He's harmless. It just frustrates him that I won't tumble for his line. He has great success with women—so he tells me—and I believe him. It just bruises his ego that he can't conquer me. It's become almost an obsession with him, or at least he pretends that it is."

He stopped walking. "Does he tempt you, *cara mia?* You work with him every day, and he is a very handsome man."

She reached up on tiptoe and kissed him softly on the mouth. "The only man that tempts me is you. You should know that. You tempt me to do things, to feel things I've never experienced before."

"Are you complaining?"

"Not for one instant."

"Can I tempt you again tonight, my sexy little one? In front of my fireplace?"

"I can't think of anyplace I'd rather be, unless it was swimming naked in a moonlit pool before the ruins of a temple." Thoughts of the night ahead brought a smoky haze of desire to her eyes as she murmured, "But since I can't have that, tell your fireplace to start warming up."

"The fireplace is not the only thing that shall warm up tonight. I promise you that, bewitching lady."

"Sounds wonderful. What time will you—"

Her question was interrupted by the ambassador's amused observation as he stepped out of his secretary's office. "I swear, I've never seen such a besotted pair. I give you the whole night, and what happens? You're still billing and cooing, and I'm still waiting."

Freya turned to face the older man. "I'm sorry, sir. We didn't mean to keep you waiting. Count Raimondi was just—"

"Yes, yes, I heard what he was just 'doing.'" Instead of being angry, Marshall beamed. "And since I've had a few great nights in front of a fireplace myself, you don't need to say anything more. I only wish there could be a few more of them in my life before Old Gabriel sends out a call for me."

Freya glanced at Antonio. Antonio smiled and nodded. "Sir, how would you like your portrait painted in the Farnese Gallery, with the documents, to commemorate this celebration?"

Thinking quickly of the quarterly check she'd received from her father, one she'd just add to the pile already deposited in the bank, she suddenly reached a decision. Wouldn't it be somehow beautifully fitting to use money from a father she hardly knew to do something special for a man who really did care for her?

"Please don't say no." Freya begged. "This is something I want to do for you. A special present for a special man to honor a special event."

Antonio turned quickly to her. *"Cara mia*, no, when I suggested this, I was not hinting for you to pay. Of course, the portrait, if everyone agrees, will be a gift from my family."

"No, it won't. It will be from me!"

When Antonio started to argue, she interrupted. "Let me do this. I can afford it and I want to do it."

"But, *cara mia* . . ."

"Children, will you stop this ridiculous bickering! I haven't even said I want a portrait of myself. I'm getting older. It's hard enough to look in a mirror, let alone to see every wrinkle immortalized on canvas for all to see."

Freya looked at the ambassador; tall, distinguished, hair a well-earned and dignified gray, he was still a handsome man.

She was about to tell him so when Antonio spoke. "You have nothing to worry about, Mr. Ambassador. The painter I'm thinking of captures the inner fire that makes a man, yet uses none of the harsh reality of a camera. No one has ever been displeased with this artist's work."

"And just who is this magician with a paintbrush?"

Expecting one answer, Freya blinked when

Antonio said the name. "The artist I'm thinking of is Signora Angelina Giorgione."

Marshall's eyes widened behind his glasses. *The* Angelina Giorgione? Everyone in Italy knows of her art, but I'd heard she'd retired from public life. Nobody in Europe has been able to entice her to work again. What makes you think she'd pick up her brushes just to do my portrait?"

"Because I'd ask her," Antonio explained. "Angelina Giorgione is the artist's maiden name. Her married name is Contessa Angelina Raimondi. She's my mother."

"Young man, you're just one surprise after another, aren't you?" Then Marshall straightened his shoulders. "Count Raimondi, if she'd come, I'd be honored. I'll have a formal invitation issued today." Then, without even being prodded, he added, "And, of course, I'd be doubly honored if she'd stay here. Do you think she might?"

Antonio and Freya exchanged a conspiratorial smile. "I am sure she'd be delighted. And better yet, Mr. Ambassador, *mio madre* plays chess."

Marshall rubbed his hands together. "Excellent! Now all we have to do is get our document into Rome safely."

"Sir, I've thought of a plan," Antonio said.

The ambassador motioned to Antonio. "Come into my office and tell me about it."

When Antonio saw Freya's expression, he asked, "You look unhappy. Are you angry that I didn't tell you my mother was Angelina Giorgione?"

"Of course not. It's just I feel rather foolish.

You're going off to discuss the security of one of America's most important documents, and what am I going to do? I'm going to taste cake."

"What's that expression of yours? Ah, yes, it's a tough job, but somebody has to do it." He patted her on the fanny. "Don't get fat. I'll see you when I'm through with the ambassador."

Freya felt slightly dejected as she headed back to her own office. When she pushed open the door, she found Emilio involved in what appeared to be a passionate conversation with a stunning blonde. Intense looks, hurried whispers, emphatic gestures; yes, it had all the earmarks of romance. They were so deeply engrossed in each other's company that they didn't notice she was standing in the doorway. For a moment she didn't interrupt, glad that Emilio had found someone else besides herself on whom to use his Latin charm. Only when the woman moved to one side did she see the tiered white cake.

When it became obvious that they weren't going to notice her presence, she raised her voice. "Emilio, shall I call Conrad to send up some coffee to go with the cake? At least I assume that's why this woman is in our office."

At the sound of her voice Emilio whirled to face her. For a second he looked startled, then he recovered. "This is the caterer I told you about, Carmen Fre—"

The woman put her hand on his arm, and instantly Emilio fell silent. "Just Carmen, if you don't mind," she said in a low voice that tended to be a little strident. "I don't like to use my last

181

name for business. I want you to think my cake is excellent for itself and not because someone with my family name baked it," she said, hinting that Freya would have no trouble recognizing the name of one of Rome's first families if she heard it.

Freya made no comment. Instead she turned to the phone. "I'll call for coffee and for Conrad. He's the embassy chef," she explained to the woman. "I'm sure he will want to sample any cake that will be the finale to one of his feasts."

Conrad swept into her office, barking orders at the waiter who was following with the silver tray of coffee. When he saw the woman standing by the cake, he declared, "You expect me to allow this woman to bake a cake to crown the feast of the century? No, not the century, the millennium! Women cook for families. Men cook for presidents and kings."

It was an argument they'd had many times before, and Freya was in no mood to repeat it. "Conrad, I asked you here only as a courtesy. You refused to bake the cake, and it is within my powers to hire whomever I choose to recreate the Victor Emmanuel II monument in pastry. So please stuff your outdated prejudices under that starched hat of yours and cut the lady's creation before I'm tempted to throw it at you."

With a hauty sniff and ill-concealed contempt he complied. When they all had plates, he drove his fork into the cake as if expecting to hit concrete, yet at one taste his face was transformed. As the last morsel slid down he bowed over

Carmen's hand. "I am humbled. This cake is ambrosia. It is a triumph! Yes, it is fit to grace the finale to even one of *my* feasts. You are to be congratulated." He paused the barest of seconds before asking, "May I have the recipe?"

Carmen smiled sweetly at his flowery compliments, then answered with a curt "No."

"But, charming lady—"

Her back stiffened. "That recipe has been in my family since the time of Clement VI, and I do not intend to share it with anyone."

After Conrad left, Carmen became all business. "You realize that I will have to visit the Farnese Gallery to see for myself where my creation will be placed."

"I don't think that's necessary. You're just baking a cake," Freya protested. "I don't think Ambassador Maromme would be too pleased if we send an endless stream of people into his embassy."

Carmen folded her arms. "If I don't see the Farnese, I don't bake the cake. There are a dozen things I must know." Suddenly, for no reason Freya could see, Carmen smiled. "As I understand Emilio's plan, my creation will be the end of the festivities. Who will wheel it in? How wide are the doors? How big is the cart?"

"It would be my pleasure to escort Camen," Emilio offered. "Ambassador Maromme knows me."

Freya shrugged her shoulders. "I don't have time to argue about it. I'll call the French embassy and see if it can be arranged." She turned to her assistant. "Emilio, after you've escorted Carmen to her car, please hurry back. The ambassador has told me that the first shipment of food is on the way, and we need to make plans."

"That's certainly not necessary," the other woman protested. "I'm quite capable of walking myself out of a building."

Freya mustered up her official smile. "I am sorry, but for security reasons strangers aren't allowed to wander around the chancellery unescorted. I'm sure you understand. And Carmen, Conrad was right. That cake you baked was fit for the gods."

Carmen didn't seem overly impressed with the compliment. "I hardly think a bunch of politicians are gods, but I thank you, anyway." Then she glanced at Emilio and smiled. "I'm sure it will be a cake they will never forget."

When Emilio returned to the office, Freya glanced up from the list of foods for the festival she was studying and commented, "A marvelous baker and a beautiful woman, that's quite a prize. Where did you find her?"

Obviously pleased at her assessment, Emilio said bragging, "I met Carmen at a political rally. We were both—"

Emilio stopped short, as if someone had put a gag in his mouth. Freya looked at him with amusement. "Emilio, I've known you for a long time, and never once have you mentioned politics, so why would you be at a political rally? Come on, fess up. I'll bet you were there for another reason."

"I never could fool you, could I? You know I think all politicians are idiots, but I discovered one of the great truths of the ages—political rallies attract beautiful women, and beautiful women attract me, so—"

"Emilio, you're incorrigible!" She laughed.

"I may be incorrigible, but at least I'm not stupid. And stupid is what *you're* being, my beautiful Freya."

Fraya sat straighter, resenting his impertinence. "I have been many things in my life, but I have never been stupid," she said, protesting.

"Well, you are being stupid now! You've picked a real winner this time. Since I've known you, you've only let one man in your life, and when you did, *Dios mio,* did you pick the wrong one!"

"Emilio, I don't think my private life is any of your business."

"You're wrong. It is. Especially when I see you falling for the wrong man."

Her emotions, her desires, lived with Antonio, yet deep within her there was some tiny part of her soul that made her listen to Emilio as he said insistently, "The one thing you told me you've always wanted was a home, right? Some security . . . a sense of permanence. And what do you do? You get involved with an Interpol agent! You and I both know what kind of life they lead. He's probably lived in a dozen countries in as many years. Is that what you want, Freya? A man who'll be gone as soon as this assignment is over?"

She wanted to throw her hands over her ears to blot out his words, yet she couldn't deny the truth he spoke as Emilio's voice hammered home an unpleasant message. "This is a man who's off to a new country, to a new challenge, probably to a new woman as soon as all this nonsense with security and documents and politicians is over. Is that what you want?"

The scream came from her heart. No, it wasn't!

CHAPTER TWELVE

Emilio forced her to look into that future, and what she saw shattered her heart. All her life she'd yearned for two simple things forever denied her: the security of love and a home. Antonio could give her neither. Freya felt the tears prickle behind her eyes, but she wouldn't let Emilio have the satisfaction of seeing her cry.

Instead she raised her chin and met her assistant's gaze. "I think we have too much to do to worry about my love life."

When he started to protest, she said insistently, "I have a meeting with the ambassador. I'll speak with you in the morning." Then she fled.

The garden, always a place of refuge before, now mocked her unhappiness with the lovely scents of its roses and the vivid glory of its azaleas, but she refused to run again. Walking aimlessly up and down the paths that wound between the flower beds, she asked herself over and over how it had happened, why she had let it happen. She'd given her heart, knowing little of the man who claimed it so easily, and now the painful day of payment had come for that foolishness.

As she paced, she tried to feel anger toward

Antonio. Was she just the last in a long list of conquests? A new assignment, a new lover? Was that why she'd fallen so easily into his bed, because his flawless technique had been perfected over time? But deep within her she knew that their passion was real. Interludes of passion, no matter how beautiful, weren't enough for her. With every breath she knew she needed more.

To be happy she needed what Antonio couldn't give her. She remembered the pride in his voice when he spoke of the Raimondi family history, of their centuries of service to his country. As he'd admitted, he couldn't escape that history, either, which meant that his life belonged to Interpol, a life destined to be nomadic. The scars left by her childhood cried that she couldn't live without a place to call home.

Freya stopped, her eye caught by a scarlet rose, a rose so like the one Antonio had used to make love to her. Without thinking, she reached for it and tore it from the bush. As the petals shredded beneath her fingers all of Antonio's words about destiny returned to haunt her. Maybe they were destined to meet, to love, to part. All her life she'd been alone. Wasn't it fitting that she'd fall in love with a man who'd leave her, so that she'd have no choice but to return to that loneliness she'd always known? To be alone; yes, that was her destiny.

Emilio was right. When this assignment was over, Antonio would be gone. It was going to end, anyway, so wasn't it better for it to be now before she could be hurt any more? Yes, it was better that it end now.

Her pace quickened. She knew Antonio would try to see her as soon as he'd finished talking with the ambassador, and she couldn't risk that. In her mind she knew that she was doing the right thing, but she feared that if she saw him again, if he had a chance to speak to her, to look at her with those dark eyes, which would always live in her dreams, that she might not have the strength to turn away. With determined steps Freya hurried through the chancellery and out onto the streets of Rome.

Walking the night away, Freya decided that only work might make her stop thinking of Antonio and what would never be. The first rosy threads of dawn touched her face as she walked wearily back into the chancellery and turned toward her office.

Several hours later Emilio arrived at the office. Surprised to see her already at work, he noticed the way she was savagely pounding the typewriter and commented, "From the way you're attacking those keys I'd say the bloom is definitely off the romance with my less-than-favorite Interpol agent. But I can't say that's bad news for me." When she didn't respond, he raised his voice. "I'm available if you need a broad shoulder to cry on."

She glanced up at him but didn't stop typing as she muttered, "I'm fine, just fine!"

"You don't look fine to me. In fact, you look like you've gone through hell and barely survived."

Rather than risk revealing too much by responding, she skirted his observation. After stopping the typing she instructed, "If I look like hell, it's because I've been here at work since dawn, and I need some coffee. Go down to the kitchen and see if Conrad can fix a breakfast tray. We have a lot of work to do today, and I don't want to hear another word about my personal life."

After Emilio left, Freya's phone rang. Automatically she picked it up and spoke. The instant Antonio heard her voice, he exploded. "Freya, where have you been? After my meeting with Ambassador Whittiker I tried to find you, and the guards said you'd gone and they didn't know where. I tried calling all night, but you never answered, and the guards said you hadn't returned. I even woke the ambassador at four in the morning to see if he knew what had happened to you."

At the sound of his voice the warmth began to curl within her, but this time, instead of letting the web of fantasy begin to spin, she let the disturbing warmth warn her, not seduce her.

"Freya, answer me!" Antonio begged when she remained silent. "I've aged ten years in this one night worrying about you. Say something. Say anything."

He sounded so concerned, so caring, Freya couldn't stop a tiny hope from stealing into her mind. Maybe he wouldn't leave. Maybe they did have a future.

"Freya, are you still there?" he demanded.

Tears choked her throat, but she forced out the

words. "Yes, I'm still here. And I have a question. Antonio, what happens after the festival?"

Her unexpected question jolted him to silence a moment, then he asked, "Why do you want to know that?"

She swallowed nervously. "Just answer me. What happens?"

She could almost see him shrug as he said, "I get another assignment, what else?"

Freya felt as if something had died inside. It had. Her hope had died, and there was nothing left to hold on to. With effort she kept her voice from breaking. "That's what I thought. Goodbye, Antonio."

From a distance she heard his anguished "Freya, wait" as she replaced the receiver.

Over the next three days, the hell she'd just visited the night before became her permanent home. Antonio called, but she ordered Emilio or the operator to tell him that she was unavailable. She didn't leave the chancellery. She didn't unlock her French doors.

The ambassador, obviously very concerned, tried to talk to her, but she would only discuss guest lists and menus with him, nothing else. She couldn't sleep. She wouldn't eat. Inside existed a huge, barren nothingness that robbed her even of tears.

She thought she'd known how much loneliness could hurt, but she was wrong. What she'd lived through before meeting Antonio was nothing compared to the bitter ache now shrouding her heart. Yet each time she admitted how much she missed him, her doubts reminded her of the future without him. Letting him back into her life would ease the pain for the moment, but later it would only make the pain that much worse. No, she'd done the right thing. But if it was the right thing to do, why did it have to hurt so damned much!

Late in the afternoon of the third day, Monday, Freya left Emilio typing up a tentative timetable for the final evening's program and walked once more into the gardens behind her office. Only there, outside, could she find any peace. As she wandered up and down the gravel paths she picked first one flower, then another, dropping each as soon as she felt the satiny softness of their petals brush against her palm.

The misery clouded her thoughts so completely, she didn't see the ambassador approaching. She was just reaching for a pale pink rose when he grabbed her hand to stop her.

"My dear, enough is enough! Look at what you've done," he ordered, sweeping his arm back over the path she'd come. "At this rate I won't have a bloom left to welcome the Contessa Raimondi when she arrives Wednesday."

Freya turned to look back over her shoulder, then unconsciously gasped when she saw the trail of tattered and mangled flowers she'd left behind. She hadn't been aware that she'd destroyed even one flower, let alone dozens.

"Sir, I'm sorry. I wasn't thinking."

"That's more than obvious!" he grumbled.

"You haven't been 'thinking' for the past three days, and I want to know why."

The pain etched deep lines across her forehead. "I can handle it," she mumbled. "Don't worry. It doesn't have anything to do with the festival. It's just a personal problem."

Marshall took her forcibly by the arm and led her to a marble bench beside a small fountain. "For the first time since I've known you, you're wrong. This is not just a personal problem between you and Antonio. It's also an embassy problem. We have the most important celebration I've ever been involved with coming up in less than two weeks, and to be blunt, you aren't functioning in anything close to top form. To make matters worse, Count Raimondi, our vaulted security expert, is as miserable and distracted as you are. I don't think he's slept in days, and that hardly makes him alert. Something has to be done or we're going to have a first-class fiasco on our hands. And that, my dear, could have very serious international repercussions!"

With fatherly concern he gave her hand a squeeze. "Ever since you met Count Raimondi you've been positively glowing, and if you'll permit an old man his prayer, I couldn't have been happier for you. Then"—he paused to snap his fingers—"all of a sudden all your joy evaporated. You disappear from the chancellery. Count Raimondi is calling me in the middle of the night to find out where you are. I try to talk to you, and I might as well be conversing in Latin, because you really don't hear a word I say. I even tried to

193

let you work this out on your own, but my patience is at an end. I want to know what happened between you two, and I want to know now."

Maybe talking would help. More than anyone she'd ever known, she trusted Marshall and his judgment. Maybe hearing him agree that she'd done the right thing would help ease the sense of aching loss that threatened to consume her.

Freya turned to look at him. When she finally spoke, her voice came out very tiny and frightened. "Antonio is an Interpol agent."

Because he cared so much, when he heard this, the ambassador's hand crashed against the marble seat in frustration. "Freya, talk sense! I know he's an Interpol agent. So what?"

"So what?" she whispered. "So when this assignment is over, he leaves."

The ambassador gathered both her hands in his. "Freya, you know what you mean to me. I would hate to lose you. I would miss you as I would miss a daughter who left, but if Antonio leaves and you must follow, I would understand."

The hurt roughened her voice. "Follow him where? To nine countries in eleven years? You know about my past. You know that more than anything I want the security of a home." Her tone rose. "No, not just want, I need a home! And with Antonio I'd never—"

Surprised by Marshall's unexpected smile, she stopped short. Then, when his smile grew into a delighted grin, she snapped, "Why are you smiling like that? This isn't funny!"

"No, my dear, it isn't. I'm smiling because I finally understand the problem and I know the solution."

"There is no solution. For Antonio, Interpol is his inescapable duty. I understand that, but I also know what I need to be happy."

"A home? Right?"

When she nodded, the ambassador continued. "Maybe it's your past that's the problem. Maybe you can't know what you've never had. But you've made a very basic mistake. You've confused *home* with a place."

Freya looked at him in confusion. "Well, what else is it? It's a place for security. It's a place for permanence." She hesitated before adding something she'd never known. "It's a place where love can grow and endure."

"Yes, in a way you're right. But what you don't seem to understand, my dear, is that all of that can be had without ever owning a single piece of real estate."

When she started to argue, he silenced her. "No, let me explain. I've spent my life in the foreign service. Amelia and I spent our lives living all over the world, but—and this is the important part—each place we lived was home."

Marshall looked more grave than she'd ever seen him as he vowed, "Home is not a place, Freya. It's not a house, an apartment, a villa. A home is where love resides, and that can be anywhere, in one place or scattered all over the world."

Freya looked at him, groping to sort her way

out of the maze of conflicting emotions warring within her. She always dreamed of a two-story white house on some quiet side street. Growing up, she'd held that image close to her heart, envying those who lived in that dream house, vowing that someday she would be the one driving in the driveway or washing the windows or planting the roses beside the sidewalk.

Now Marshall's words cracked all those cherished images. Was he right? Was what she'd dreamed of for years a meaningless shell, covering what truly was real? She just didn't know.

Her confusion must have shown in her eyes, because the ambassador's tone became even more solicitous. "My dear, take your time. Think of what I've said. Then let your instincts lead you. As I observed when we first suspected Count Raimondi and you defended him, so far your instincts have always been right. They were then. I'm sure they will be now."

He paused, then added, "I believe your future is entwined with Count Raimondi. I remember the look in Amelia's eyes when we fell in love, and you had that same look. But if things don't work out, I want you to know that there will always be a place in *my home* for you."

Tears blurred her vision as she leaned over and kissed him on the cheek. "And I want you to know that I hope your *home* will again be filled with love someday, a love like you and Amelia once shared."

"Freya, I appreciate those hopes, but right now I'm concerned about you." As if he didn't know what else to say to help her out of her misery, the ambassador gave her a reassuring hug, then left her alone with her thoughts.

Again she walked the streets of Rome. The ambassador's words had shaken her. She'd been so sure that she'd made the right decision by saying good-bye to Antonio. Now she wasn't sure at all.

Dusk came and went, and still she walked, not even noticing where her steps were taking her. Then suddenly she heard a familiar sound, the sound of splashing water. It cut through her muddled thoughts, and she knew what was around the next corner. Was it chance that had brought her back to the Trevi Fountain? Or was it the memories of another night that had brought her here, a night on which she'd given her heart?

Her steps slowed as she neared the fountain. Mirroring the splashing water, tears splashed down her cheeks as she looked at the lovely fountain . . . and remembered. Maybe it meant she wanted to stay, maybe it was a way to finally say good-bye, but without even realizing what she was doing, Freya searched, then found a coin.

The blue water beckoned, wanting her coin. Closing her eyes, she deliberately let no wish form as she drew back her hand, ready to toss it into the waiting water below. Warm fingers closed over her hand, stopping her. She didn't need to see to know that it was Antonio. His touch, the touch that filled her dreams, was enough to tell her who had come for her.

Her eyes fluttered open, and the instant she

197

saw his haggard face, she reached for him. His skin, once gold, now looked dull, as if tarnished by sadness; and his eyes, once sparkling with life, now were haunted. Lines scarred his forehead. With a fingertip she tried to smooth them away, but they wouldn't fade.

And in that moment, in that moment when she touched him, she knew that Marshall was right. She knew that being with Antonio, if he'd have her, was all that mattered. Whether it lasted for a day, a week, or forever, loving him was all she needed to be happy.

He looked down at the hand trapping hers. Then, when he looked back up at her, his eyes were more serious than she'd ever seen them. In a voice husky with longing he confessed, "Freya, I love you. I've loved you from the first moment I saw you. And I hope what I see shining in your eyes reflects a love as strong and binding as mine."

His grasp released her. "Be sure of your heart, because if you drop that coin, I'll never let you leave me again."

Her heart knew. At the splash of the coin hitting the water Antonio grabbed her up in his arms and yanked her almost roughly against him, as if afraid that if he didn't hold her tight, she'd slip away from him again.

At the touch of his kiss Freya, for the first time in her life, knew what having a home felt like. Her lips parted eagerly to accept him. Her arms wound around his neck to bind him. Her heart thudded against the hardness of his chest, telling her with each beat that this fantasy was real. Time or place meant nothing as the kiss flowed on and on. The only reality was that they were together.

Each wanted to blot out the agony of the last three days with that kiss. With their arms around each other, body touching body, slowly the pain eased. The kiss deepened, becoming more delightfully satisfying and infinitely more intimate.

The passion denied for the last several days ignited as each yearned to feel the warmth suddenly reborn and to taste the desire building with each thrust of their tongues and each caress of their lips. They wanted to engrave the moment forever in their memories with that special kiss.

When they finally broke for air, they found themselves in the middle of a group of admirers, all smiling, while a few said, sighing in envy, "Ahhhh, *amore, bollo amore.*"

Freya felt her face flame at the unexpected audience, but Antonio seemed unconcerned as he bent toward her and whispered, "They're just jealous of what I have and they can only dream of."

The crowd drifted away, leaving them alone once more. Lost in each other, neither was even aware that the gawkers had gone.

"How did you find me? I didn't even realize I was heading here until I heard the splashing water." Suddenly she smiled, remembering all his words. "I'll bet it was just fate. Right?"

Antonio's fist clenched. "Not this time. Fate may have brought us together in the beginning, but it had nothing to do with my finding you tonight."

He pulled her gently to him once again. This time not in passion, but just to reassure himself that she really was there and not some fleeting part of a dream.

"When you said good-bye, I almost went crazy. I called and you wouldn't talk to me. I tried to see you, and they always said you were out. I even lurked below your bedroom in the garden, but you never came out on the balcony. You never even opened your doors. So I came here to the Trevi Fountain, where we'd first kissed, hoping, praying that you'd come. I didn't know what else to do."

His embrace tightened painfully around her. "Freya, why? Why did you put us through this hell?"

Her long hair brushed across his chest as she shook her head. "Because I was a fool. Until I talked to the ambassador, I didn't realize what I'd been searching for my whole life wasn't a thing. It wasn't a place at all. It was an emotion. Antonio, I said good-bye because I didn't think we could have a future."

He tilted her chin up so that she had to look at him. "But why? I don't understand. I told you you were my destiny. Couldn't you believe me?"

"Destiny, fate; Antonio, those were just words. They couldn't compete with needs, or at least what I thought were needs." Fresh tears scalded her eyes as she tried to make him understand. "I told you about my father. I told you I never had the security of a home. I thought that to be happy I needed that."

With infinite gentleness he wiped the tears away. "And because you know how committed I am to my career at Interpol, you thought I could never give you that."

"It seems so simple now. Marshall made me see the truth. He and Amelia had lived all over the world, and yet, because they loved each other, each place was home."

"Freya, the scars from the past always cloud how you see the world. Don't you know that?"

"That may be, but I still feel like a fool."

She snuggled deeper into his embrace and looked up at him. "Can you love a fool, Antonio?"

"Cara mia, you know I can!" he vowed. "And I intend to prove it several ways tonight. Freya, I've been in hell for three days. It's time you showed me heaven, the heaven I can find only in your arms."

The instant Antonio turned the key to start the car, Freya slid over to cuddle next to him. She turned her head, letting her eyes roam over the face that had haunted her dreams. But just looking wasn't enough, and her hands reached for him. One button on his shirt came free, and with a sigh her hand slid across his chest to lie over his heart.

A second button parted, then a third, letting her other hand begin exploring the ripple of muscles of his broad chest. A low moan escaped from Antonio as her fingertips trailed a path down to caress the hard muscles of his stomach.

"Freya," he said with a gasp, "I am going to wreck this car if you keep doing that."

Enjoying the way his breathing was becoming more ragged by the moment, she nestled even closer. "Then I guess I'd better stop. Maybe this won't bother you," she murmured, reaching up to take the lobe of his ear between her teeth. As she tugged gently and blew soft words of love in his ear, the car swerved slightly.

Antonio didn't take his eyes off the street ahead, but, unable to resist, one hand left the steering wheel. Sliding rapidly up her silken thigh, his hand moved between her legs, not stopping until he reached the silk of her panties. Freya's head fell back against the leather of his seat as his touch made her helpless to do anything but let him have his way. The barrier of silk keeping his fingers just a breath away taunted her, yet at the same time teased her as his fingers stroked first in rapid circles at the spot now on fire, then thrust hungrily against the silk, rubbing it against her, exciting her until she whimpered with need.

Unconsciously her hand reached to share the pleasure with him. Even in the dim light of the passing streetlights there was no doubt of his arousal, and her fingers easily found the evidence of his desire.

By now Antonio's breathing was coming out in short gasps, and the knuckles on his hand, still on the steering wheel, went white as he fought for control. "Freya, don't."

She wiggled beneath his probing hand but didn't stop her own caresses as she felt him swell

202

even larger. "Don't what, Antonio?" she murmured, arching against him to find his ear again. "Do you want me to stop touching you? Do you want me to stop kissing you?" Her fingers curled tightly around him, squeezing gently. "Do you want me to—"

"What I want is to be inside of you! Right now!" he said, interrupting almost harshly.

"Antonio, please drive faster." She blew the words into his ear. "I can't wait much longer."

His fingers slid inside the silk of her panties. For a second, as his fingers moved inside her, he glanced at her out of the corner of his eye and smiled. "It won't be long, little one."

Freya expected to be swept up in his arms and carried to his bed the moment they entered his apartment, but Antonio surprised her. Instead he drew her gently to him and sighed. "I've dreamed of nothing else but this moment for three days, and I want it to be perfect."

"If you make love to me, Antonio, it will be perfect. That's all I want. I want you."

His deep chuckle echoed through the room. "You'll have me, little one, again and again until I've driven the memory of these last days from my mind, but not quite yet."

Hating the thought of being apart even for a moment, Freya tried to hold on to him as he drew away, but he removed her clinging hand. "Patience, little one. You'll have me, all of me, and very soon."

Freya's eyes never left him as he knelt to light the fire. When the blaze began to crackle, sending out dancing golden flickers to light the lush Oriental rug laid before the hearth, she went to him, but still he held her off. "Wait. I must get one more thing."

When he returned, he held the white silk gown in his hands. For a moment he buried his face in the soft fabric, inhaling deeply, then he glanced up at her. "This is the only thing that has kept me sane the last couple of days. The scent of you, the memories of how you looked coming toward me in that olive grove; somehow, touching this, I knew I would see you in it again."

Slowly he came to her, his dark eyes never leaving her face. He draped her gown lovingly across a chair, then with gentle hands he unbuttoned her blouse. Her skirt quickly followed, and soon she stood naked before him. Antonio's breath caught as he looked at her, but he didn't reach to touch her. Instead he slipped the sheer silk gown over her head. As it floated down around her he lifted her into his arms.

As he laid her back against the silken lushness of the Oriental rug, she smiled up at him. "You dreamed of me in silk. I dreamed of you standing splendidly naked before me, looking like a Roman god, like you did the night by the pool."

"Anything to please," he murmured, unbuttoning the last two buttons of his shirt.

Soon he towered above her as she wanted to see him, and her eyes feasted on the obvious arousal that would soon give her such pleasure.

Without another word Freya opened her arms, and he came. Keeping the silk of her gown between them, he lay upon her, undulating his body, up and down upon her, until the exquisite friction of feeling his hard masculinity but not being able to possess it almost drove her crazy. From a distance she heard soft moans and only vaguely realized that they were coming from her parted lips. Then the moan became a cry as he arched back, pressing harder into her but still not driving into her body like she wanted.

She had never felt such waves of sensation before. First hot, then cold, she trembled, clutching at him, trying to draw him closer, wanting him, but he resisted taking her. Instead he bent toward her. Through the sheer silk of her gown he began to suck on the aroused peak, pulling it into his mouth, lifting her breast with his hands so he could taste more and more of her.

The delicious torture seemed to go on for hours as she twisted beneath him, her head thrashing from side to side as the fire exploded into flame.

"Antonio . . . please," she said with a moan, her hand desperately reaching to hold him. "Now! I want you now!"

In one swift motion Antonio shoved the silk up above her waist. Fearing that he'd escaped, Freya guided him into her, then wrapped her legs around his waist.

"Now, Antonio . . . now," she chanted almost incoherently as he drove hard and deep into her body.

At that first magical touch a shudder of pleasure rocked through them. Intensely beautiful and satisfying yet still they wanted more, much more! Letting that be just the first of many, each tried to prove the power of their love by pleasing the other in every way they could think of. No exhaustion slowed them as kiss followed kiss, as tongues mated, as caress upon caress turned already hot bodies into raging fires, fires that only possessing each other could cool.

CHAPTER THIRTEEN

The bright Italian sun warmed the morning air as Antonio and Freya arrived at the chancellery the next morning. As they entered her office Emilio glanced up from the notes he was making, took one look at her radiant smile, and spat out, *"Dios, mio,* I should have known my luck wouldn't hold when it comes to you."

The long hours the night before in Antonio's arms had been incredibly sweet but tiring, so she was in no mood to tolerate his flippant attitude. "Emilio, it's much too early in the morning to try to argue with you. We need to see the ambassador. Do you know where he is?"

"As a matter of fact, I do. He stopped in here earlier to speak with you. He seemed very concerned."

Emilio's eyes narrowed to dark slits as he glanced from Freya to Antonio. "I can see now that he had no reason to worry. Anyway, when I told him you hadn't appeared yet, he said that when you did arrive, to tell you he was waiting in the garden."

When they walked outside, they found the ambassador with a huge arm load of roses, boughs of mock orange, and even some sprays of yellow jasmine he'd cut. When he saw her happy face, he let out a huge sigh. "Well, I can see all of this early-morning work of mine wasn't the least bit necessary. The blooms would have been safe."

When he saw Antonio's confused frown, he explained, "Count Raimondi, you should have seen her yesterday. She was so upset that she shredded every flower in sight. If things hadn't worked out, as they obviously have, I was afraid the contessa would have been greeted with a barren room when she arrives tomorrow. Barren, that is, unless I salvaged these flowers now."

"Well, I'm especially glad that Freya is no longer upset, and that you have some flowers left, because last night my mother called. All the plans are set. She'll arrive by plane about noon tomorrow."

"Then we must plan a festive luncheon to welcome her," the ambassador suggested. "Freya, pull out all the stops. I want her to know how honored the embassy is to have her visit us. And I'll call Ambassador Maromme and make arrangements for us to tour the Farnese Gallery later in the afternoon. I know she is anxious to see that marvelous fresco. Count Raimondi, of course I insist that you come with us."

"That should present no problem. In the morning I must check the security arrangements where the ship carrying the Declaration of Independence will dock, but after that I am free."

Antonio paused, then added, "Everything seems so bright with hope this morning, I almost hate to tell you this, but the rumors of a possible terrorist strike are increasing. The target you've created may be too tempting to ignore." His mouth firmed into a taut line. "But we'll be ready. Nothing must be left to chance."

"It won't be," the ambassador vowed. "By the way, Count Raimondi, I received word this morning from the carrier, the *Constitution*. The navy brass thinks you're crazy, but they've done what you requested."

"Hey, wait a minute," Freya said, interrupting. "What is your crazy idea? Won't you tell me?"

"No, I won't. Nor shall I," Antonio insisted. "The fewer people who know about the security measures I've devised, the better."

"You act like I can't be trusted." She pouted for a second, then shrugged. "I'm sorry. I know you're right."

When Antonio didn't disagree, the ambassador hurried to bridge the awkward pause by asking, "Have your arrangements for the armored car been completed?"

"Yes. When we find out the exact time the *Constitution* will dock, it will meet the ship and transport the document back here. To use one of your American expressions, I will ride shotgun."

Freya twisted her hands together, hearing his words, understanding yet hating them. She'd just found Antonio again, and the thought that he might be placing himself in danger tore at her heart.

"Must you do that? Won't it be dangerous?"

"Don't worry, *cara mia*. I'll be all right. If you

think of it, what safer place could I be than in an armored car?"

"I still don't like it!" she muttered.

"My dear, I'm sure there's nothing to worry about," the ambassador said, trying to reassure her. "But just so you can see for yourself, I want you to be with me to receive that great document when it arrives here at the chancellery. Then you will know that both it and Count Raimondi are safe. In fact, come to think of it, we should have some sort of fancy welcoming celebration when it arrives. Freya, why don't you—"

"Don't you think the next day might be better, Mr. Ambassador?" Antonio said, quickly interrupting.

Freya looked at him in surprise that he'd make such a suggestion. But before she could question his curious intervention, Marshall agreed.

"Ah, ah, yes, I forgot. That's an excellent idea, Count Raimondi."

Freya looked from one man to the other, completely confused. "Delaying the celebration doesn't make much sense, at least not to me."

"My dear, logical or not, that is what I want to do, and that's what we shall do. Draw up a guest list of people to invite. I know it would thrill any American living in Rome to see the Declaration of Independence, written in Jefferson's own hand, unveiled." He winked. "And don't forget to invite the British ambassador. I enjoy reminding our pompous friend how his country lost the colonies. Now, children, I must go get these flowers into water. I want everything to be per-

210

fect when the contessa arrives. With all you young people around, it will be nice to have someone more my own age to talk to. Oh, one last thing, Count Raimondi. Does your mother speak English?"

"Of course. Like I, she studied in both England and France."

Before turning to go, Marshall sighed. "Makes my four years at the University of Nebraska sound rather provincial, doesn't it?"

When they were alone, Antonio pulled her gently into his arms. "Ah, Freya, if I could just go on holding you like this forever . . . but I can't."

She lifted her head from the warmth of his shoulder. "That sounds suspiciously like there is something you haven't told me."

With a huge sigh of regret Antonio admitted the truth. "I have to fly to Paris this afternoon to confer with my superiors at Interpol headquarters. They want to be briefed on the security measures I am planning. I won't be back till morning. Then I must go to Civitavecchia and check the docks. I'm afraid I won't be able to see you again until after *mio madre* arrives."

He gazed down at her with such longing, it brought a glistening of tears to her blue eyes. "How cruel is fate to give you back to me one moment, then force me away the next."

She smiled sadly. "Come back to me soon. I'll miss you."

He kissed her softly on the mouth. "*Cara mia*, tomorrow night seems like an eternity away. I can't wait to have you before the fireplace again.

211

I can't wait to slip the clothes from your body. I can't wait to fill you with my love again and again and again."

"Maybe the waiting will make our loving even better," she murmured, trying to find some good in his leaving.

"*Cara mia,* that isn't possible. Each time I take you in my arms we can equal the beauty we found last night, but it never could be better than it was, because what we shared was perfection."

Her embrace tightened around him. "Antonio, how come you always say the very words that are in my heart?"

"Because we think and feel as one. It can be no other way between us. It has been that way from the first, and it shall be that way for all eternity."

She frowned, thinking of the night ahead. "Maybe I should be jealous. Paris is a romantic city, full of beautiful women. With me miles away, you might be tempted to sample some of those Parisian delights."

Antonio shook his head as he smiled down at her. "I won't even see those other women, no matter how beautiful. Remember your name, my precious Freya. When a man has tasted of the goddess of love, as I have with you, he can't be tempted by any other woman."

A delighted smile touched her lips. "I'm awfully glad to hear that. Think of me tonight. Promise."

"I have no choice, little one. You fill all my thoughts."

He leaned down and kissed her again. "*Cara*

mia, I must go. Think of me as well, through the long hours of the night, and dream of the pleasure and joy tomorrow night shall bring us."

The touch of his lips lingered on hers as she turned back toward the chancellery to start planning both the special luncheon for the contessa and the welcoming party for the Declaration of Independence.

The next morning, having been exhausted by the emotional storm she'd endured for the three previous days, Freya slept late. With a lazy stretch she threw back the covers, then padded out onto her balcony. The crisp breeze brought the scent of the garden wafting up to her, and a delightfully wicked idea stirred.

Dressing quickly, she slipped downstairs and then hurried outside. Her rampage through the flowers the day before and the ambassador's cuttings left little, but after searching, she finally managed to find about two dozen roses worthy of being picked. A happy smile touched her mouth as she thought of the surprise she'd planned. She could just see the fire blaze in Antonio's eyes when he carried her into his apartment and saw the rose petals scattered invitingly over the Oriental carpet in front of his fireplace.

After tossing a few last instructions to Emilio about the luncheon for the contessa, she glanced at her watch, then she hurried out of the chancellery with the roses in her arms. The contessa wasn't due to arrive for about another two hours, and from what he'd told her, Antonio would be tied up at the docks checking on security for the arrival of the Declaration of Independence, so she had time to arrange everything.

The doorman hesitated only a minute as her big smile and her bigger tip produced the key to Antonio's apartment. Each time she'd come up these steps, happiness had followed. This time felt no different as she thought of the evening ahead, an evening of fire, an evening of roses, and another evening of love.

Quickly Freya laid a new fire, then gathered up the roses. Gently picking off the petals, she began to scatter them on the Oriental carpet. Soon the heady scent filled her senses as red petals followed pink petals, to mix with the yellow ones already there. She was so intent on her surprise for Antonio that she didn't hear the door open.

"Antonio, I see that someone else knows how much you love roses. You must introduce us."

At the sound of the rich contralto voice, bearing only the slightest hint of an accent, Freya whirled around. A scarlet blush to rival the reddest rose flamed across her cheeks as she looked first from Antonio, then to the woman beside him, then guiltily down at the rose petals at her feet. The remaining four roses fell from her fingers as she cried, "Antonio, I'm so sorry. I didn't know . . . I wanted to surprise you but . . ."

"But it is we who surprise you, no?" the older woman said. "Antonio, mind your manners. Introduce me to your lovely visitor."

"As you wish." His tone became formal. "Contessa Angelina Raimondi, I would like you to meet Freya Davidson, social secretary to the

American ambassador and"—he paused, his voice growing infinitely tender—"and a very special friend."

Soft, dark eyes, still hinting of a personal sorrow, met the blue of Freya's as he moved aside so the two women could see each other for the first time. Freya hoped the surprise didn't register on her face as she looked at the other woman.

An Italian contessa, descended from an ancient noble family—the image that conveyed had formed a picture in her mind of what Antonio's mother would look like. Tall, like him, and regally slender; a brittle, aristocratic manner coupled with a sharp artistic temperment; yes, that's what she'd look like. Freya could see her clearly. The only problem was that it bore absolutely no resemblance to the woman before her. No taller than she and delightfully plump with gentle features and soft gray hair, Antonio's mother looked nothing like her mental picture, and she was glad. This woman looked much more approachable than the contessa she'd created in her imagination.

As the silence stretched, Freya was aware that she was undergoing a similiar appraisal, and she held her breath until the other woman smiled warmly and she started toward her.

After brushing a kiss on each of Freya's cheeks, the older woman smiled again as she insisted, "Yes, I can see that you're a very special friend to my Antonio. This is good. I think anyone who can make my Antonio this happy must be a wonderful person."

As Antonio moved slightly away he kicked some of the fallen blooms. His eyes sparkled with mischief as he asked, "Did you bring these to welcome *mio madre*, Freya? How thoughtful."

His question caught her off-guard, and the truth slipped out before she could stop it. "Ah, not exactly. I thought . . . well, I thought . . ."

"I know exactly what you thought, little one," he said teasing her.

Freya ignored his mischief-making as she firmly changed the subject. "I'm confused. Weren't you supposed to inspect the security at the docks this morning? And for that matter, wasn't your mother supposed to arrive around noon?" She glanced at her watch. "Unless this thing has stopped, it's only a little after ten. That's why I came. I didn't think anyone would be here."

He shrugged. "In Italy plans change easily. We're not as tied to schedules as you Americans."

"Actually all of this is my fault," the contessa admitted as she started across the room. "Come, sit with me and I will explain while my Antonio picks up the beautiful flowers you brought to brighten his apartment.

"I fear that all of this tumult is my fault," Antonio's mother continued. "When I spoke with my son two days ago, I heard such unhappiness in his voice that I decided I must come to Rome early to see if I could help."

The contessa patted Freya's hand, reminding her of the ambassador's favorite gesture. "Then my Antonio came forward to meet me as I got off the airplane, and I knew I had put the extra gray in my hair for nothing. Ah, so happy I have never seen him. And I can see that you are the light behind his smile."

Antonio, after putting the roses she'd dropped in a cut-crystal vase, joined them. He smiled fondly at his mother. "Don't let her fool you, Freya. She just came early to meddle in my life. Like all Italians, it is her favorite hobby."

The contessa squared her shoulders. "Meddling is a mother's duty. You were unhappy. I intended to find out why, but I can see that you children settled your problems without my help." Then her gaze wandered off into her world of personal sadness. "You didn't need me. I could have stayed at the villa. I need never have left."

Freya glanced at Antonio and saw his pain as he looked at his mother. Quickly she gathered the contessa's hands in hers. "No, you are wrong. We do need you here. Your country needs you here. My country and Ambassador Whittiker need you here. Only someone with your talent can do justice to this special celebration."

The contessa glanced down at her hands, still held in Freya's. "Your words echo Antonio's when he convinced me that I must do my duty and come. Yet I wonder. It's been a long time since I touched a brush. Maybe I can't—"

Antonio's authoritative voice cut through her indecision. "*Mio madre,* the gifts of one so great as Angelina Georgione cannot die. It's time to let

217

them live again. Now come, we must go. I know that the ambassador is anxious to meet you."

Two hours later the ambassador stood up after a luncheon of treasures mostly stolen from the sea. The special luncheon had ranged from fresh crab salad continuing through abalone simmered in wine, to the perfect ending of a sorbet made of tart Italian persimmons.

Marshall raised his glass of California champagne to the contessa. "We are honored not only to have a great artist here to commemorate this historic event, but also to have a beautiful woman to grace our chancellery. Thank you for agreeing to come."

He nodded to the French ambassador, who'd joined them for the luncheon. "And a toast to the Farnese Gallery, a fabulous work of art by a great Italian artist, and to the French, who own it and have so generously agreed to share it with the world on this historic occasion."

Freya was sitting next to Ambassador Maromme, so only she heard him mutter, "Your flattery means nothing. We'd better keep the Farnese safe, or we both shall know the agony of exile to our own personal Elba."

Yet nothing of his concern appeared on the French ambassador's face as he rose to return an equally flowery toast.

The Italian sun was high and warm when they finished the luncheon and were finally free to visit the place everyone had toasted. Once at the French embassy, Marshall gallantly held out his arm to the contessa as they stood outside the magnificently carved doors leading to the forbidden gallery. "I'm delighted I can be the one to escort you in to see Annibale Carracci's greatest work. Freya has spent hours telling me about its mythological wonder, but I must admit that this is the first time I've seen it for myself." Then, with a flourish, he pushed open the great doors and they entered.

Freya enjoyed watching the expressions on Marshall's and the contessa's faces as they both lost themselves in the overwhelming fresco. Around and around the gallery they walked, absolutely transfixed, staring upward as scene after scene of the love stories of the gods unfurled, each one more beautiful than the last.

Finally the ambassador stopped beneath the central fresco of *The Triumph of Bacchus and Ariadne.* After studying the painting a long moment he turned to the contessa and smiled. "I have one thing to say about the way you Italians view life. It makes me believe we Americans are dead wrong about one thing. Concerning our women, we are taught to treasure a reed-slender figure, more bone than flesh."

His glance flowed over her generous figure, then returned upward again to view the well-endowed goddess. He smiled. "When I take a woman in my arms, I'll be darned if I don't want to feel more than skin and bones beneath my touch. I want a woman to feel like a woman."

Then, as if suddenly aware of what he'd said, Marshall coughed to hide his discomfort. When his throat cleared, he rushed to apologize. "Contessa, I'm so sorry. I can't imagine what made me make a personal remark like that! I hope that didn't embarrass you."

Angelina's sparkling laugh floated through the vaulted gallery. "I can't think of a nicer thing a man has said to me in ages."

With obvious relief Marshall patted her hand that still rested on his arm. "My favorite of the pictures is *Jupiter and Juno.* Shall we go view it again before we leave? It's reassuring to know, at least where the gods are concerned, that not all lovers have to be young."

The contessa smiled up at him. "The gods are not the only ones who know that secret."

From the doorway Antonio and Freya watched the ambassador and the contessa move through the gallery. Antonio looked down at the woman by his side and smiled. "I knew it was time for *mio madre* to escape from that villa."

"They do seem to be having a good time, don't they?" Freya agreed as the other couple moved back toward the painting of Jupiter.

"A good time? Those words are hardly adequate." Antonio's eyes, a moment ago alight with happiness, dimmed. "It's a lot more than just a good time that. You heard her laugh, didn't you?"

"Yes, but . . ."

"She's hardly laughed in six years, Freya. It's good to see some happiness return."

CHAPTER FOURTEEN

While Freya and Antonio watched in amusement, the contessa and the ambassador stopped again beneath the huge central painting showing Bacchus and Ariadne's triumphant arrival in a gilded chariot. Marshall sighed. "That's the way a beautiful and talented woman like you should be greeted—with music and dancing, with luscious fruit and flowing wine. That makes my welcoming luncheon for you seem most inadequate."

"No, no, your welcome was perfect for me," the contessa argued. "I fear I am much to old to go riding around in an open chariot, even if it is a golden one."

"Then how about some entertainment that's a bit more sedate." The ambassador pulled two tickets from his pocket. "They are featuring Verdi's *Rigoletto* at the opera this evening, and I took the liberty of purchasing two tickets just in case you might consent to go with me. Since Verdi's a compatriot of yours from the north, I thought you might enjoy attending."

When the contessa didn't answer, Marshall rushed on. "Now, I don't wish to pressure you,

Contessa, so if you would rather not go with me, I assure you that it will not hurt my feelings."

As Freya and Antonio approached, the contessa looked back at the ambassador. Apparently seeing the doubt on her face, he hastened to add, "For someone who's been a diplomat for more years than I care to remember, sometimes I can be very undiplomatic. I shouldn't have sprung an unexpected invitation on you like that. I can see that I've embarrassed you. Please forgive me."

The contessa reached one jeweled hand to touch his arm. "No, it is I who should be forgiven. I hesitate, but not for the reason you think. I love the opera, and *Rigoletto* is one of my favorites. I just wondered if it would be proper for a mother to desert her only son on the first night they are together in many months."

Reaching her side, Antonio bent down and gave her a kiss on the cheek. *"Mio madre,* forgive me for saying this, but you are being a little foolish. I can take care of myself, and if I can't, Freya can."

The contessa glanced from one to the other. "Ah, yes, of course, you are right. I am being foolish. I should have realized that when a beautiful woman comes carrying arm loads of roses into my Antonio's apartment, it means they have plans for the evening."

For a long, awkward moment, as the blush raged across her face, Freya could think of absolutely nothing to say. They were interrupted by the sound of angry voices.

Turning, Freya was surprised to see Emilio and

Carmen, the caterer, slamming into the gallery. They were so intent on their argument, they didn't realize that there was anyone else present.

The blond tossed her head impatiently as she said insistently, "Emilio, stop seeing problems where none exist. The plan you've devised is foolproof. It can't fail! It will be a day the world will remember forever." She spread her arms wide as her eyes swept upward to embrace the gallery. "Behold, the scene of our greatest triumph."

Obviously Emilio wasn't impressed by her excitement as he countered, "But what if—"

Suddenly Carmen noticed the group standing across the chamber. Poking Emilio sharply in the ribs with her elbow, she snapped, "Emilio, *silenzio!*

At her prod Emilio's head snapped up, and he looked across the gallery. For an instant his gaze tangled with Freya's. Seeing the expression in his eyes, she frowned. Instead of looking surprised, he seemed momentarily startled. No, she decided it was more than just startled; he seemed almost afraid. Then, in a flash, his usual cocky smile was firmly back in place.

Carmen walked toward them. "You must excuse us. Emilio and I can never talk without emotion. We did not realize anyone else would be in the gallery to overhear our quarrel."

"We also expected to be alone," Freya admitted. "Emilio, what are you doing here? I left you with instructions to finalize the menu plans with Conrad."

Her assistant shifted from one foot to the other.

"I know you did, but then Carmen came and . . . and . . ."

"And I insisted that we come here to check on all the arrangements," Carmen explained, finishing his sentence for him.

Freya turned to the ambassador. "This is Carmen. She is going to bake the monument cake for us." Freya then introduced her to Antonio and the contessa.

As the ambassador and the contessa wandered off to take one last look at the fresco, Freya turned to her assistant. "If you were going to come here, I wish you would have consulted me."

"You must not blame him," Carmen urged. "I insisted that we come, and he agreed, since he is as concerned as I that everything will go as we've planned. I wanted to check for myself on the kitchen facilities, and I assure you that everything is fine. In fact, it's more than fine; it's a perfect arrangement for what we have in mind. As for Emilio, you know that when it's something as important as this celebration, he's not satisfied until he's checked on every last detail."

Freya looked a bit skeptical. That didn't sound like the Emilio she knew. Instead of being a perfectionist, her assistant tended to slide by with doing as little as possible. No doubt he was just trying to impress Carmen with his dedication to his work. Or maybe because the festival honored his country, he was concerned that it come off perfectly.

"I'm glad you're pleased with the arrangements. Your cake should be the highlight of the evening," Freya said, graciously reassuring her.

Carmen didn't look at her. Instead she smiled at Emilio. "*Si*, my cake will be a finale no one will ever forget."

She took Emilio's arm. "We are done here. Can you drive me back to the bakery?"

Her assistant glanced at her, and Freya nodded. "Certainly. Take Carmen back." Then an idea pricked. "In fact, since it's already getting late, why don't you skip coming back to work and instead take her out to dinner, at embassy expense, of course, to let her know how much we appreciate everything she's doing."

"What an ironically appropriate idea." Emilio smiled. "Carmen, shall we go?"

Freya watched them as they walked across the gallery. Near the door Emilio leaned down to say something that brought an outburst of laughter. When Carmen stopped laughing, her glance swept once more over the gallery, then they left.

"What do you suppose he said to her?" Antonio asked.

"Who knows and who cares?" Freya shrugged. "I'm just delighted that he's found someone else to flirt with. His persistence was getting quite irritating."

Antonio's voice dropped to a husky purr. "And do you find my persistence irritating, *cara mia?*"

She smiled up at him. "No, I'd be unhappy if you didn't persist."

"I wish I had time to show you just now 'persistent' I could be." Antonio glanced at his watch.

"But unfortunately that demonstration will have to wait until this evening. Since I missed checking the docks this morning, I must go now." He lifted her hand to his lips. After a lingering kiss he murmured, "Tonight—the roses and you."

They were so absorbed in each other, they didn't hear the ambassador and the contessa approach. Marshall cleared his throat. "I think we'd better get these two children out of here. Apparently Carracci's *Loves of the Gods* is giving them ideas."

Antonio and Freya turned just in time to catch his tender smile. "And speaking of ideas, Contessa, you never did tell me if you would honor me by accompanying me to the opera this evening."

Angelina's smile warmed to his. "Obviously my Antonio shall have a pleasant evening. Why shouldn't I? But first I'd like to do a few preliminary sketches of you."

"Can you do them while I work?" Marshall asked. "I can hardly find the top of my desk."

"Of course," the contessa agreed with a smile. The ambassador looked startled when she reached up to trace fingertips over the contours of his face. Then he relaxed, realizing that it was the touch of an artist, not of a flirtatious woman.

The contessa's dark eyes reminded Freya of Antonio's at his most serious moments. "It is the character, the strength of your face I wish to capture," the older woman explained. "And I can do that easily while you're reading dispatches or whatever it is you ambassadors do. I don't like posing sessions. One is never natural just sitting before an artist."

The ambassador looked uncertain. "I'm still not sure I want the scars of a lifetime preserved forever on canvas. Paintings should be of the young and beautiful."

The contessa tapped him on the arm. "If the soul is beautiful, and I sense that yours is, the painting will reflect that beauty."

"You see, Mr. Ambassador, I told you, you had nothing to worry about. *Mio madre* can be trusted." Then Antonio's jovial expression faded as his Interpol demeanor slipped back into place. "At least nothing to worry about where the painting is concerned. The celebration is another matter. I am leaving now for Civitavecchia to inspect the docks. I will report back to you when I return."

"Excellent idea," Marshall agreed. "Mind you, no official word has come yet, but the *Constitution* should be arriving in the next day or two."

No smile touched Antonio's lips. "Everything will be ready, I promise you."

"It had better!" the ambassador muttered. "Or we'd all better grab our passports and head for Brazil. And that is no joke!"

Two hours later Freya hung up the receiver in exasperation. It was the sixth phone call in less than thirty minutes. Pushing back her chair, she grabbed a yellow legal pad and headed for the ambassador's office to lay her troubles on his desk.

When she pushed open the door, her step

faltered at the unexpected domestic scene she encountered. Marshall was leaning back in his chair, his feet propped up on his desk, reading a report. The contessa was sitting at his side, a pad of paper on her lap, humming happily to herself as she quickly drew sketch after sketch of his face. Sitting between them was a coffeepot merrily perking away.

The ambassador's smile was one she'd never seen as he greeted her. "My dear, come in. The coffee's almost done. You must join us. We're having a grand time!"

Before Freya could sit down, the contessa rose gracefully to her feet. "I see that I must leave you. You have official business, and I have taken too much of your time already."

"Nonsense. You couldn't have finished with your work yet." Marshall gestured for her to sit back down. "I don't think Freya will mind having you here. I know I don't. Besides, the troubles of the social office are hardly a top-secret matter."

The contessa seemed reassured by Freya's smile. "All right I'll finish the sketches, but first I must go and get some paints." She held up her art pencil. "Charcoal is fine for the rough contours but not for the subtle details. I will not be long."

When the door closed, Freya commented, adopting a teasingly formal tone, "Mr. Ambassador, I do believe you are smitten."

Marshall gazed at the closed door. "Freya, you do read me like a book. Isn't she wonderful?"

But then Marshall straightened his shoulders,

deliberately shoving aside his personal feelings. "Now, how can I help you?"

Freya smiled. His words were very ambassadorial in tone, but she wasn't fooled. She detected the pleased gleam in his eye.

"I've had six phone calls in thirty minutes. Every newspaper and magazine in the States wants press credentials issued so that they can cover this celebration." She started ticking them off on her fingers. *The New York Times, The Washington Post, Time, Newsweek . . .*"

"So what?" The ambassador shrugged. "What's so unusual about that? They all have foreign desks in Rome."

"Wait, it gets better. I've also heard from the *Topeka Daily Capital* and a dozen others. It seems that all of America wants a firsthand report on how the food they sent has been received. But there's just no way we can—"

Freya stopped when a knock at the door halted her words. The ambassador called, "Come in."

As the contessa entered with her paints she commented, "Mr. Ambassador, it may be none of my business, but—"

"Contessa, I thought we'd agreed that you'd call me Marshall," he said, interrupting, then smiled at her.

Freya smiled, too, when she saw the blush pinken Antonio's mother's cheeks. Her voice was low, almost uncertain, as she replied, "And I thought you'd agreed to call me Angelina. In Italy titles mean little."

"All right, Angelina, what is the problem?"

"There is a young man outside. Obviously he has something to tell you, and just as obviously he's afraid to come in. I just thought—"

Marshall grimaced. "No doubt you're talking about Charles McFee, the junior press attaché. He always acts like a scared rabbit. Charles, you can come in."

A nervous young man in a pin-striped suit and wingtip shoes shuffled into the room. He glanced at the two women, and the press release in his hands got twisted into even a tighter knot. "Mr. Ambassa—" He had to stop to clear his throat. "Mr. Ambassador, this just came over the wire. I thought you'd want to know about it."

He thrust the printout at him, then backed away quickly. Marshall smoothed out the dispatch and began reading. With each line the set to his mouth grew tighter and tighter.

Finally his explosive "damn!" rocked the room.

CHAPTER FIFTEEN

"Damn!" the ambassador repeated, angrily crushing the dispatch into a tight ball.

The young press attaché took one look at his scowl and fled.

Freya took a deep breath, steadying herself for what she knew was bad news. "I assume this has something to do with the festival. What's gone wrong now?"

Jabbing the dispatch with one finger, he snapped, "The Italian government has announced that the *Constitution* will arrive tomorrow afternoon, Thursday, at two o'clock at pier nineteen. They were even so kind as to print a map to show everyone how to get to Civitavecchia and, once there, how to find the right berth. They're urging everyone to travel to the docks and give it an enthusiastic Italian welcome."

Freya had never seen the ambassador so distraught. "In other words, they've set the Declaration of Independence up like a sitting duck for anyone who might want to take a shot at it. And unfortunately we know that there are those who'd like nothing better."

"I couldn't have summed it up better myself."

He rubbed his fingers hard across his forehead, trying to ease the tension. "Damn those idiots at the State Department. I swear, it almost makes me want to retire right now and return to Nebraska and grow corn! Nobody throws bombs at a cornfield."

She came around the desk and started massaging some of the tightness out of his shoulders. "You know as well as I do that after a life in the foreign service you'd find farming stupefyingly dull. After all, you told me that's why you left Nebraska in the first place."

"Maybe," he grumbled, "but right now a dull life looks vastly appealing."

A knock on the door brought another frown. "Now what?" the ambassador muttered irritably. "Probably another problem." Still, he raised his voice to yell, "Come in."

As Antonio entered, he smiled at his mother, then raised an eyebrow in mock disapproval at the sight of Freya massaging the ambassador's back.

"Do you see now, *mio madre,* why I wanted you to come? Someone needs to distract the ambassador. I've only been gone for a couple of hours, and already he's enticed Freya to rub his back." He winked at Freya. "I thought your backrubs were reserved for me. We'll have to talk about that tonight, little one."

Then, noticing the ambassador's frown, Antonio quickly changed the direction of the conversation. "It looks like you could use some good news, and I've got some. The armored car has been reserved, and the security at the docks appears to be excellent. I don't see any problem with unloading and transporting your Declaration of Independence to the safety of this chancellery."

Freya moved around the desk and resumed her seat as Marshall growled, "If you think that, then you haven't seen the latest newspapers or listened to the TV."

After Marshall had explained what the Italian government had done, Antonio slapped his forehead. "I don't believe it!"

As always, when worried, he started pacing the floor. "Well, this certainly alters all my plans. I'd planned to have it unloaded in secret, then slipped into Rome before anyone was aware that it had even arrived. Now not only do we have to worry about security on the docks, but also we have to worry about an ambush along the highway. I think I'd better arrange for a police escort."

Freya tried to soothe the situation. "I'm sure the only reason the Italian government did it was as a gesture to honor the United States in thanks for our honoring Italy."

"I'm sure you're right," Antonio muttered. "I just wish they'd thought of the possible consequences before they decided to be so diplomatically polite."

"That's why your secondary plan is so important, Count Raimondi," Marshall said reassuringly.

"I know, but I'm still worried!"

"What secondary plan?" the contessa asked, glancing up from her painting.

"You don't even need to ask," Freya told her. "These two are keeping their secrets to themselves. They won't even tell me."

The ambassador pushed back his chair. "This is all in your hands, Antonio. As for me, I think I'll go drown my worries in a bottle of wine and a pre-opera dinner."

He crossed the office and gently removed the brush from Angelina's hand. "Contessa, I'd be honored if you would accompany me. You can finish your preliminary work another day. Tonight I'd like to forget the celebration, the Declaration of Independence, the Italian government, and, most of all, the State Department!"

When they had left, Freya looked at Antonio. "Your mother really seems happy here. When I came in earlier, she was humming merrily as she sketched."

"Humming; yes, that's a sure sign that she is enjoying her visit to Rome. Even if it's only for a few days, I think she's ready to relax and have a little fun. Maybe for her the past is now only a memory instead of a living pain."

Thinking of the heartbreak of her own childhood, Freya sighed. "I think that's an excellent place for the past to reside. For it to be just a memory that can't cloud the present."

Gently Antonio drew her into his arms. "I think the ambassador had an excellent idea. Tonight we are going to savor every minute, from the Filetto di Sogliola Margherita I'm going to cook for you, to the roses in front of the fireplace, to our night of love—and that is all! Promise that you will forget that any other reality exists."

Freya smiled at him, knowing that his wish was easy to grant. "Don't you know when I am with you, when you kiss me and touch me, there is no other reality for me?"

When they reached his apartment above the Piazza Navona, he poured her a glass of Chianti, then led her to the sofa. After gently brushing her lips with a kiss, he straightened. "Sip your wine and relax while I fix our dinner. I won't be long."

"Are you serious? I thought you were kidding." Remembering a remark Emilio had made, she observed, "I didn't think Italian men cooked. Isn't that rather an unmacho thing to do? Think of your image," she said, teasing.

He bent toward her and traced one fingertip over her nipple. Under the sheer chiffon of her blouse it instantly responded to his touch. He glanced down and smiled when he saw how it thrust hungrily against the silk material. "I can think of much better ways to prove that I am a man than by disdaining cooking." His hand softly cupped her breast. "Would you like a more complete demonstration of just how 'macho' I can be?"

The question stirred her blood, yet the evening was too special to rush. Instead of rising eagerly into his arms, as part of her wanted desperately to do, she demurred. "Yes, I do indeed want to see how completely 'macho' you can be; first with your culinary achievement, then later with your loving. Both will make tonight an evening I'll never forget."

Antonio's voice dropped to a purr. *"Cara mia,* I never forget any moment I spend with you."

Then he reluctantly moved away from her. "But as the infamous Nero used to say, you need energy to make Rome burn, and tonight I intend to 'burn,' so I guess I'll go start dinner."

"Nero never said that," Freya said, challenging him as he headed toward the back of the apartment where the kitchen was located.

Antonio glanced over his shoulder. "Probably not, but on the other hand, Nero never had a chance to spend a night with a woman like you. Can you blame me that I want all the energy I can get to enjoy everything the evening and you will offer?"

Quickly Freya rose to her feet to follow him. "Can't I help you?"

He grinned at her. "All right, come with me to the kitchen. There you can supervise while the chef creates."

"That sounds like a polite way of saying, 'Stay out of my way,'" Freya said protesting with a smile.

The large kitchen, made cheerful with copper pots hanging from hooks and painted pottery bowls on every counter, greeted her like a favored friend. From the doorway she silently watched as Antonio meticulously chopped the shrimp, clams, and mussels to adorn the filet of sole she could see marinating in a lemon-butter sauce by his side.

Finally she ventured to say, "Hmmm, your macho-chef act is making me hungry. How soon does this feast begin? I can hardly wait!"

Antonio bent over and twisted the heel off a loaf of Italian bread. Handing it to her, he said, scolding her, "Here, this should hold off your starvation for a while. Save that delicious greed for later this evening . . . after we've eaten. I don't want your passion wasted on fish with a seafood topping."

That dinner was the most sensuous meal Freya had ever experienced. The food was delicious. The salad was crisp, and the wine, chilled and dry, added to the pleasure, as did the sweetness of the chocolate gelato Antonio served for dessert, yet each spoonful touching her lips tasted less of food and more of Antonio's kisses.

She looked across the table, and seeing the heat in his gaze, she knew that with each bite he was feeling the same magic as she. He was tasting her with each morsel of food he consumed.

Slowly, enjoying the way his eyes burned as he looked at her, she toyed with the gelato he'd placed before her. Eyes meeting eyes, she challenged him as she provocatively licked the spoon. Then her tongue slowly escaped from her mouth to lick over her lips, to explore the last drops of sweetness lurking in the corners . . . and finally, as if to invite his to follow, her lips parted, and with tantalizing slowness her tongue slipped back into the warm moistness of her mouth.

At that Antonio abruptly shoved back his chair. "Freya, you would tempt a saint, and I don't aspire to that calling." Almost roughly he yanked her up into his arms. "Come, I've waited long enough tonight to have you."

No protest touched her lips as he swept her up in his strong arms and turned toward the living room. Once there, seeing again the roses scattered before the fire, his kiss, both conquering and grateful, swooped down to capture her mouth. Sweeter than all the gelato in the world, she welcomed him with parted lips. As his kiss pressed harder she welcomed the thrust of his tongue, welcomed the fire he lit within her—a fire she knew his powerful possession would soon satisfy.

"I hope you don't mind about the petals," she whispered. "Waking up to you and that rose is something I will never forget."

"I can't think of anything I would rather do than make love to you on a pallet of roses."

To prove his point Antonio carried her quickly to the bed of flower petals she'd prepared. As he let her slide from his arms she brushed against his body, felt its tantalizing hardness, and knew how hotly his desire burned. Her own desire, already hot now, exploded when she felt how ready he was to love her.

No time for caresses, no time for long, lingering kisses, his hands couldn't find her flesh fast enough as her skirt fell to the carpet, followed by the last wisp of silk guarding the most intimate valley of warmth. But he wasn't the only one eager for love as her hands performed a similiar dance, freeing his chest from his shirt.

Their passion exploded as never before. Partly clothed, partly naked, lying on a bed heady with crushed rose petals, they came together, needing to prove their love with savage intensity.

Neither spoke, but they desperately tried to ignore the danger the next day might bring. They desperately needed this night of love. . . .

Over and over they came together as one, loved to a beautiful climax, then rested, knowing that desire would soon come again. Finally, near dawn, when Antonio's fingers found the warmest, most intimate part of her being for the dozenth time, Freya sighed in pleasure, then sighed again in resolve.

"Antonio, we must rest. We have loved the night away. And we must"—the words choked in her throat, but she forced them out—"and we must remember that tomorrow is almost here. A tomorrow when you must be sharp and alert." She swallowed back tears. "A tomorrow when I could lose you."

"*Cara mia,* you won't lose me. Not tomorrow. Not ever!"

Yet even as he said it his actions seemed to agree as he cradled her warmly in his arms and, upon their bed of rose petals, they slept.

Saying good-bye the next morning hurt more than anything Freya had ever endured. Instinct told her to hold him in her arms and never let him leave her, but she knew she couldn't do that no matter how much she wanted to. Even at the door she couldn't resist one last, long hug, as if she wanted to imprint the feel of his body upon hers.

When his car pulled to a stop on the drive in front of the chancellery, she made no move to open the door. "I wish you'd let me go with you to pick up that document."

Antonio had a strange look on his face as he considered her question, then he smiled. "Maybe you can someday, but not now."

"There you go with double talk again," she said, grumbling. "I suppose you mean I can go with you when the Declaration of Independence is delivered to the Farnese."

"That trip will be a lot safer than the one from Civitavecchia."

"But, Antonio—"

"No, Freya, you can't come with me."

His tone allowed no argument, so with a sigh she opened the door and stepped out onto the drive that sliced through the courtyard in front of the loggia. Tears prickled behind her eyelids as she whispered, "I'll be waiting for you."

"Don't worry, Freya. I'll be all right, I promise. If all goes as planned, I should be back between three-thirty and four this afternoon."

With a jaunty wave Antonio drove away.

As she watched his car melt into the traffic she bit her lip, wishing with all her heart that she could believe him.

Her concern must have been etched clearly on her face because the instant Emilio saw her, he demanded, "What's the matter? Did you and your count have another fight?"

"Haven't you read the newspapers?" she retorted. "I should think what's wrong with me is obvious."

When he looked blank, she snapped, "I am not happy to have the details of the arrival of the Declaration of Independence splashed all over the Italian press!"

"I thought you'd be pleased it was going to be greeted with such a warm welcome."

"I just hope one of those greeting it doesn't 'welcome' it with a bomb."

Finally Emilio understood. "I never thought of it that way." Then he smiled. "But you can relax. Any smart terrorist would wait until all three documents were in the Farnese Palazzo before tossing in a Molotov cocktail. That way they could strike at four countries instead of just one."

He rubbed his hands together eagerly, concocting an imaginary scenario. "Just think of the headlines it would generate. Those terrorists would be famous! It might even bring down the government, which, since it's almost tax time, wouldn't necessarily be a bad thing."

"Emilio, I'm worried, and you're cracking jokes. This isn't a funny matter!"

Quickly his smile disappeared. "No, I agree that it isn't. I don't want anything to prevent this festival from taking place any more than you do."

She glanced at her watch. Three-thirty seemed an eternity away. Maybe work would help. "Why don't you come into my office and let's try to finalize the menu for the banquet. By the way, have we heard back yet from the governor of Louisiana? Wasn't he the last one who hadn't replied to our telegrams?"

Emilio nodded. "The wires came in late yesterday afternoon." The glint in his eyes was disapproving. "I tried to find you, but apparently you decided to quit early. I suppose you had plans with your precious count."

She ignored his comment, as she ordered, "Call Conrad and tell him we need to meet later, then bring in that wire from the governor."

Emilio didn't look happy at her instructions. As he turned to leave, she heard him mutter, "One day you'll realize that I'm more than an errand boy!"

Freya shook her head. Emilio's ego grated, and unfortunately his wasn't the only monumental ego she had to deal with. After taking a fortifying sip of her coffee she waited for Conrad and the inevitable battle a meeting with him always meant.

The meeting was worse than she expected. An hour later, as a headache pounded, her control finally snapped. Slapping her palm down on the top of her desk, she insisted, "Conrad, I don't care if you do think English cheese is superior to American. You will use what comes from Wisconsin or, to be blunt, you can look for another job."

After he'd flounced out, angry, but still on the payroll, Freya glanced again at her watch. One good thing could be said for Conrad's flights of temperament: While she was arguing with him she didn't have energy to worry about Antonio. But once she was alone, the thoughts started coming, followed by horrible visions, followed by tears.

Finally Freya wiped them away with the back of her hand. She was being ridiculous to cry over the imaginary fears of a remote possibility.

Luckily, before the argument could go any further, her phone rang. Picking it up, she smiled when she heard the enthusiasm in the ambassador's voice.

"My dear, I just had to call you and tell you that the veal scallopini was topped only by *Rigoletto!* Without doubt one of the most memorable evenings I've spent in many a year."

"And I have no doubt that the contessa's presence helped make it so enjoyable," Freya added teasingly.

"A remarkable woman!" Marshall boomed. "Why, do you know she's not only an artist of note, but also an accomplished pianist? After the opera she played several of Chopin's sonatas for me. As I said, a truly remarkable woman!"

Unexpectedly Marshall's voice sobered. "Which brings me to the purpose of this conversation. Angelina is concerned for her son, and I thought that having a pleasant lunch together might help the hours pass more quickly."

"I can't think of anything I'd rather do," she admitted, speaking from her heart.

"Good. Then the three of us will drink a toast to Antonio and to the future."

CHAPTER SIXTEEN

The lunch served by Conrad thrilled the taste buds but couldn't lift the anxiety that all three were feeling. The ambassador tried to ease the contessa's and Freya's fears, but neither the delicious food nor his light banter could make the clock hurry.

With the meal finally over, the ambassador poured the coffee. Just as he was filling Angelina's cup someone knocked on the door.

Automatically Freya glanced at her watch. It read two-thirty. The rich sauce Conrad had served over the sirloin steak suddenly felt like a lump of concrete in her stomach, and her thoughts leapt to Civitavecchia and Antonio. The docking, the crowds, what if someone had— The thought was too painful to complete as she twisted her linen napkin into a wadded ball.

One of the young military attachés poked his head in the door. "Mr. Ambassador, I just thought you would want to know that the communications officer from the *Constitution* has just informed us that the welcome the Declaration received was a spectacular success, complete with balloons and confetti and two local bands playing 'America the Beautiful.' "

"And?" Marshall urged, demanding the rest of the report.

The aide stiffened to attention. "And I am happy to report, sir, that the armored car, the police escort, that Interpol agent, and our priceless Declaration of Independence are safely on their way to Rome. Their ETA at the chancellery is four o'clock."

Marshall's smile softened as he looked at the young man. Remembering the obvious pride in his voice when he spoke of the song "America the Beautiful," he instructed, "I realize that you are on security duty this afternoon, but I have a direct order for you. I want you to join us, be on guard so to speak, in the courtyard to receive that document."

Marshall was rewarded with a blazing smile as the young man backed out of the room after uttering a snappy, "Yes, sir. Delighted, sir! You can count on me, sir."

Minutes seemed like days, hours like years, but finally the clock moved toward four. Out in the courtyard in front of the chancellery's loggia, the staff gathered. Emilio hovered near Freya's side as she paced nervously. The contessa, obviously worried, never strayed far from the ambassador. Unconsciously, as if drawn by a magnet, first their hands brushed as if by accident, then twined. When Freya saw them drawing closer, she smiled. Then her thoughts turned again to the man she loved.

The young military attaché was the first to hear the approaching sirens. He tapped the ambassador's arm. "Mr. Ambassador, do you hear that? Unless I'm mistaken, that means that the armored truck is almost here."

Luckily for Freya's taut nerves he was right. As everyone watched, with lights flashing and sirens wailing, the Italian police ceremoniously escorted the armored truck to the entrance of the chancellery's drive. As the truck pulled to a stop in front of the chancellery, a huge cheer went up from the crowd. Freya's heart tumbled when she saw the broad smile of satisfaction on Antonio's face as he stepped to the ground. Acknowledging the tribute with a wave, he walked toward the ambassador.

Stopping in front of him Antonio said, "Mr. Ambassador, I am delighted to report that the Declaration of Independence has arrived." Antonio held out a key. "Would you like the great honor of removing it from the truck to show it to your staff? The case is quite heavy, sir. You'll need some help lifting it out."

Freya glanced at the older man, then blinked. She could understand why Marshall might look solemn for this occasion. Or she could understand why he might look pleased. But why in the world did he look amused?

Shaking off the confusing thoughts, she watched the ambassador take the key from Antonio. "Young man, it would take an army to keep me from being the first to see that piece of parchment."

Then he turned and held out his arm to Angelina. "And because you represent Italy so graciously, Contessa Raimondi, I would like you to accompany me for this unique unveiling."

As Freya moved to join Antonio, the ambassador and the contessa moved to the rear of the armored truck. All eyes were riveted on him as he unlocked the double doors. After throwing them open with a flourish he reached inside, and with the help of a couple of strong Marines, they slowly started to draw the heavy wooden case out of the truck. So electrifying was the moment, no one noticed the van idling at the corner.

Suddenly their world exploded when, without warning, the van leapt forward, not stopping until it came skidding into the driveway. Before it even came to a stop, the doors flew open, and armed men leapt from it.

By instinct Antonio shoved Freya to the ground, but she could still see the horror. A thousand images of the next awful moments burned into Freya's mind. Images she'd never forget. Images of a man throwing a fiery bottle toward the open doors of the armored truck. Missing, it rolled beneath and exploded. Images of the ambassador shielding the contessa's body with his. Images of Antonio, his gun out, winging one of the gunmen. Images of the Marine guards joined by the Italian police in front, in the street, returning fire, felling another one of the terrorists. Then, most horrifyingly of all, the young military attaché falling with a stain of red blood staining the front of his uniform.

Then the terror became personal . . . terrifyingly personal. His gun spent, Antonio paused to reload. She watched him, for a moment feeling safe. Then her eyes widened in horror as she saw one of the terrorists running toward them, his submachine gun lowered, aiming directly at them. And in that awful split second only one thought echoed in her head, and she prayed, "If I have to die, thank you, God, for sending me Antonio."

The terrorist seemed to relish the look of pure terror on her face as he fingered the trigger. Then he pointed the gun directly at Antonio and . . . click. Miraculously his magazine of ammunition was empty.

Images that had a moment ago seared into her mind now became a kaleidoscope of impressions. Everything seemed to happen at once. The terrorist, only yards away, ejected the used magazine and rammed another one home at the same instant that Antonio got his gun reloaded. Both aimed, then, in a flash, from behind the man a fist crashed down on the terrorist's arm. With a yowl of pain he doubled over, and his submachine gun fell to the ground, skidding toward her over the concrete. As the terrorist bent to grab the fallen weapon another crushing blow across the back of his neck sent him sprawling to the ground. Stunned, she saw Emilio standing behind the fallen man.

Antonio, in a crouch, ran toward the man as Emilio jammed his foot down hard on the gunman's back, holding him until Antonio could get there.

More shots, more screams, then Freya saw two of the terrorists retreating toward the van. A white-hot rage boiled up within her at the thought that they might escape. Without thinking, she rolled across the concrete and grabbed the terrorist's fallen submachine gun. It was so hot, it burned her hands; but she didn't drop it as she braced herself up on one elbow. She didn't even stop to realize that she'd never fired a gun before as she aimed and pressed the trigger. The recoil almost knocked it from her hands, but she didn't stop firing as she emptied the thirty-two-round magazine into the van and its tires, shredding the tires into a hundred pieces.

Then, as suddenly as it started, it was over. Seeing that no escape was possible, the terrorists dropped their guns and raised their hands high. Freya got quickly to her feet as a distant scream of sirens told her that, gratefully, ambulances were on the way. Her first thought was of the fallen Marine. Others were bending over him as she shoved her way through. With relief she saw that his eyes, while glazed with pain, were open. The bullet had hit high, missing his heart by inches.

Out of the corner of her eye she saw that Antonio was busy handling the terrorists, and since she knew the ambassador would be concerned about the fate of the young military attaché, she turned toward him. He was helping Angelina to her feet as she approached.

Freya had never seen him look grimmer. "Freya, thank God you weren't hurt. Take the contessa inside where you'll both be safe," he ordered. "There could be a second attack." He beckoned imperiously to some of the Marines. "Get this case inside now!"

"Don't you think you should come with us," Freya suggested. "You're as tempting a target as the Declaration of Independence."

"Nonsense, I'm too tough to kill. Besides, after what's happened, I want the pleasure of watching these terrorists carted off to the nearest Italian jail where I assure you they will stay a long, long time if I have anything to say about it! Now please get inside. I'll join you as soon as I'm sure it's safe."

Half an hour later Antonio and the ambassador entered the chancellery. As Angelina rushed to meet them Freya saw something she'd never seen before. The ambassador was blushing!

Obviously noticing the rents and tears in her dress for the first time, he rushed to her with an embarrassed apology. "Contessa, you must forgive me. I don't know what to say. I knocked you to the ground then fell on you like a sack of potatoes. And I've positively ruined your dress. What a wonderful welcome to Rome!"

Surprisingly the contessa smiled up at Marshall. "My Antonio, he said it was time I started living again, and what's happened is certainly a lot more exciting than pruning roses at our villa."

Taken off-guard by her mild response, the ambassador said, sputtering, "But my actions . . . your dress . . ."

One jeweled hand reached out to touch his arm. "In a more innocent age gallantry meant carrying a woman's handkerchief into the tilt yard as your talisman. In today's rough world what you did was equally as gallant. You risked your life to save mine. I thank you."

Antonio could see that the ambassador was at a loss for words, so he stepped forward. "Sir, you'll be happy to know that the young Marine is going to be all right. He's hurt, but I don't think it's too serious."

"Thank God for that! After ordering him out here, if he'd been seriously wounded, I would never have forgiven myself," Marshall vowed, then he returned to a more businesslike tone. "Come on, let's get that document uncrated. I think we've earned a look at it."

After all the excitement, actually seeing the Declaration of Independence was almost a letdown. Encased in glass, it looked just like the copy she'd bought when a group from one of her boarding schools had toured Philadelphia.

They were studying it when Antonio and Emilio joined them. She had never seen such pride shining in Antonio's eyes as he looked at her. "Mr. Ambassador, I'm tempted to try to recruit these two here for Interpol."

"What do you mean, Count Raimondi? I was so busy protecting the contessa, I didn't see what happened."

"To put it briefly, Emilio may well have saved

our lives, and Freya kept the terrorists from escaping." After filling him in on the rest of the details of their heroics, Antonio asked, "I know you want Freya to help with the details for the reception you've planned, but I wonder if I might borrow her for the rest of the afternoon. As you know, there's something else I have to do."

The ambassador hesitated, then, with obvious reluctance, agreed, "If you think it's safe, I suppose I won't object. We'll be waiting for you when you return."

To Freya's surprise, when they walked out of the back door of the chancellery, they headed for a large delivery truck, not his car. "This isn't exactly riding in style," she muttered, climbing into the cab. "Where are we going, and why do we need the truck?"

Antonio smiled mysteriously. "You'll see," he answered vaguely, turning the key in the ignition.

She started to demand an answer, then relaxed. After the turmoil of the afternoon she was just glad that he was beside her and that she could finally relax. With a contented sigh she slid over next to him, cuddling close as they headed northwest out of Rome. Sleeping little the night before, coupled with the tension of the day, had made her eyelids droop. She tried to stay awake, but finally the effort was too much, so she rested her head on his shoulder and slept.

An hour later his kiss brought her back to the world as he whispered, "We're here, my sleeping beauty."

Slowly Freya lifted her head, then blinked. Night had fallen, but even in the darkness she could make out the lines of the American ship, the *Constitution.*

"Antonio, what are we doing at the docks? Isn't that the ship that brought the Declaration over?"

"Yes, it is, and what we're doing here is picking up the food for the banquet that's aboard."

She looked at him suspiciously. "Why is an Interpol agent delivering food?"

"Because the ambassador asked me to take care of this. Now come on, the captain is waiting for us."

They were piped aboard to be greeted by the captain and several of his officers. "We heard what happened in Rome, Count Raimondi. May I offer the gratitude of the United States Navy that you were able to protect the ambassador? Now, if you will follow us, we will escort you to the food cases."

With a brisk snap the men wheeled around and marched ahead of them in parade formation. "Isn't all this ceremony a bit much for cases of food?" she whispered.

Antonio's only answer was a long "Shhhhhh."

Her confusion increased when they arrived in the hold of the ship. The captain turned to his military aide. "See that the boxes are loaded into the truck and post guard. We're not taking any chances with this cargo. Count Raimondi, Miss Davidson, will you please follow me? There is one special case I want you to see."

Off to one side lay a large wooden box. Antonio

253

smiled when he saw the shock of wheat painted on it beneath the words "To our Italian allies, the best wheat Kansas has to offer."

The captain smiled. "Take special care of this one. You know how Italians love bread."

"Trust me, we shall," Antonio promised with a fervency she didn't understand.

Once they were back in the truck, Freya protested, "Antonio, I don't understand any of this!"

"Just relax and enjoy the ride," he answered unhelpfully.

Then, before she could ask any more questions, he commented, "In case you're interested, those terrorists weren't Italians. They were Palestinians."

"I don't care who they were. I'm just glad it's over. The rumors were true. There was an attack. But thank God we survived." She sighed with relief. "Now the only thing I need to worry about is Conrad throwing another temper tantrum."

The surprises continued as they arrived back at the chancellery. The instant Antonio pulled to a stop, they were surrounded by Marines with guns drawn.

"I know Italians love to eat, but aren't these security measures excessive?"

Antonio shrugged. "I guess that after this afternoon the ambassador isn't taking chances that anything else can go wrong."

The ambassador walked out of the back entrance to meet them. "I'm glad you're back. We've been worried."

"The only thing you needed to worry about on

this trip was some weevils getting into the wheat," Freya muttered in disgust at all their cloak-and-dagger antics.

"Take everything to the kitchen," Marshall ordered to one of the guards. "We'll follow."

"Just the way I want to spend the evening, uncrating food," Freya complained.

Conrad was equally unhappy with the thought. As the Marines started carrying the boxes and crates into his kitchen, he raged, "I won't have that trash in here! I insist that you take those to the storeroom!"

"Conrad, be quiet," the ambassador insisted. "Your kitchen is being honored. You just don't know it." He turned to one of the guards. "Please go and get me a hammer."

When the hammer arrived, the ambassador glanced at Antonio. "Mr. Ambassador, knowing how the Italians love bread, the captain of the *Constitution* suggested that I take special care with the wheat shipment from Kansas."

He nodded. "Would everyone mind standing back?"

He worked quickly, prying the wooden lid off the crate. When all the nails were out, he slipped it off the box. Then, like a magician conjuring up a rabbit, he swept his hand over the box and announced, "Ladies and gentlemen, the Declaration of Independence."

With a gasp everyone pressed forward. If the earlier copy had left Freya unmoved, this one did not. As she stared down at it, encased under hermetically sealed glass, the words, Jefferson's handwritten corrections, and the signatures of brave men, so real, so meaningful, reached toward her, sending a chill up her spine.

She turned toward Antonio. "So this was your plan."

"Yes, it was vital for us to keep the real document safe. And with all the publicity we were afraid that there'd be an attack. There was, but I figured, who's going to bomb a crate of Kansas wheat? I'm sorry I couldn't tell you what was really going on. I hope you understand."

"The only thing that's important is that the Declaration of Independence is here and safe."

His arm swept around her waist. "Correction. The only thing that's important to me is that *you're* here and safe!"

The next eight days were some of the most exhausting, exciting and passionate Freya had ever lived through. The days were filled with work, but Freya lived only for the nights to come; nights spent in Antonio's arms, nights where pleasure topped exquisite pleasure, until she didn't think desire could be any more beautiful. But the next time he touched her, it always was. Still there was a part of her that wished he'd speak of the future, yet he didn't.

Two days before the Friday opening of the festival, the Declaration of Independence was moved again. This time under heavy guard, it was transported to the Farnese. At the same time it was being mounted on the wall, the British arrived with their copy of the Magna Carta.

Watching all the dignitaries scurrying about, Emilio turned to her. "As Shakespeare would say, it seems much ado about nothing. Why all fuss over a couple of pieces of parchment? They mean nothing. In today's world action counts, not meaningless words."

"Sometimes, as in America, ideas have the power to change history," she countered.

Emilio wouldn't back down. "I've studied your American history. And as I recall, your vaulted leaders backed those ideas with bullets and cannon fire. It's always easier to destroy and build anew than to change from within."

"Well, maybe," Freya conceded. "But to be blunt, neither you nor I have time to debate the issue. I want you to check with Carmen on the status of the Victor Emmanuel II cake she's baking, and I need to talk with Conrad."

She rubbed her fingertips across her forehead where lately a headache had taken up permanent residency. The last days of preparation were filled with frantic activity and a million small decisions. Then finally Friday arrived, the kickoff of the three-day celebration of Italian republican liberty.

The French had the honor of hosting the first day's festivities at the Farnese. After unveiling the documents for the press and the attending dignitaries, they staged a fashion show of the best of Paris haute couture. The evening ended with a splendid feast, featuring everything from pâté de foie gras to truffles, all of which was washed down with magnums of the finest French champagne.

The British followed the next evening with a performance given by the Royal Shakespearean Company of selected scenes from plays the great bard had set in Italy.

That night even Antonio's lovemaking couldn't quiet Freya's nerves. Sleep just wouldn't come as she worried over the countless things that could go wrong the next evening. Conrad had been cooking for days, but would he be able to get everything done? Would the cake be as impressive as Carmen promised? Would the opera singer, the only American ever to star on the opening night at La Scala, whom the ambassador had invited to come and sing some Italian arias, come down with laryngitis? Over and over the questions swirled in her mind, finally spinning slower and slower until she dropped into an uneasy sleep in his arms.

The next day she arrived at the Farnese early. Even though she had a hundred things to do, she couldn't resist spending just a few moments longer gazing at the wondrous fresco she might never get to see again. Emilio found her gazing up at the dozing Endymion.

He looked at her in distaste. "Freya, haven't you got better things to do than gaze at that disgusting trash?"

"You're wrong Emilio. This fresco is a fabulous piece of art."

Then, as quickly as it came, his anger faded and he smiled. "Why argue about it? It won't be an irritant for long."

Suspicious, she demanded, "What do you mean by that? This fresco isn't going to disappear."

Emilio paused, as if considering his answer, then explained, "I just meant that after tonight it won't irritate me, because I won't have to look at it, that's all. The French will simply seal this gallery up again and I won't have to think about it."

Something in his tone bothered her, but she had too much to do to probe further. An hour later Conrad and his staff arrived to start arranging the food for the banquet. One glance at the chef and she knew what she'd forgotten. "Oh, damn!" she muttered.

"What's wrong?" Emilio asked, surprised at her unusual outburst.

"What's wrong is that I left the place cards with the state's names on my desk at the chancellery."

"Well, don't just stand there." Emilio started for the door. "I'll drive you back to get them."

"Maybe getting out of here wouldn't be such a bad idea," Freya agreed. "We can go over the final details on the way, and that'll be easier to do without Conrad raging in the background."

The parking lot behind the chancellery was almost empty, and Emilio was able to park right by the kitchen entrance, which was the closest one to her office. With most of the staff over at the French embassy, the chancellery seemed strangely deserted as she and Emilio walked down the empty halls. Even most of the Marine guards weren't on duty.

Freya unlocked her office. After grabbing the place cards she turned to her assistant. "Oh, there's one thing I forgot. I want you to take the responsibility of wheeling that cake in, then staying while the waiters cut it. I don't trust them to — Why are you shaking your head?"

Emilio shuffled his feet on her carpet. "I'll wheel the cake in, but I can't stay to supervise the serving. I just can't. I have to leave."

"Emilio, this is the most important party of the year. As my assistant I expect you to be there until after the last guest leaves. You know that's my rule for all parties, and it goes double for this one."

"I can't stay," he mumbled, not meeting her eyes.

"Why?" she demanded sharply.

"Ah . . . I have to . . . ah, I have to attend my niece's baptism tonight." He raised his head, more confident now. "It's my sister Rosa's son. It's family, you understand. It's taking place . . ."

Freya hardly heard him as he named a church close by. His story didn't make sense. And when she admitted that, suddenly she was bombarded with thoughts, thoughts so awful that she wanted to ignore them but couldn't.

She remembered a meeting when they were first discussing the festival. All along she'd thought she was the one to think of using the Farnese, but now the memory of Emilio voicing the suggestion echoed clearly in her mind. She remembered his bitterness over Italy's fall from power. She remembered his scorn that ideas written into documents could be more powerful

260

than action. Then Antonio's words returned. "We suspect that some terrorists groups have recruits on some of the embassy staffs."

Emilio, he couldn't be! Could he? The risks ran too high to take any chance, even if her vague suspicions turned out to be ridiculous.

"Freya, why are you staring at me that way?" Emilio demanded, uncomfortably aware of her scrutiny. "You look like you've seen a ghost."

She yanked up her thoughts. If he was dangerous, she couldn't warn him that she was on to his game. If he wasn't, she didn't want him ever to know that she'd even suspected him for a moment. At the very least that would add an intolerable strain to their working relationship.

She cleared her throat. "I'm sorry Emilio, my thoughts had wandered. I was just envisioning Conrad's wrath if I failed to bring him the special knife he wanted from the kitchen." Trying to appear as casual as possible, she pushed her chair back. "Why don't you wait here while I run down and fetch it. Then we can go back to the Farnese."

Her heart felt like it was going to pound through the walls of her chest as she left the office. Antonio—she had to talk to Antonio! He would know what to do. But he was at the luncheon with the ambassador. Once she was around the corner, out of sight of her office, she ran toward the kitchen.

Freya's hands were shaking so hard, she could hardly dial the phone. Then the agonized wait began until she finally heard Antonio's voice.

"Freya, what is it? What's happened? Nothing's happened to *mio madre,* has it?"

"Antonio, be quiet and listen." Her voice, low and urgent, continued. "Remember when you told me Interpol suspected that a terrorist group might have either infiltrated an embassy staff or recruited someone inside?"

"Of course, but—"

"Antonio, this may sound crazy, but I think I might know who it is. At least I'm suspicious enough that I want you to know what's happened."

"Look, Freya, no idea is too wild to check out when it's an event this important. Whom do you suspect?"

Now that the moment had arrived, she almost couldn't force the words out. The idea was so preposterous, he'd probably have her committed.

Finally she took a deep breath. "All right. You're not going to believe this, but I think it's—"

Suddenly there was nothing but a sickening silence. The line went dead. If her heart had pounded before, now it galloped out of control. Fear hit her stomach like a sledgehammer as she turned and saw an Emilio she'd never seen before. His mouth was twisted in a knot of fury, his eyes blazed with the wild glow of a fanatic—and in his hand dangled the telephone line he had ripped from the wall.

As he leapt for her, her mouth opened to scream, but he was too quick as he ruthlessly jammed a handkerchief down her throat. Gagging, suffocating, struggling for breath, she tried to break his grip, tried to keep him from tying her hands with the telephone cord, tried to run, but he yanked her long hair, savagely pulling her back . . . then slowly everything went black.

CHAPTER SEVENTEEN

The nightmare gripped her with such awful force, she could feel the handkerchief choking her, could feel the bite of the cord cutting into her wrists and her ankles. She wanted to scream through the blackness, but no sound would come. Then slowly the blackness started to recede. Thank heavens! With the dawn she'd wake and . . . oh, dear God! It wasn't a nightmare! She twisted her hands, and the cords cut deeply until they drew blood. She wasn't dreaming at all. This was real!

Everything came back in a rush. Her suspicions of Emilio, trying to reach Antonio, the kidnapping! Painfully her eyes opened. Emilio had jammed her unconscious body down on the floor of the passenger side of his car, but Freya could still see out of the window, and what she saw flashing by was the railing of a bridge. That meant they were crossing the Tiber. Dear God, where was he taking her? Then tears scalded as a worse question stabbed her mind. What was he going to do with her once they got there?

Emilio noticed her movement out of the corner of his eye. Glancing down, he sneered. "For once my brilliant boss was too smart for her own good. And you'll pay for that. You'll all pay!"

Once across the Tiber, the streets narrowed. Through the window she could see the decaying medieval and Renaissance palazzos and knew that they were driving through an older area of Rome called the Trastevere. Finally he pulled to a stop in a dark, narrow alley. Her eyes, already wide with fear, grew even wider when she saw him pull a gun from beneath his jacket.

Ice chilled his voice as he explained, "You're going to pay a nice long visit to our headquarters here while I complete my assignment. Now I'm going to untie your ankles so you can walk. But don't try to run, or I swear I'll put a bullet in the middle of that beautiful back of yours."

Bending down, he untied the cord from her ankles. Then, keeping the gun trained on her, he walked around the car and opened her door. Roughly he hauled her to her feet. After what she'd been through Freya could hardly stand, but he did not wait for her to steady herself. Instead he jabbed the gun in the small of her back and shoved her toward a door opening into the back of one of the ancient palazzos.

Once inside the dim corridor, Emilio grabbed her shoulder, pulling her to a stop. "Turn around and I'll take the gag out. In here you can scream all you want, because there's nobody but our people around." His glance raked suggestively over her. "And I assure you that they won't help you."

A wave of nausea hit her as he pulled the soggy handkerchief out of her mouth. Her throat muscles cried in pain, but she forced the words out. "Emilio why are you doing this?"

"Because you know too much. No one is going to stop our plans."

"What are you going to do?"

He smiled. It was a smile that turned her blood to ice. "Trust me, you don't want to know. All I will say is that the revolution begins tonight. Once Italy was great. Now we're nothing, but that will change. We will change it. And it's easier to build a new Italy on ashes than to wait for those fools in the government to take action. Government!" He spat out the word. "We have no need of it."

Desperately stalling for time, hoping she could think of some plan of escape, she tried to keep him talking. "But you helped stop that terrorist attack. Why? I don't understand."

"It's simple. That wasn't our group. Besides, if they had succeeded in ruining that worthless piece of paper you call a precious document of liberty, Britian and France might have called off this 'great' celebration, and all of our plans would have been destroyed."

At the word *liberty* his mouth twisted into a contorted sneer. "Now we will bring everything down, and no one can stop us."

"But—"

"No, we've talked enough. Now move."

When she hesitated, he brought the gun up level with her chest. "The walls of this palazzo are thick. No one would hear the shot, but I'd hate to shoot you . . . at least right now."

266

Reluctantly she turned around. "Up the stairs," he ordered. "We have a special room reserved for troublemakers like you."

Up and up they climbed, two stories, then four, not stopping until they reached the eighth floor of the old building. As they started down the hall someone stepped from the shadows.

"Emilio, what in the hell are you doing? What is she doing here?"

Freya couldn't see her face, but she recognized the voice. It was Carmen. To Freya's horror the other woman had a semiautomatic cradled in her arms.

"I'm afraid she discovered my little secret, and since we obviously don't want her talking to anyone, I brought her here."

With a hard push he shoved her into a small bedroom. Stumbling, Freya fell across the hard cot.

Emilio handed his gun to Carmen. "Here, keep her covered while I untie her hands."

"Are you an idiot?" Carmen demanded harshly. "Leave her tied up. Why take chances?"

"You're the idiot," Emilio countered, quickly freeing Freya's hands. "You know that this room is especially prepared for unwelcome 'visitors.' That door is solid oak, and the bolt is four inches of steel. As for the window, we're eight stories up. If she wants to jump, it'll save us the trouble of killing her later."

"Emilio, I tell you she's trouble! Get rid of her now," Carmen said insistently.

Freya trembled when she saw the look in his

eyes. As his gaze raked over her again, mentally ripping the clothes from her body, she shuddered, knowing what his words were going to be even before he spoke.

"I'm not going to get rid of her yet. She's said no to me too often. This time she won't be able to argue when I want to have a little *fun.*"

He looked down at her helpless figure. "Think about that, Freya. Think about me as the night approaches. Think about what I will do. Think about what I can make you do as you wait to hear my footsteps coming. This time you won't say no." His voice harshened. "You won't say no to anything I ask!"

He glanced back at Carmen. "When I tire of her, then you can have the pleasure of getting rid of her."

"I still say we should do it now," the other woman argued.

"And I say no!"

Emilio turned and walked out of the room. As the heavy door closed, Freya heard Carmen make one last protest. "You're a fool, Emilio!"

"So I'm a fool, am I?" His cruel laugh echoed as the bolt shot home. "Would a fool think of a finale that's really final?"

Then there was silence.

In desperation Freya hurled herself against the door. Like hitting a wall of solid concrete, the door didn't budge. Wildly her eyes searched the room, looking for another way out. A thousand fears churned within her as she rushed to the window. There was nothing but air outside and hard concrete below. For a terrified moment she thought of jumping. Wouldn't death now be better than the fate Emilio promised?

The horror of that idea finally sliced through the curtain of fear shrouding her thoughts. With effort Freya forced her breathing to slow. If she was going to find any way out of this, she had to think logically and not panic. The door—maybe it had a weakness. Quickly she ran to it, but it was hopeless. Obviously it had been installed to keep people in.

She turned back toward the window. Maybe she could smash it. Maybe she could scream for help. As she examined it more closely this time, she felt the first stab of hope. In her panic before, she hadn't noticed the narrow ledge below the window, a ledge that looked to be about the width of the balance beam she'd practiced on when she'd done her gymnastic routine. After saying a prayer for all those years of training, Freya kicked off her shoes.

Glancing down at the red silk dress she had on, she knew the skirt was too narrow to allow her the movement she needed. With a twinge of regret because it was one of her favorites, she ripped the side seam all the way to her waist. The window was sealed, but Freya didn't hesitate as she wrapped her hand in the blanket and slashed it through the glass, shattering it into a thousand pieces.

Then she took a deep breath and eased out of the window onto the narrow ledge below. Keeping her eyes straight ahead, she silently repeated over and over again the instructions she'd received while training on the balance beam. One step at a time she carefully edged along the ledge. At first she thought she'd slip in another window and try to escape through the palazzo, but once outside, when she saw the sturdy drainpipe at the corner of the building, she had a better idea.

Step by step, not looking down, she neared it. Never before had anything felt quite as good as touching that drainpipe. Then borrowing on another skill from her past, she wrapped her legs about the exposed surface of the pipe and told herself that it was just a fat rope, similiar to the ones she slid down many times before. Slowly she started down. It seemed to take forever as story by story she eased toward the hard concrete below.

A dozen dangers threatened, but she didn't stop. Down, down, inch by inch, the ground edged closer. Then finally, a few feet above the street, she let go and dropped to the sidewalk. Not pausing even to let her pounding heart quiet, she dashed around the corner, running as fast as she could to lose herself amid the narrow, twisting streets of the Trastevere.

Only when she was blocks away did her run slow to a walk. Night had fallen while she'd made her escape, and she didn't need a watch to know that the festivities at the Farnese were already under way. She had to find a telephone! She had to warn Antonio, or he and a lot of other people including the ambassador and the president of Italy were going to die.

Then, with a sickening lurch in the stomach, she realized that she had no money to make the call. And who could she trust? It was Sunday. The streets were deserted. And if she stayed in the area, searching for a safe phone, some of Emilio's terrorist friends might recapture her. Or Emilio or Carmen might intercept the call. But if she didn't try . . .

Then she heard it! From behind she heard a motorcycle roaring up. As it skidded to a stop her heart pounded once more in fear. Was this one of Emilio's men? Had they discovered that she'd escaped and come after her? Bravely wanting to know her fate, she turned to face the man.

Only the rider wasn't a man. He was much younger than she expected, really not much more than a boy, but he knew the typical macho line. He was leering, and his eyes roamed over the high split in her skirt. In Italian he asked her how much she charged for a night of fun.

Slipping quickly into Italian, she snapped, "You're got to help me!"

"Sure, baby, if you help me. Together we can 'help' each other to a lot of fun."

"Look, I'm serious. If you don't help me, a lot of people are going to die."

The smile faded from his face. "You're not kidding are you, *signorina?*"

"No, I'm not! Right now a group of anarchists are planning to destroy the French embassy and everyone inside."

"Isn't that where that big celebration is tonight? I saw something about it on the television." His dark eyes popped wider. "Our president is there!"

Freya nodded. "Yes, he is, and so are a lot of other important people. I've got to warn them."

He patted the seat behind him. "Climb on. This is the fastest motorcycle in Rome."

She believed him as they roared through the dark streets. Silently she prayed that she had not risked death climbing from an eighth-story window, only to die in a motorcycle crash. Then she put her fears away as she began to plan what she must do. With Emilio, Carmen, and who knew how many other terrorists in the French embassy, she couldn't risk going in herself, so when they neared the Farnese, she tapped the young man on the shoulder. Over the air rushing by she yelled, "Stop at that taverna."

When he shut off the motor, he helped her alight. "Look," she explained quickly, "I can't go into that embassy. I'm afraid that the terrorists will stop me before I can get help, but they don't know you. You've got to get in there and find a man named Count Antonio Raimondi. He'll know what to do. It's a matter of life and death."

"What if they won't let me in? Don't I need an invitation or something?"

She grabbed a menu off a nearby table. Quickly she wrote a message. "Give him this. If he has any doubts, have him look over here where he can see me. Now hurry! I don't know how long we have."

The waiting topped the agony of Emilio's kidnapping. She felt almost faint when she finally saw Antonio emerging from the Farnese with the young man at his side.

The relief in his eyes when he saw her touched her heart. He couldn't seem to run fast enough to reach her. Sweeping her up in his arms, he lifted her off her feet as he vowed, "Thank God you're here, Freya. I've been so worried! Dear God, where have you been? Emilio had some story about problems holding you up at the chancellery, but I didn't—"

"Antonio," she said, interrupting him, "we can talk about all that later. Right now we've got to stop a horrible tragedy."

Instantly he reverted to the cool Interpol agent as she quickly spelled out her suspicions. When she finished, he doubled up his fist. "We'll have to alert the French police inside the Farnese, and we'll have to do it without arousing Emilio's suspicions. We have to take him off-guard. I don't want him rushing his attack."

"Can I help?" the young man asked, his eyes shining with excitement.

"It could be dangerous," Antonio argued. "I don't think you should—"

"Antonio, let him if he wants to. Without his help I might not have made it in time."

Without wasting any more words, Antonio nodded.

Quickly they crossed to the Farnese. A few hurried words later the doorman's face went white, but he didn't hesitate as he hurried inside to sum-

273

mon the French police. Soon six officers of the Sûreté slipped out into the darkness to meet them.

After Freya's explanation the captain took control. "Here is our plan. This assistant of yours and the woman are in the kitchen. We'll go in the back way and surprise them before they can act."

With the captain leading the way the group silently rounded the embassy. Gun drawn, the captain took a deep breath, then threw open the door to the vast kitchen.

Seeing them, Conrad raised the cleaver he was holding, as if to fend them off. "What is this?" he said, raging. "You can't invade my kitchen. I won't have it. There's mud on your boots!"

Over his shoulder Freya saw both Emilio and Carmen spin toward the doorway. The captain brushed past the fuming chef. "One more step and it will be your last!" he yelled at the fleeing pair.

"How dare you threaten me?" the chef sputtered.

Freya's nerves, overly taut by all that had happened to her, finally snapped as she exploded, "Conrad, for once just shut up! It's Emilio and Carmen they want, not you. Antonio, Emilio has a gun. It's under his jacket."

Disarmed, surrounded, escape impossible, Emilio snarled back at them like a trapped animal. "Go ahead arrest me. It won't do any good. The bomb's on a timer, and you don't know where it is." He raised his fist in the air. "The cause will triumph, even if I fall!"

"No, it won't." Freya's soft voice cut through the tension. She watched her assistant's face turn to ash as she repeated his words, " 'Would a fool think of a finale that's really final?' That's why you wouldn't stay, isn't it, Emilio? The bomb is in the cake."

The unnatural pallor of Emilio's face spoke the truth. Antonio didn't hesitate. Glancing at Carmen's four-foot confection of cake and icing sitting in the corner, he ordered, "We've got to evacuate the Farnese and call the bomb squad."

The captain stepped forward again. "Unnecessary. Two of my officers here are trained demolition experts." He waved imperiously toward the towering cake. "Get to it."

"We've still got to clear the Farnese," Antonio insisted.

"No, wait, Antonio," Freya urged, glancing quickly at her watch. "This banquet is scheduled down to the last minute, and I know Emilio would not have set the timer to go off on that bomb until after the dinner was finished and he had time to get away. He would sacrifice a lot for a cause he believed in, but not his life. I think we have time to handle this quietly."

"How can you be sure?" Antonio asked.

"Because this afternoon I asked him to wheel in the cake, and he agreed," she explained. "Then he insisted he'd have to leave after that. That's what tipped me off about him. So if we can settle this without causing an international incident by clearing the gallery, I know the ambassador would be grateful."

275

Antonio's lips tightened to a harsh line. "Captain, tell your men to hurry!"

Agonizing minutes later, after carefully stripping layer after layer from the huge cake, one of the officers raised his hand to signal that they'd found Emilio's bomb. It seemed like Freya held her breath for hours as they slipped it out of the middle of the cake, then studied it, making sure which wire would deactivate it.

From a distance she heard a formal drumroll. Antonio glanced at her, one eyebrow raised in question. "That was Emilio's signal to wheel in the cake," she explained.

The drumroll came again, this time louder. "Maybe I'd better slip in and tell the ambassador what's happening." Then she glanced down at her bare feet and torn dress. "On second thought maybe you'd better do it."

Antonio nodded. Just as he turned toward the door, Marshall burst into the kitchen. "What in the hell is going on here? Where is Emilio and the—"

As his glance swept over the scene of Emilio and Carmen in handcuffs, Freya in rags, the cake torn to smithereens, and the officers cutting the wires of the bomb, he turned as white as a ghost.

He froze in his spot until the officer announced that the bomb was safe, then he hurried to Freya. "My dear, are you all right? Antonio told me that your phone call had been cut off, then when you didn't appear, we were afraid something awful had happened to you. Obviously it had. Did Emilio do this to you?"

276

"Yes, but I'm all right now," she replied, reassuring him. "It's quite a story, and I'll give you all the details later. But now that the crisis is over, shouldn't you get back to the gallery and your guests?"

Marshall bent over and kissed her on the forehead. "Even after all that has happened, you remain the perfect social secretary." He looked around the kitchen, still a bit dazed by the scene. "Knowing how close we came to disaster, it seems a little anticlimactic to have to return and make a round of meaningless diplomatic toasts, but it has to be done. I'll wrap it up as soon as I can. I want to hear all of the story."

After Marshall had departed, the young motorcycle rider had been profusely thanked by everyone, and the police had marched Emilio and Carmen away, Antonio took her in his arms. He held her, not with passion but more to reassure himself that he hadn't lost her. They didn't speak for long moments. It was enough just to be together and safe.

Then he sighed deeply. "I wish I could hold you like this forever. I never want to let you go."

Knowing his thoughts so well, she sensed that there was a *but* on the end of that sentence. "But you can't, can you?"

"I'm afraid not. I have to go with the Italian police to raid that palazzo where you were held captive. I have no choice."

She smiled wanly. "I know, it's your duty. Right?"

No more happy than she, he nodded.

"I guess that's what happens when you fall in love with an Interpol agent. Duty comes first. Antonio, I understand. I really do."

"Are you sure?"

This time it was her turn to nod.

He gazed down at her with such love in his eyes that it brought tears. "You know, even when we're apart, my heart never leaves you," he whispered, pulling her close.

"Nor can mine leave you," she admitted.

"I'll come to the chancellery as soon as I can. Will you wait for me?" he asked, obviously hating the thought of leaving her.

"Forever, if I have to, Antonio."

An hour later she was sitting with the ambassador and the contessa in the library of the chancellery. Filled with books, a fire crackling in the hearth, it was her favorite room of all.

While she told the tale of her kidnapping and escape, the ambassador paced the room and then exploded in anger when she finished. "I wish that traitor Emilio was here right now. After what he did to you I'd like to show him how I feel with one or two well-aimed punches! I hope he rots in prison!"

"Knowing how our Italian courts feel about terrorists, I'm sure he will," the contessa said, reassuring him.

"What I still don't understand is why he did it," Marshall said. "He's been on the staff for years. I would have sworn he was loyal."

"No doubt he was at first. But I think over the years his beliefs became more radical, and that

278

made him an easy recruit," Freya said speculatively. "I don't know everything that went on in his head, but I do know that he wanted Italy to be as great as it had under the Caesars. When the present government couldn't do that, he probably began to hate all authority."

"In the end I suppose it doesn't really matter," Marshall observed. "I'm just glad you discovered the truth in time, then acted to save everyone. Which reminds me, don't let me forget to have a medal presented to that young man who helped you. He risked his life."

Thinking of him, Freya suddenly laughed. "I'll tell you the truth. Riding behind him on that motorcycle was almost as scary as crawling out of that window!"

The door opened. "Ah, how good to hear you laugh again, my little one," Antonio said from the doorway.

The ambassador stood up. "Angelina, I think we should leave them alone, don't you?"

She rose and moved beside him. "Certainly. The last thing young lovers want are a couple of chaperons underfoot."

The ambassador winked at her in secret meaning. "For that matter, older lovers don't care much for them, either, as I've discovered." He held out his arm. "Shall we go?"

Freya looked at Antonio in surprise when he said insistently, "Sir, I must speak with you and *mio madre* first." He glanced back at her. "Freya, I won't be long."

She stared at him in confusion as he escorted

them from the library, shutting the door firmly as he left.

Left alone, Freya paced the room. What was going on? Why had he left her? What had he wanted to talk to the ambassador about that couldn't wait? Half irritated that their reunion had been interrupted, she sank down before the fireplace to stare at the flames, as if they might explain the mystery.

When Antonio reentered the library, she heard the ambassador say from the hallway outside, "Come on, Angelina, we have a lot to do." Then Antonio closed the door and they were alone.

He moved quickly to her side and knelt beside her. "Forgive me for leaving you, but I needed their help with my plans."

"Plans?" she whispered.

Tenderly Antonio picked up her left hand. A delicious flutter of joy sparkled through as he slid the huge diamond and emerald ring on her fourth finger.

She looked questioningly at him. "But this is your mother's ring."

"No, my love. This ring has been in the Raimondi family for generations. It is given to each new Raimondi bride and is hers until her child marries."

Freya could hardly believe her ears. "Raimondi bride?" she repeated. "Antonio, do you mean—"

His kiss stole her words from her lips, and she didn't mind; she didn't mind at all. For a long time the only sound in the room was the popping of the burning wood, then he drew away. His dark eyes were serious yet, at the same time, filled with longing. "When I thought I might have lost you, it felt like something died within me. I knew that only making you my wife would make me feel whole again. And I shall do that this night."

"Tonight? But your job—"

"Freya, shhh. That raid on Emilio's palazzo was the last duty I'll perform for Interpol. I'm quitting the agency."

"But your duty?"

He gathered her hands within his. "I can still serve my land and not be with Interpol. It'll be on a smaller scale, but it will still be important. The villa needs renovating, and I want to reestablish the Raimondi vineyards." He smiled tenderly at her. "Besides, if I'm honest, part of the reason I joined Interpol was for excitement, but I think you can give me all the 'excitement' I'll ever need."

Antonio took a deep breath, then spoke from his heart. "Besides, I want to give you that home, that security you've always wanted, and I can't do that dragging you from country to country."

He lifted her hand to his lips and kissed the ring. "Freya, will you marry me? Will you let my home be the one you've been searching a lifetime for?"

She wound her arms around his neck. "Since the first moment I saw you I had no other destiny. You've told me that often enough, and finally I believe it. Yes, Antonio I'll marry you, anytime, anyplace."

Their kiss sealed the vow.

A discreet knock interrupted the beautiful moment. "Don't answer it," Freya urged, nestling deeper into his embrace.

"I have to, my love." He rose and helped her to her feet. "Come, the knock tells me that everything is ready for me to make you my bride."

To her surprise the ambassador and the contessa were standing outside the door holding suitcases. "The airport just called Count Raimondi," Marshall explained. "The private jet is fueled and ready to go."

"The jet?" Freya asked. "Where are we going?"

Antonio smiled tenderly down at her. "To the place where all Raimondi brides are married, and we're taking along two very special people to witness the binding of our love."

An hour later the chauffeured car pulled to a stop on a graveled drive. At the first sight of his villa Freya gasped. There was no mistaking the master's touch. Gleaming white marble, the classic pediments over the windows, the elegant columns, no hand but Palladio's could have created such beauty.

She turned toward the contessa. "No wonder you couldn't bear to leave this place. Even in my wildest dreams I never would have dared to think that a villa designed by Palladio might one day be my home."

Antonio squeezed her hand. "To be surrounded by beauty, that's how I want every day to be for you."

Freya felt like the beautiful dream would never end as the contessa led her up the sweeping marble staircase and into the most elegant bedroom she'd ever seen. Woven tapestries on the wall, hand-carved furniture, the plushest Oriental carpets underfoot, but Freya saw little as her eyes were riveted to the bed and the gown that lay upon it.

The contessa took her arm. "My child, my Antonio can't bear for another night to pass before he makes you his bride, so there is no time to find you a wedding gown of your own." She patted her ample middle. "You may not believe this, but as a bride I was as tiny as you. Would you do me the honor of wearing my wedding gown to be joined with my son?"

When Freya hesitated, Angelina rushed on, "I know every woman dreams of her own wedding gown, but—"

"No, you don't understand," Freya interrupted, her eyes shining as she looked at the exquisite gown laid before her. "I was silent because I could hardly believe such a thing of beauty might be mine to wear."

Moments later Freya turned to look at herself in the cheval glass. The gown might have been created just for her. Hand-embroidered lace, turned to a rich ivory by time, lay over a sheaf of satin. But what made the gown so special were the thousands of silver threads woven through the fabric. Those threads gave it an ethereal look, reminiscent of moonlight on a secluded pool.

She raised her hand and looked at the golden ring Antonio had placed on her finger, and she smiled. Silver and gold, entwined forever. It had been that way since the first night they'd loved. Like everything else, the gown seemed destined to be the one she'd be wed in.

The contessa settled the gossamer veil against the silver of her hair, then lowered it to shield her face. There were tears of happiness in the older woman's eyes as she looked at her daughter-to-be. "Come, child, my Antonio is waiting."

The night air nipped, but Freya felt only warmth as they walked outside. Nestled amid the trees, glowing softly like a jewel in the moonlight, she saw the tiny chapel. The doors were open, welcoming her. And inside, lit only by candle-light, Antonio waited for his bride. As she walked toward him down the aisle, toward the destiny meant only for her, somewhere the goddess of love smiled.